M000198261

Men without Bliss

CHICANA & CHICANO VISIONS OF THE AMÉRICAS

CHICANA & CHICANO VISIONS OF THE AMÉRICAS

Series Editor

Robert Con Davis-Undiano

Editorial Board

Rudolfo Anaya

Denise Chávez

David Draper Clark

María Amparo Escandón

María Herrera-Sobek

Rolando Hinojosa-Smith

Demetria Martínez

Carlos Monsiváis

Rafael Pérez-Torres

Leroy V. Quintana

José Davíd Saldívar

Ramón Saldívar

Men without Bliss

Rigoberto González

UNIVERSITY OF OKLAHOMA PRESS : NORMAN

ALSO BY RIGOBERTO GONZÁLEZ

So Often the Pitcher Goes to Water until It Breaks (1999)

Soledad Sigh-Sighs (2003)

Crossing Vines (2003)

Antonio's Card (2005)

Other Fugitives and Other Strangers (2006)

Butterfly Boy: Memories of a Chicano Mariposa (2006)

Library of Congress Cataloging-in-Publication Data

González, Rigoberto.
   Men without bliss / Rigoberto González.
      p.   cm. — (Chicana & Chicano visions of the Américas ; v. 6)
   ISBN 978-0-8061-3945-6 (alk. paper)
   1. Mexican Americans—Fiction. 2. Men—Fiction. I. Title.
   PS3557.O4695M46 2008
   813'.54—dc22

                                                            2008005981

Men without Bliss is Volume 6 in the Chicana & Chicano Visions of the Américas series.

The paper in this book meets the guidelines for permanence and durability of the Committee on Production Guidelines for Book Longevity of the Council on Library Resources. ∞

Copyright © 2008 by the University of Oklahoma Press, Norman, Publishing Division of the University. Manufactured in the U.S.A.

All rights reserved. No part of this publication may be reproduced, stored in a retrieval system, or transmitted, in any form or by any means, electronic, mechanical, photocopying, recording, or otherwise—except as permitted under Section 107 or 108 of the United States Copyright Act—without the prior written permission of the University of Oklahoma Press.

1 2 3 4 5 6 7 8 9 10

For Lauro and Christine,
who always believed

Contents

Acknowledgments   ix

Part One: Men in the Caliente Valley

Mexican Gold   3

Your Malicious Moons   23

Cactus Flower   33

Plums   41

Good Boys   58

The Call   90

Confessions of a Drowning Man   105

Men without Bliss   115

Part Two: Men in Other Places

Nayarita Blues   137

Día de las Madres   148

Haunting José   165

Road to Enchantment   174

The Abortionist's Lover   193

Acknowledgments

"The Abortionist's Lover" was published in *Inside Him: Best New Gay Erotica*, ed. Joel B. Tan, New York: Carroll & Graf, 2006.

"Cactus Flower" appears in the online anthology *Cortland Review*, ed. Guy Shahar, 2001.

"The Call" appears in *Americas Review*, ed. Lauro Flores, 1999.

"Confessions of a Drowning Man" was published in *Palabra: A Magazine of Chicano/Latino Literary Art*, ed. Elena Minor, vol. 1, 2006.

"Día de las Madres" was published in *Latinos in Lotus Land: An Anthology of Contemporary Southern California Literature*, ed. Daniel A. Olivas, Tempe, AZ: Bilingual Press, 2008.

"Men without Bliss" was published in *Everything I Have Is Blue: Short Fiction by Working-Class Men About More-or-Less Gay Life,* ed. Wendell Ricketts, San Francisco: Suspect Thoughts Press, 2005.

"Road to Enchantment," originally appeared as "Dependable" in the *Colorado Review*, ed. Stephanie G'Schwind, Fort Collins: Colorado State University, 2000.

"Your Malicious Moons" appears in the online anthology *Blithe House Quarterly*, eds. Jarrett Walker, Tisa Bryant, and Aldo Alvarez, 2001.

With special thanks and much gratitude to Robert Con Davis-Undiano, an important champion of Chicano letters, for having faith in my work. With affection y mil gracias to my New York City padrinos Scott Hightower and José Fernández.

Part One

Men in the Caliente Valley

Mexican Gold

A cockroach fights to free itself from a tiny pool of water in the tub. Moonlight beams through the window, strikes the insect and makes it sparkle like Mexican gold, like a cheap Guadalupe medal, the kind that dulls and loses luster. Marcos leans forward on the toilet lid to watch the insect spin with its legs in the air. One, two, three, four, five. Where's number six? Does it make a difference to a roach when it has five others to carry that burden of an egg tube from one dark place to another? Tonight it does. Faucet on, faucet off. The small flood spirals the cockroach into the mouth of the drain.

He spots a second roach twitching its antennae from the dirty tile on the wall. Want to be next?

Someone's at the door. Someone tests the doorknob. Someone walks away. It's not Abuelo because he's snoring in his room, dreaming he's a muffler, and it's not Abuelo because there's a piss pot beneath his bed, the water in the basin rippling each time Abuelo exhales. Marcos fades into the background and holds his breath. He bites on the joint, keeps the silver lighter steady as the flame trembles. The soft sound of the gas jet amplifies in the silence. When he takes a lengthy drag, he imagines the burning tip makes his face glow in the dark. He's all acne scars and a pock-marked forehead and long black strands of sweaty hair. He's a wall of ugly with a face coming through it.

Marilú opens the front entrance and steps out. The air pressure coming in rattles the bathroom door. Marcos holds back a cough. He reaches over to the sink to pour some water into the small cup of his hand and coats his mouth. Marilú shoos the cats away. They leap through the plants, rustle the leaves. Marcos pulls the shower curtain just in case Marilú wants to peek through the window. But she won't. She knows he's inside and what he's doing because it's not the first time he locks himself in late at night. He's surprised to hear her pull her panties down and squat. She farts, drops a stream of piss. He imagines the small mud puddle beneath her in the garden as the urine trickles down. After a faint sniffle comes the sound of the elastic of her panties as she snaps them back over her waist.

He sticks the joint between his lips again. He knows his mother pisses, but at this proximity he feels she's telling him a secret. She's human, vulnerable, like the times he hears her fuck, or like the times he hears her cry. At times like these when she leaves some evidence behind.

Once his mother goes back to bed, Marcos returns to his own room. The scent of marijuana trails behind like the black veil of his hair. There's something about smoking out in the bathroom, perhaps the claustrophobia of it that gives him a quicker, stronger high. He drops his body heavily on the mattress and rolls himself into the striped blankets. Of course the joint has failed him and his mind keeps spinning the same name like a pair of dice inside an anxious fist. *Roger Roger Roger.* Another reason Marcos likes the bathroom—the only space they never shared at the same time. Dear Roger. Dear dead Roger. *Roger Roger Roger.* Jolly jolly Roger—the rusty metal embedded in the center of Marcos' heart that poisons him a little more each night.

Last week he came across one of Roger's notebooks. Roger's handwriting a little too faggy for Marcos: the *i*'s dotted with pregnant circles, the final strokes of the *a*'s and *s*'s curled like a strand of kinky hair. The notebook is proof of Roger's average grades in high school history. The class notes, scribbles and doodles fill page after page, using more ink on the weak illustrations than on jotting down dates and names. Except for the girlish handwriting, Marcos discovers that his own history notebook is no different. He also takes sparse notes, the writing moving away from the left margin each time he skips to the next line. He also makes pathetic drawings and inks them in obsessively. It saddens him to have found common ground with his brother too late. And yet, leafing through months of Roger's notes does nothing to shrink the distance that was always there, between them.

Roger Roger Roger. Dear dead Roger. Now there's only Marilú, who's alive and sleeping in the next room, but who's just as far away as the brother he doesn't have anymore. In spite of himself, Marcos cries beneath the blankets, the tears roll down heavy and hot. Grieving inside the dark and in such silence is the same as if not grieving at all.

The next morning Marcos' back aches from zoning in and out on the toilet lid for hours. His mouth is dry, not cotton-mouthed like the night before but still sticky. He doesn't want to fetch something from the kitchen. He wants to stay beneath the blankets. The blankets are dusty and stink of sweaty feet. He feels heavy, especially above the neck, as if he's wearing the tight football helmet from high school. Annoyed by the cartoon voices on the TV, he peers over the blanket to find his young cousin sprawled across the floor.

"Turn it off, Richie," he says. "Who said you could come into my room? Go home."

"Ma doesn't like me watching TV too early in the morning," Richie says. He crunches on a chocolate bar.

"Then watch the TV in the living room. Shit."

"What's wrong with *your* TV?"

"Leave me alone, Richie," Marcos pleads, bothered that his voice is weak. Resigned, he adds lazily, "Turn it down at least."

"Abuelo made me come in to wish you a sapo verde. So, sapo verde." Richie's face is smeared in chocolate and a peanut crumb sticks to the corner of his lip.

Marcos glares at him, pulls the blankets back over his head and then shifts his body around with his back to the TV. Moments later, Richie turns off the set and leaves, slamming the bedroom door shut. The smell of peanuts and chocolate lingers behind, and Marcos takes the odor with him to his sleep.

Waking up the second time, completely drained, Marcos rises slowly in his pearl-colored boxers. His balance falters because he hasn't eaten since yesterday morning. The chocolate bar he consumed in his dream didn't trick his stomach and now it grumbles for attention. A bitter taste coats the back of his throat but the spit he swallows goes down clean. He manages the walk to the mirror. He brushes his hair aside; his lower lids are dry and bloodred. The clock on the opposite wall claims it's two in the afternoon.

Abuelo turns the living room stereo on, playing his brass band music loud enough for the windows to shake. In this shoddy housing project even the concrete walls vibrate. Abuelo recently bought the stereo from the guys who drive around in a van stuffed with stolen merchandise. There are two stereos in the house now: the one in the living room and the one still in its box, Marilú's purchase for Roger the week before he was killed. They didn't buy any more TVs; they already had four: in the living room, in Abuelo's room, in Marilú's, and in this room, for Marcos and Roger.

"Lower that thing, Papa, I'm using the phone!" Marilú yells out. The windows stop shaking but a steady hum still runs through the walls.

Marcos opens the dresser drawer and fumbles among the clutter for a cigarette and matches. The lighter's still sitting on the bathroom sink, and though it's only a few feet away he doesn't want to bump into Marilú. Not yet. He shoves aside crushed Winston boxes, loose change, crumpled zigzags, a few condoms, number two pencils he never used for school, and snapshots of the old football team taken during practice. In the photographs the grass emits a bright green glow he doesn't remember seeing on the field. A fake ruby stud rolls out into view—the companion to the one Roger wore on his ear. It had maddened Marcos that his brother had thought to pierce his ear first, which kept him from piercing his. Finally he comes across a wrinkled Camel with a small tear near the filter, probably bummed since this isn't his brand. *Do you have to smoke in the room while I'm fucking eating?* The phrase suddenly comes alive with the scent of the tobacco as Marcos sniffs at the tear. Marcos remembers those Friday nights, Roger complaining over his pizza, Marcos coming home alone from yet another game because no one in the family ever goes to watch him play.

He bites into the unlit cigarette, making it bounce between his teeth as he licks the butt. "After I find me some matches," he answers Roger. But when he looks back Roger isn't there.

"You fool," Marcos says.

"What did you say?" Marilú asks. She has poked her head in. In the crook of her arm hangs a stack of used towels.

"Nothing," says Marcos, then adds: "Did you see my lighter in the bathroom?"

Marilú holds out her hand. Marcos takes the lighter. "I'm doing laundry. Do you have anything else that needs cleaning besides the mess you left in there?" she says.

Without pause Marcos peels off his boxers and hands them to Marilú, whose face reddens. Naked, he lights his cigarette. "Thanks for the lighter, Mom," he manages to say before she flees.

Marilú doesn't like Mom. It was Roger's idea to call her Marilú, and Marilú's to call Rogelio Roger. Marilú and Roger were always improving each other, like the time Roger said Marilú should wear her hair loose because it made her look younger. Marcos couldn't tell the difference, but she stopped tying it back and since then none of her plastic hair clips have reappeared. Marilú had wanted to change Marcos to Mark, but Marcos, dark and acne-scarred, scoffed because he didn't look white like Roger, so why the hell put on a white boy's name?

Marcos sticks the cigarette in the Budweiser ashtray on the dresser, his mouth too dry to suck smoke into it. He turns eighteen today and he has slept through most of the day. Roger will always be seventeen. *Roger Roger Roger.* Where would Roger be if not for the knife in the gut? Marcos is punishing himself, but the urge is uncontrollable. Dear dead Roger.

"Tino's out to get you," Marcos had warned Roger. A warning was fair enough, and Marcos gave him the chance to do something, maybe run off with Tino's girl the way he had been threatening to do all month. Roger was sitting in his precious Mustang, pretending to know about fuses.

"I can kick his ass. Why should you give a shit anyhow?" Roger said.

"I don't give half a shit," Marcos said, "and that's not the right fuse."

Roger got up and let Marcos take over. Marcos inspected the fuse box beneath the panel and quickly replaced the one burnt out. He let Roger take back his seat.

"Thanks," Roger said. "For the fuse, not for being all up in my Kool-Aid. I know what I'm doing and I can take care of myself. Got that?" Roger's eyebrows arched from fear.

Marcos shook his head. "Look," he said, "you're the one who's going to get it if you don't quit fucking around with this girl. What the hell are you thinking?"

"What's really eating you, Marcos?" Roger's pupils dilated when he got angry, darkening the iris. His face looked larger, powerful. "Are you pissed that Susie chose Tino over you and then me over you? Is that it? Huh?"

Marcos didn't respond, embarrassed into silence because Roger had it right. For the first time Roger had named the jealousy. Marcos could've done something more—like recruit Marilú into talking Roger out of the fight—but he didn't. Instead he watched in silence as Roger drove off that afternoon. Dear dead Roger, stubborn Roger. He accepted Tino's challenge to a brawl and lost.

Brawls in the Caliente Valley were the best public theater, because they were so frequent and well attended. But Roger's will always stand out because he died in one. At the end of a fight, both the winner and the loser are supposed to make peace through the exhaustion of their bodies. A quick fist-to-fist tap signals the end of the show, but also of the conflict. They had it out, they moved on. And then their friends stepped into the arena to hold up the winner, to keep him from stumbling down on the sand the way the loser had, the guy whose friends had stepped forward to help up, to let him know he did good even though this night was not his night, and that there was no shame in that. Shame would be not showing up, or getting beat before the excitement of the crowd reached its peak.

What should have happened was this: Tino knocks Roger around for a few minutes, plays with him, lets him think he actually stands a chance to come out of the fight with his dignity intact. And when he gets tired of watching Roger's bloody face wave in front of him he euthanizes him with a solid right hook and a swift kick in the stomach. It's how a real man puts his competitor out of his misery, and it's considered honorable. And Roger writhes in pain a bit and then the crowd loses interest quickly and disperses, some guys complaining this wasn't much of a match.

But Roger fucked it up by sneaking a switchblade into the mix, breaking the code of fair fighting. When it gleamed with the headlights illuminating the ring, Marcos recognized it as his and instinctively reached back to feel the emptiness of his pocket, though he wouldn't have brought it to a brawl in the first place. And just as impulsively he yelled out, "Tino!" to let him know what was coming.

Why had he done that? To keep Roger from making a big mistake? Or to protect himself from the accusation later that he had supplied Roger with the switchblade in the first place? Or maybe he knew that Tino, infuriated by the weakness of his rival, the same guy who had taken away his girl, would grab Roger's wrist and turn the blade around to finish him off with one quick thrust.

Roger's mouth opened up so wide it looked as if the knife had sliced a vertical line across his cheeks. And then it swallowed every sound and movement. The fake ruby stud glared on his left earlobe like the first drop of blood. When he plunged, spilling blood like no one before him had, the fury of fear and flight took over, and everyone disappeared, except for Marcos and Tino, who stood paralyzed over Roger's body as if waiting for him to get up and do this right this time, fight fair and keep everyone from getting into trouble.

And when Marcos dared to say, "Roger," the sound came out so brittle it crumbled on his lips.

In one quick move, Marcos takes the cigarette out of the ashtray and puts it out on the back of his left hand, at the base of his left thumb. The intensity weakens his grip and he releases. The hot tip slides smoothly on the surface, exposing white flesh beneath the dark skin.

"Shit!" he yells, covering the flesh wound with his right hand.

Marilú sticks her head into the room again. "Are you going to walk around naked all day or are you putting some clothes on soon?"

Surprised, Marcos reaches for his jeans. "Jesus! Can't a guy have some privacy?" Abuelo turns on the stereo in the living room up to full volume again. Marcos yells out, "And some fucking peace and quiet!"

"Papa," Marilú calls out. She presses her fist to her forehead. "Lower that thing!"

Abuelo appears at the door after lowering the volume, the hairs in his nose wiry and gray. "Are you awake finally? Richie came in this morning to wish you a sapo verde, did you see him?"

"I told him to get lost," Marcos says, rummaging through the closet for a shirt.

"He's in one of his moods, Papa," Marilú says.

Abuelo steps back, shaking his head as he shuts the door.

Marcos stares at the burn on his hand. Blood collects in the dimples of the knuckle. His hand trembles as he bandages himself with a blue bandanna. He uses his teeth to secure the knot. He anticipates the curious look on the postal worker when he shows up to register. The clock on the wall makes him quicken his pace; he has two hours before the post office closes.

Both the shower and the sink are running as Marcos bandages his hand with a piece of gauze. Black spots stain the basin from Marilú's hair dye. Cockroaches have dotted the mirror with their tracks, yet Marcos sees his acne scars clearly enough. They darken when he gets stoned. Roger pointed that out. *Roger Roger Roger.* Dear dead Roger.

Roger's skin was always clean and smooth, not even marked by adolescent pimples. He grew out of the precious little boy into the tall, precious teenager. Marilú's Roger. When they were children, Marilú took only Roger by the hand, scolding Marcos for lagging behind. When Roger turned his head to stick his tongue out, Marcos gave him the finger, a comeback his father had taught him.

"You're going to turn Rogelio into a sissy," his father once warned Marilú. Marilú said nothing, making matters worse by pressing Roger tightly against her and planting a kiss on his head.

"The other kids are going to kick his ass for being a mama's boy," his father said, a third or fourth beer shaking in his hand. "I should take him to work with me. Make a man out of him. Marcos knows what it's all about, don't you, Junior?" The young Marcos froze, careful not to shudder.

Marcos wraps a plastic bag over his hand to keep the gauze dry, and then steps into the shower, watching the darkness of his skinny foot descend into the white tub. Since Roger's death he has been losing weight. That and his depression got him benched most of the season in his final year of high school.

The truth is Marcos didn't like going to work with his father. He only pretended. He knew nothing more painful than getting up at dawn to go to the desert, where his father drove the bull-dozers and cleared the ground for new roads. It wouldn't have been so bad if his father didn't insist on forcing the pedals and gearshifts on him while he had a beer. Marcos hated that, especially when he forgot which lever did what and his father slapped him on the head, sometimes knocking him off the bulldozer and into the stones the machine had broken down to sharp gravel.

His father taught him to drive at age nine just so he could have Marcos drive him home drunk from the bar. Marcos had to wait for his father to get drunk first. He waited in the car for hours, slumped on the seat to avoid being seen, afraid someone would walk by, break in and take the car keys away from him. He chewed on the key chain with the taste of his father's hands, with the taste of shiny pennies.

The truth is, when his father left for good, after years of threatening to do so, Marcos was glad. But he never shared that relief with Roger or Marilú. Marcos never told them that his father had tried to take him away that night, and that he had squeezed against the wall beneath the bed, out of reach of his father's hands. "Come on!" His father's voice was a desperate whisper rough with smoke and alcohol. Marcos hugged himself tightly. He found a penny beneath the bed. His father's hand waved above the coin as if he were doing a magic trick, perhaps trying to make the penny levitate. Marcos nearly brushed against his father's fingertips when he jerked his arm out to sweep the penny clean off the carpet. Seconds later his father gave up and sat on the bed, his weight lowering the weak mattress on top of Marcos. Drained of strength, Marcos fell asleep with the coin clutched against his chest and when he woke up later, his father was gone.

After showering and throwing on a pair of jeans and a t-shirt, Marcos decides to check the oil in the Mustang before driving off. Technically, he has inherited Roger's car. Abuelo has the old Ford station wagon and Marilú drives a Toyota truck. They never go anywhere together and they prefer it that way, especially Abuelo, who complains that Marcos and Marilú drive too fast.

Marcos learned from Abuelo the basics of car maintenance; he learned the more advanced stuff—alternator adjustments, radiator cleanings—from the guys on the team, Tino and them. Especially from Tino, whose father's a mechanic at Pep Boys. Tino taught him to clean the battery terminals on a budget, with only baking soda and a lemon.

Though the raised hood is in the way, Marcos knows Abuelo's near. Abuelo smells like brilliantine and cigarette smoke. A few yards back, Marilú hangs jeans on the clothesline.

"What happened to your hand?" Abuelo asks.

"Nothing," Marcos replies.

"Giving the Mustang a tune-up?" Abuelo persists.

"Just wiping off the terminals before I go to the post office," says Marcos. "How's your car running?"

"Not too good," Abuelo says. He gives a lengthy and scattered update on his car troubles, which Marcos half-listens to until Abuelo asks, "So you're going to register?"

Marcos glances at Marilú, at her slim legs glistening with perspiration at the calves. He tries to remember her boyfriend's name: Germán or Jacobo or Esteban.

"I'm going to do more than register. I'm going to enlist," Marcos dares to say in a voice loud enough to carry the message over to Marilú. She looks over her shoulder, briefly.

"In the military?" Abuelo asks, alarmed.

"Yes, sir," Marcos says.

"What for?" Abuelo says. "Remember Chano's boy? Got kicked out. You boys don't like to take orders. You boys like to stay in bed all day."

"Did you hear that, Mom?" Marcos calls out. "The military."

"Don't start something, Marcos," Abuelo warns.

"I'm serious, Mom. Getting the hell out."

Marilú loads the washing machine with the white shirts she left bleaching in a green bucket. She takes her time starting the cycle.

"Yes, sir, I'm ditching this dump," Marcos says, weakly. "Going to Iraq."

"Stop it," Abuelo says.

Marilú walks over slowly and surprises Marcos by leaning on the Mustang and pulling the cigarette box out of Abuelo's pocket. She's not a smoker. Abuelo fumbles with the matches and speaks nervously as he lights the cigarette for Marilú, "Well, what else is the boy going to do now that he's out of school? Sell drugs? Pick grapes? The military will do him good. The war needs more dead kids, I suppose."

"Yeah, that's right," says Marcos. "I'm a dead kid all right."

"Don't be stupid, son," Abuelo says. "All those boys are coming home in bags. And all for what? It's just another senseless war, and a waste of life."

"Well, maybe I want that," Marcos says.

"Shut up with this nonsense," Abuelo says.

"Don't let him do this to you, Papa," Marilú says. She then stares at Marcos. "Go ahead. Run away. You get that from your father," she says. Marcos blushes. "You're old enough to do whatever the hell you want," she continues.

"I always have," Marcos snaps back.

"You don't give a shit about anybody but yourself."

Marilú's response startles Marcos at first, but slowly his mouth shapes a smile as he realizes she's performing, just as he is.

"And who do I get that from, Mom?" he says, snidely.

"Enough!" Abuelo says, putting his hand up between them. "Stop it! You two embarrass me." Both Marcos and Marilú notice Roger's class ring showing brightly on Abuelo's finger. Marcos puts his head down in shame.

Marilú puts out her cigarette on the ground and follows Abuelo inside. As she walks into the house she shoves the green bucket out of the way and knocks it off balance. Marcos responds by slamming the car hood down, determined to make it to the recruitment office before it closes.

On the way out of the housing project he passes Lety's apartment. Lety and his mother are cousins, but Marcos never bothered to map out the family tree to find out how that's true. He slows down enough for Richie to jump out of a game of marbles and run toward the car.

"Can I go with you, Marcos?" Richie asks. "Please?"

Marcos' instinct is to say: "No way!" But Richie doesn't have a father, either, and at this moment that fact means something to Marcos, so he assents.

"Just tell your mom," Marcos says.

"Ma!" Richie yells out. "I'll be right back, I'm going with Marcos."

Lety sticks her head out of the front door and waves at them. "When will you be back?" she asks.

"A few hours," Marcos replies.

"I don't have any money, Richie," she says, and before Richie has time to become dejected, Marcos chimes in: "I've got him covered, Lety." She shrugs and steps back inside the apartment. As Marcos drives out, he warns Richie, "And only I touch the radio," though today he doesn't feel like listening to music, and he speeds out of the neighborhood in a quiet ride, a rarity in that part of town.

"Where are we going?" Richie asks.

"To hell," Marcos says.

"Ma says Bush already took us there," Richie says.

"Alrighty then," Marcos says, smiling.

In the south side of the Caliente Valley, the housing projects border the crop fields, and to get anywhere that matters to Marcos he has to drive alongside acres of grape and beet and lettuce. The high school is located to the east, the small cluster of business buildings and eateries, which passes for downtown, is located to the north, and to the west, where the sun sets like a spoiled apricot inside a honey jar, is the post office.

"I need to register," Marcos tells the plump redhead behind the counter. She looks put out by his sudden appearance at the empty postal station and watches with slight disdain as Marcos fills out the small card. He's out of the post office in less than five minutes. Richie follows along in silence, trained well by his mother, just like Marcos was by Marilú, about how to behave in public spaces. And this irritates Marcos.

"Hey," Marcos says, "I have to go do something boring right now, but after that we can do something cool, okay."

"Okay," Richie says. "Like what?"

In that inquisitive look Marcos recognizes something of his younger self, and it's only then that he realizes that he and Richie are blood relations and not just an invented extended family, what many of the Mexicans who end up in the housing project do to keep their numbers large, their safety net wide.

"Like the arcade?" Marcos says, hopefully.

"Yeah!" Richie says, and for some reason his display of genuine excitement chokes Marcos up.

The recruitment office has always been next to the unemployment office downtown. Marcos remembers all those times he accompanied his mother or Abuelo out here, only to be struck by the romantic portraits of young military personnel in pressed outfits and perfect posture. When he ran into boys he knew, they'd stare at the posters and choose a future in the service based on the uniform. He always chose the army because he couldn't see himself keeping the white navy uniform clean, and he didn't imagine himself brave enough to handle flying. He still hasn't flown, he thinks as he opens the door.

"I have to babysit," he explains to the recruitment officer, a man in a beige uniform behind a desk. Richie knows about the white lies grown-ups tell and doesn't betray Marcos. When the officer looks down at Marcos' bandage, Marcos quickly adds, "Car maintenance injury."

"That's fine, son," the recruitment officer says. He has his hair cropped close on the sides and his Adam's apple bobs whenever he breathes. "Your little brother can sit over there while we talk. Would you like to read a magazine, son?" Richie looks puzzled as the recruitment officer hands him a glossy propaganda pamphlet.

"Before we have our sit-down," says the recruitment officer. "Step over here a minute."

From the corner of his eye, Marcos notices Richie looking more confused as the officer weighs and measures Marcos, just like at a doctor's office. The officer mumbles under his breath: "No piercings, no visible tattoos. Good."

"A bit on the thin side, aren't we?" the officer says. "Your mama not feeding you enough frijoles or something?" The officer chuckles; Marcos keeps a stoic expression. They sit with a large metal desk between them.

"The military is the cornerstone of this great nation of ours," the officer begins his speech, slipping into scripted lecture mode, which triggers the daydreaming nerve in Marcos. He has had plenty of practice in high school, pretending to be paying attention with his face upright and directed straight at the speaker. He can hear Richie ripping the pages out of the pamphlet, and minutes later he catches a peripheral glimpse of a flying object—a paper airplane no less, that both he and the officer ignore.

And then Roger steps forward. The shock is enough to make Marcos go pale, and for the officer to pause to offer him a glass of water.

"I'm fine," Marcos says, but he doesn't unlock his gaze from the poster behind the officer's desk of a fair skinned officer in a blue uniform, a dead ringer for Roger. *Roger Roger Roger.* Dear dead ringer Roger.

"Are you sure you're all right, son?" the officer asks, looking over his shoulder.

"Yes," Marcos says. The officer continues his speech, uncertainly. *National security. Terrorists.*

By the time they walk out of the office, Richie has constructed an entire fleet of warplanes, which he leaves scattered on the waiting room carpet, some of them under the chairs turned hangars. Marcos carries a stack of reading material under his arm.

"I'll be here when you've have a chance to think carefully about your options," the recruitment officer says. "I'll be here to welcome you to your home away from home."

"What a weirdo," Richie says as soon as they're outside. "And he didn't have a thumb."

"What?" Marcos says.

"That man in there," Richie says, holding up his own thumb. "He didn't have one of these."

Marcos drives out of the parking lot and heads toward the arcade next to the miniature golf course. He exchanges five dollars for tokens and spends the next hour and a half keeping up with Richie at the race-car simulator. Marcos gets distracted each time he surrenders to the screen's illusion of high-speed motion, as if he has indeed been sucked into the two-dimensional animation—a city of bright color and no depth. No history.

"Pay attention!" Richie commands. "I'm creaming you!"

Halfway through their stay, he springs for a couple of hot dogs and sodas. Richie eats quickly, anxious to get back to the simulator.

Although it's only been a few months since high school graduation, the crowd at the arcade has changed, as if there's some unwritten rule about excluding recent graduates. Marcos suddenly feels self-conscious, as if his presence here means that he hasn't grown out of his childhood. But he's a man now at eighteen. And he's here for his little cousin Richie, not for himself. Yet the nostalgia is unmistakable. He wishes he were still in those days when all he had to do was long for the freedom from school. But those moments of puffing on cigarettes with urgency between classes and the defiance of sitting in the back of the classroom, making the substitute teachers nervous, seem so stupid now. Now. The present—this was a terrible place to be in.

They drive back to the housing project and Marcos pulls over to drop off Richie. Richie is slow to open the door.

"Okay, stupid," Marcos tells him, "don't ruin it. Your quarter's up."

"You're not really going to the army, right? Mom says everyone who goes there gets killed," Richie says.

Marcos chuckles. "Not everybody," he says, and imagines those personnel who come home without a limb or two. "And what's it to you, anyway?"

Richie's head drops.

"Hey," Marcos says, softly this time. "Sorry, man." He reaches over to tussle Richie's hair, but Richie pulls back and leaps out of the car. And just before he slams the door shut he yells out: "Maybe I don't want to lose another big brother!"

Marcos watches him run past the small window of the rearview mirror.

Marilú's taking one of her hot showers when Marcos enters the apartment. The pipes bang and the sweat from the steam collects outside of the bathroom door. Marcos picks up the telephone, changes his mind, and replaces the receiver. He turns the ringer off, then switches it back on, then off again. He hasn't heard from the guys in the team since graduation, except for Paul and Frankie. He will tell them later he made up his mind to enlist with them after all. But he doesn't want anybody calling him tonight. All week the guys have been talking about getting together for a few beers to celebrate his birthday.

When Marcos walks into his room he finds a package on the bed—a gift from Marilú. That's how she gave him gifts, in unwrapped boxes. He hates the look of new clothes: too clean, smelling of cardboard, the creases too sharp and defined, and the colors too deep and vibrant. That sets you apart right away at the housing project. You have to shove your new shirt in the washer a few times before you can wear it to the school bus stop or else you get shit from the guys. He recalls that time back in junior high.

"Why're you messing up your shoes, fool?" Roger asked. It was just after Christmas break and Roger and Marcos had each received a new pair of shoes. Marcos had taken them off on the way to the bus stop and was hammering them against the ground.

"Shut your mouth and don't tell Mom, either," Marcos warned Roger.

"Like she's not going to notice them all scuffed? Retard."

And Roger walked straight to the bus stop in his brand new shoes, prepared for the teasing and spit-wad throwing. Marcos watched from a distance, resisting the urge to admire his brother's courage.

Marcos empties the box on the bed. The dark blue shirt has a black diamond pattern, a print he would never wear.

Marilú knocks on the open door. "Well?"

"It's all right," Marcos answers, sheepishly. He folds the shirt up awkwardly and stuffs it back in the box.

Marilú combs out her wet hair. Drops of water fly out, a few drops striking Marcos on the arm. "Are you going out tonight?" she asks.

"Probably. With Paul and Frankie."

"I'll be gone for a few days with Esteban," she says. "Pick up some fried chicken or something for your grandfather to snack on. He'll be having his meals over at Lety's." Marilú grabs her hair with one hand and pulls down at the glistening ends with the other. "If you need some money I'll leave a few twenties on the TV in my bedroom. You know where."

Marcos suddenly pictures the porcelain jewelry box with the secret compartment at the bottom. He discovered the cache long ago and has been pilfering money from it since.

Marilú is about to turn away when Marcos blurts out, "I miss him too, believe it or not."

Marilú stiffens, and then shakes her head. "Not now, Marcos," she says

"I should have stopped him, I should have told you."

They remain frozen for a few seconds, Marcos staring at Marilú, Marilú staring into space.

"What are you doing?" Marilú asks after she breaks the spell.

"What?" Marcos asks.

"Why are you telling me this? What does it matter what you should or shouldn't have done? It's not going to change anything. Roger is dead and that boy is rotting away in prison, just like he deserves. So what do you want, Marcos, huh? Do you want me to tell you it's all right? That I forgive you? Jesus Christ. For the last year I've been going crazy, trying not to think about it. I don't need to hear any more, especially not from you."

Marcos' throat tightens. "Well, you won't even have to see me anymore," he manages to say without coughing. "I enlisted this afternoon."

"Well, good for you," Marilú responds. "Take off. Go away. Disappear."

Marilú's makes another attempt at walking off, but Marcos won't let her. He's struck by the sudden burst of urgency to keep her close so he pulls her back by the arm.

"Let go of me," she says.

"I could have left a long time ago, you know," he stammers. "My father came for me that night, you know, when he went away. But I was hiding. And I've regretted it every fucking minute since, putting up with your shit. And Roger's." He adds the last two words as an afterthought. He anticipates a slap in the face; he would have welcomed it. Instead Marilú lets out an unsure chuckle, which feels worse.

Marilú finally speaks after a brief silence. "Nobody was more surprised than me when you were still around after your father left, Marcos. He was *supposed* to take you with him." Marcos' face turns cold. Marilú shakes her head, leaning against the wall. "And all this time I thought he had chickened out. Jesus Christ, this is perfect." She wipes her face. "But you're here and Roger's not. I guess we all deserve—" Marilú doesn't finish her sentence. She bursts into tears and rushes into her own bedroom across the hall.

Speechless, Marcos steps back and shuts the door. He opens the dresser drawer with a violent motion that knocks the ashtray off. Maybe he shouldn't smoke in the room anymore. Roger hates the smell. *Roger Roger Roger.* Dear dead Roger.

He doesn't have a picture of Roger. He has pictures of the football team, of old girlfriends, of Benito, the Doberman he had to give up when the projects passed an ordinance against pet dogs. The bottom of the dresser rattles with change, mostly pennies. His gauze comes undone but he continues his search. Why is it that nobody likes pennies and yet the coins keep popping up by the dozens?

He imagines himself in those army movies where the cropped-haired privates take a handful of photographs out of their footlockers when they get homesick. He imagines himself in the barracks of some other part of the world, wondering how Abuelo's adjusting to living with Lety. Maybe Lety or Richie will write him. And if the grunts in the quarters ask him about his family, he will tell them about his brother Roger, show them a picture so that they know what his brother looks like, never mind that they might not believe he's a flesh and blood relation. They will see the resemblance despite the different skins.

But that scene in the army movie fades quickly as Marcos struggles to find a picture of Roger at the zoo, or Roger at the park, or at the fair. Marcos has seen those photographs; he was there, standing behind the camera because he was asked to take most of them. He tosses things out faster. He pulls out the dresser drawer completely, spilling the coins around him and a few roaches scurry out. His impulse is to crush the insects, to chase them down before they disappear beneath the bed, but he doesn't move. His arms tremble. Roger isn't anywhere anymore. Not in the house, not in the room, not in the top dresser drawer, or in the second one, or in the third. But the real surprise comes when he realizes that neither is his mother, the woman standing beside Roger in those photographs taken at the zoo, or at the park, or at the fair. She has faded from his personal belongings, having made herself irreversibly invisible as if she too were dead.

Marcos squats down over the drawer and plucks out the fake ruby stud. The guys on the team had used ice cubes to numb their earlobes and heated the sharp tip to sanitize the pin. He darkens the pin with the lighter. He stretches his earlobe out and aims. The tip stings a little, but when he pushes it through he doesn't feel any pain other than the brief surprise of the warm penetration of metal.

Your Malicious Moons

You're on your way, you're almost there, and it's going to happen, this tête-à-tête, this tit-for-tat meeting with your half brother at the Mexican restaurant. You'll finally, openly and without room for backing out, tell Víctor what he's suspected all along. By default it's the perfect time since on Sunday your smile will be plastered like an orthodontist ad on the newspaper's human interest feature profiling the gay experience in the Caliente Valley. At tonight's event you're positive someone from the press will mention it, and even though you'd get a good kick out of shocking, surprising, and outright appalling Víctor in public, you don't want to let the cameras turn the moment into unbreakable stone. That would be too cruel, even for you.

You know your revelation will piss off and antagonize your little brother, but he can't afford to write you off completely either. He agreed to meet because (you know this, you sense this) he wants to hit you up for a loan. Again. He's gathering funds for the campaign he's going to launch after he makes his big announcement tonight. You're both comfortable with this game of strained compromise. Once, while you were visiting from college, you fought over the use of your mother's car. Víctor won because your mother voted in his favor, so he drove you to a friend's house to cool off for the night, only to come knocking the following morning to offer you the car. You walked out of Steve's, making up a story to explain the hickeys on your neck, which Víctor didn't question. You know he didn't quite believe you but he had no choice—he needed money. On the way to the bank he even advised you on how to cover up the blemishes. "Rub the back of a spoon against them," he said with a nervous chuckle. You handed him the cash; he handed you the keys. Today's exchange will be no different: he needs you and the favor will cost him.

You're twenty minutes early to the Mexican restaurant, so you wait in the parking lot of Las Cazuelas. You straighten the collar on your black suit; the cempasúchil in the lapel has spread its heavy fragrance in the car. Your nose twitches so you pinch it looking into the rearview mirror. When you're stressed you feel like a Dalmatian. You pull back the birthmarks on your skin as if smoothing them out will make the flesh swallow them into your face. You got the birthmarks from your mother's side of the family: all your tíos in Michoacán have brown and black moles on their cheeks, chins, and foreheads. Tío Eddie has a big one the size of a fly on his nose. This is why you chose never to pierce your ears like every other fag you know. You were born with too many accessories on your face already. Your mother's were beauty marks. She called them "lunas" because they were feminine and pleasant as the moon. Before you got too big, before Víctor, she used to let you play connect-the-dots on her, drawing invisible figures that found their way to your skin when you compared the birthmark patterns. You still carry them. That and the memory of the playful fingertips that made your mother coo each time they pressed down on her skin. *Coo coo*, the big dove nestling against the little dove in the corner of the cage in Tía Cristina's garden in Morelia. *Coo coo*, the morning showers cool and the hanging pots making music on the courtyard tiles as they overflow with water. *Coo coo*, the memory of mother.

The cempasúchil was your mother's favorite flower—the flower of the dead. And now she's dead, which makes it all the more appropriate to wear one to Teresa Talmontes Remembered. In a few short hours begins the function commemorating the fourth anniversary of your mother's death. Víctor and his wife Pamela Jean, former homecoming queen and star of the local McSorley Hot Dog commercials that make you want to puke because you know she's a sell-out vegetarian and will do anything to stand in front of the cameras, organize celebrations for the deceased: Día de los Muertos, César Chávez Day, and Teresa Talamontes Remembered. The lettering on every banner in italics. All three events take place in the Woodrow Wilson High School auditorium, where you lost your virginity to the chorus teacher. The auditorium can be decked with skulls, red United Farm Worker Union flags, or enlarged portraits of your dead mother, who's a former mayor of the town, and all you can think about during the speeches and school band recitals is Ms. Symington going down on you as you perch like a nervous pigeon on the piano bench. Since that day you have discovered that you like men, but thinking about Ms. Symington with her whitish-blonde helmet hair and pink pearl necklace still gives you a hard on. So do piano benches.

Your eyes jump as Las Cazuelas' entrance lights come on in the twilight. A wagon wheel and a piñata shaped like a burro swing from the building's eaves. You start the ignition. One time around the block, you promise yourself, and then you go in. You're anxious, not about Víctor, but about your mother—dead four years and you still carry her coffin on your shoulders. You imagine a snail, a turtle, an armadillo. Each time Teresa Talamontes Remembered comes around, you feel like the rebellious boy she criticized for being self-absorbed. You must admit she was right. You are vain, selfish, and self-centered. You only think about yourself. But who else is there to think about when you're boyfriendless, fatherless, motherless, and most of the time brotherless. You refuse to change because you want to spite her, and even with this firm conviction you can't help but wonder if it's still her power and not yours.

You make a U-turn at the traffic light and drive up to the Texaco to buy bottled water and a pack of cigarettes. The town's gas station attendants have always been high school kids with cheap shoes and tight Dickeys. You were one of them once, minus the cheap shoes because your mother was dating the manager of a Reebok outlet store at the time. White, balding, and with an irritating lisp, he was the one, your mother kept proclaiming until she found out he was gay. You could have told her that.

Inside the convenience store you feel out of place wearing a tailored J. C. Penney's suit. You opt for the generic brand of water.

You buy Benson & Hedges, menthols. You ask for matches, though you carry a goldplated monogrammed lighter in your coat. How to explain to the guy in the tacky red company shirt that the suit is borrowed and that the lighter is pilfered from the lost-and-found drawer of the hotel where you're the morning concierge.

"Hey, man, spare a smoke?" A doped-out woman with a bad perm taps your arm. She's holding the pay phone receiver with the other hand.

After tapping the box five times against your palm, you open the pack and pluck a cigarette out. You give it to her, trying to show no interest in her cocky gestures.

"Can I pay you for a ride, man?" she asks.

"I didn't drive here, honey," you tell her as you walk away and snap your fingers, "I flew in on a one-passenger broom."

"Hey, fuck you, asshole," she spits out; then adds, "Fucking faggot!"

The phone in her hand reminds you you have to turn the cell phone on. It's usually turned off because the only people who call are your desperate Internet hookups. And your brother. Now that you're aware of it, the cell feels heavy in your coat pocket, so you take it out and stuff it in the glove compartment. You don't turn it on.

You back out between the service islands, cigarette in your left hand to expel the smoke through the window, and then merge into the boulevard traffic. This was one of former Mayor Talamontes' strokes of genius: rerouting the boulevard to benefit the business district. Now there's more noise, more pollution, and a string of potholes that, once covered up, reappear overnight. To her credit, the influx of outsiders warranted the construction of a fancier hotel, which supplied you with a job after you dropped out of college. You're due for a promotion soon: evening concierge.

You could live on what your mother left you in her will, but she didn't want you to have it easy, so you get your yearly modest allowance only if you're steadily employed in her town—an odd provision, but she wanted to force you into an unrewarding life in the place you always said you hated. That's how she's getting back at you. That's how she wants to hurt you for not being Víctor since, unlike your gullible half brother, your mother figured out long ago you are just like the shoe-store boyfriend. The hickeys on your neck—man bites through and through. She always knew. She was Teresa Talamontes, mother, mayor, sage.

You've been hoarding your inheritance, living frugally until you have enough to flee and forfeit the allowance, which will automatically be given to your half brother, who waits patiently for you to give up on the Caliente Valley and leave. In another time, you might have called this battle a "stare down." Your brother wouldn't, because he always loses such a duel. He's going to lose this one as well. You will lend him the money, but only if he gives you a job once he makes mayor. You can already see your future: a bogus office for a dummy adviser who spends most of the term sipping margaritas in Acapulco. Technically, you'll remain employed in your mother's town. You grin at your own cleverness. Just as quickly you lament that you're not as good a driver as you are a scheming bitch.

You've never mastered two driving maneuvers: parallel parking and cutting off other drivers. Instead of interrupting the steady flow in the next lane to make a left into Las Cazuelas, you decide to keep going, make a right at the next light, turn the car around, and then take the left turn arrow back down the boulevard. You don't count on the pedestrians at the intersection, especially not the old lady in a pink sweat suit that makes her look like a giant bottle of Pepto Bismol. You put your cigarette out in the panel ash-tray. Pepto Bismol is going to take her time across, even though you give her an anxious stare through the windshield. The light changes to red, but you manage to make your turn so you lift the curse you've placed on Pepto Bismol: that she will trip at the next curb and break her dentures.

The detour runs smoothly, but just before you reach the parking lot entrance, two cars down a van with engine trouble brings your lane to a stop. You take this as a sign. You can't spot your brother's car from where you're sitting and the lights to the restaurant entrance look brighter. You're now ten minutes late. Between jerks of the car moving forward, you could grab the cell phone out of the glove compartment, call him to tell him you're within spitting distance, but you've never been that nimble, you don't want to risk a distraction, an accident, another point on your pathetic driving record. You can't afford a jump in your insurance. Excuses, excuses, you just don't want to call him, that's all.

The male passenger in the car to your left takes a good long look at you before the car speeds up and leaves you comparing him to Guillermo, a former lover: similar stubby nose, similar cleft on the chin. Maybe they're related. They had to be: Guillermo came in and out of your life just as quickly, carried off by another pretty face. Currently boyfriendless, you spend too much time fending off the drunken patrons at the hotel, male and female. At first you found it flattering, but with time you realized they found you convenient. Only once did you consider accepting an offer, but the handsome man had squeezed in the come-on between a request for a wake-up call and a query on late-night food service hours, so in the end you politely declined.

In the station wagon in front of you, a young boy rides in the back seat. He picks his nose staring at you. Behind him, another child throws an object at his head; the boy, undaunted, simply moves to the side and continues to pick his nose.

That's nothing like the times you struck your brother from behind, when he thought he was safe—pardoned from your longing to attack. Patience is your revenge tactic. You're the seasoned predator, stalking your prey until the timing's right for the kill. You waited an entire week before you reminded Víctor of the damage to your Spirograph: he had launched the plastic drawing wheels out the window of the car, and they flew into the road in the path of old trucks and Memo's ice cream wagon. Seven days later Víctor was snacking with the refrigerator door open. His neck smooth and brown—exposed. You swung your fist so hard he crashed into the metal compartment dividers, knocking down the lettuce, the ripe tomatoes, and those rum cherry chocolates your mother served up at her council meetings. Supine on the linoleum, Víctor turned blue, his mouth covered in melted chocolate. You knelt down and stuck your fingers down his mouth but you couldn't get at the slippery lump. You envisioned his burial, the house in mourning, and then the clouds opening for the world that was now yours alone. But there was no death, no grief and no new sky, because Víctor dug the piece of chocolate out of his throat himself. Víctor would do that—be his own hero just to piss you off.

Víctor should have never lived in the first place. You knew the story of the premature birth, the lengthy postpartum hospitalization, and the subsequent revelation that his father was that celebrated plastic surgeon to the aging movie stars. Víctor doesn't like to mention his father, but neither will he refuse the money that comes his way once in a blue moon. Your father, on the other hand, was the guy who played Joseph at the Pastorela, the year your mother played Mary. You were conceived during an uncontrollable urge behind the manger, consummated with your parents still in costume. Your mother told the story without a hint of nostalgia the day you turned fifteen and finally confronted her about your father, whom you've never met. "Ours was just a fuck," she declared. Always aiming between the eyes, she explained that the quickie with the father of Christ is also why she named you Jesse.

Víctor will say that your coming out is all part of some plot to dampen his small-fry political career. He's right of course, but nothing can stop him from getting elected mayor. At twenty-five he's the youngest executive board member on both the Town Council and Latinos Unidos. The town cherishes the Talamontes name. When Teresa Talamontes died of an aneurysm while in office, she became an instant saint. For the next four years, the town council groomed Víctor, the former high school football star and present high school football coach. The town wants a Talamontes in office again. Those were the days of family values, ethnic pride, bilingualism, and public service. You were never considered a worthy candidate. You left home and majored in philosophy and minored in French. After five years you dropped out, far from achieving the necessary credits toward a degree.

You like Machiavelli. You dislike Socrates. You can understand Baudelaire titles but not poems. You can French kiss and ménage à trois. You can hear your mother's voice declare: "And so what? How is any of that going to change the lives of the people in this community?" You promised your mother you would return home and do something useful for a change, but you stayed away until her death and that will with its hard-edged condition—her final kick in the groin because she wanted you to admit defeat, to concede that she was always right and that you should have done something more noble like becoming a politician and marrying your high school sweetheart. Yours was really Jimmy Peña and not the girl you took to the prom, so your mother's plan wouldn't have worked out either. In the meantime Víctor has been taking care of himself. He's a winner and the son of a prominent citizen from Palm Springs, who watches over him from a distance. Your father was a bit player in a mystery play. You don't even know his real name.

The van with engine trouble is pushed aside to the curb and the two cars in front of you switch lanes, so you quickly move forward and into the parking lot. When you finally enter the restaurant, you rush up to a podium decked in green, white, and red. Nearly out of breath, you tell the hostess, an awkward white girl in a señorita outfit, "I'm late for a reservation, but my date might still be here. Talamontes?"

You crane your neck to look around the crowded room while the young woman checks her reservation book.

"He was here," she tells you, "but he said he was stood up. I'm so sorry."

Your look of anguish is hard to disguise. She quickly adds, "But I assure you your date didn't look that upset. Don't worry, everything will turn out fine."

You stare into her eyes. They're hazel. She smiles. She's young and pretty, probably funding her tuition at the junior college. You decide not to tell her that Víctor is your brother and not really your date. You will let her keep the satisfaction of having offered a total stranger, a gay man, compassion and understanding.

To thank her, you remove the cempasúchil from your lapel and hand it to her. She blushes as she takes it. Her smile widens. You want to kiss it. You want to show up to Teresa Talamontes Remembered, unconditionally, with your birthmarks alive with the patterns of happier times.

Once in the car you dig out the cell phone and turn it on: Víctor didn't bother with a message, which means he's really pissed. But Lewis from Cathedral City—the guy who drives an old beat-up convertible that he's been wanting to fix up for the last ten years—he left two.

When you finally arrive at the Wilson High auditorium, your mother's blown-up portraits stir the bile in your stomach. You look like her; you're as beautiful as she, but no matter how you move across the room you know she's watching over Víctor, the champion and true successor of her energy and drive. Her darker side is all yours; the misery of her loneliness, of crappy romances and loser boyfriends, belongs to you. You stand at the cold wings ready to push out your face into the light for Víctor to see you. You want to show Víctor your malicious moons, no different from your mother's, but hers have been enlarged to look like bullet holes.

Víctor's wife comes up behind you and places her hand on your shoulder. Pamela Jean's touch is heavy with pride. The glaring lights blind you as your half brother takes center stage to test the sound system. You can't help but feel the bottom of your bitter heart grow suddenly warm. Maybe it's Pamela Jean's breath thawing the left side of your face, but in that moment you make up your mind to disappear after all, to spin your moons out of their axes and shift your life into a new direction. The tension between you and your dead mother is not really Víctor's fault. Víctor is your little brother, caught in the merciless crossfire. And soon your little brother will be mayor, all adult and professional.

You think maybe it's time you grew up as well. More importantly, you think it's time to bury the dead, to leave, to live and let live. But then Víctor turns his head. He winks at Pamela Jean and then scowls accusingly at you, narrowing his eyes in that all too familiar way that says: "Wait, you just you wait, Jesse, I'm going to get you back." And suddenly the order of things becomes clear again. You look down at your watch. Your mother has been dead four years and five days—your prison term and counting. Critical decisions are still being made: pardons denied and sentences extended.

Víctor begins to mumble a few words of his speech at the podium, his shoulders squared and back straight as a surfboard, as if at any moment someone's going to step up to the stage and take his photograph for posterity. He will remain that way regardless, because in a few hours the auditorium will fill with people, the evening will settle into the warmth of a communal nostalgia, and you will sit slumped on the sidelines as blank and expressionless as your dead mother's picture. In the meantime you too begin to rehearse your words: *Víctor, kiss my faggoty brown ass.* In the meantime both of your lives continue to be fucked.

Cactus Flower

Going from the main road to the wooden shack takes about a forty-minute walk through the desert. Though the desert is flat and Rolando thinks he can see for miles into the faded blue horizon, the shack remains invisible until it shoots upward suddenly from the ground, becoming distinguishable from the clumps of golden tumbleweeds and the sand hill leading up the ravine, everything blanketed by the brightness of the sun. The outer leaves of the fresh head of lettuce he brings from the fields wilt in his oily fingers. He thinks about his toes shrinking back from the steel-tipped boots, his scrotum pulling away from his sticky underwear. The smell of dirt rises pure off the ground as if there weren't any other human around. Suddenly his hand trembles at the thought of an empty shack, of nobody inside to open the door for him and take the lettuce from his hands, of no one to gasp in gratitude to assure him that, despite the journey through the sweltering heat, the leaves at the center are cool and crisp. His fears dissipate with the presence of his wife, Mirinda, standing at the doorway, still as a cactus flower in her diaphanous white blouse, which she wears not so he can peek at her small white bra or at the pudgy abdomen he likes to grab while she's washing her hair bent over a bucket of water. She wears it, she tells him, to let the faintest breeze blow on her blouse, so she can spread her arms and cool her sweaty undersides. She's posing that way now, arms outstretched, but this far back it's hard to tell if it's the desert breeze coming her way or if she's greeting him. He looks forward to tonight when they'll feed each other lettuce leaves and devour the moisture as slowly as caterpillars, when they will play the question-and-answer game. Suddenly his eyes clamp shut, victims to the beads of sweat mixed into the dust he carries on his face from the fields, giving the sweat a more powerful sting. He rubs his eyes with the sleeve of the blue flannel shirt. The smooth cloth contrasts sharply with the coarse skin of his dark hand. Out of focus, he tries to reclaim the image of his wife in her white blouse and then saddens, realizing that Mirinda wasn't standing at the entrance to the shack because the door is shut. The padlock hangs heavy like a heart gone solid and cold. But that's when the rose on his shoulder grows warm—the tattoo with a banner wrapped around the thorny stem. He had her name inked in red, like the petals of the rose, so that the letters were visible on his dark skin, so that she could see that she was permanently needled into his body, never to be erased again.

What's a kiss?
The sound loneliness makes when it dies.

The candle flame twitches violently, threatening to leave him blind. The weather changed during his nap and he woke up surprised in the dark. The wind hurls small stones against the wooden walls and bumps the window shutters repeatedly. Only when the wind blows is Rolando painfully aware of the imperfections in the small one-room home he built for himself in the middle of the desert, what the residents of the nearby town call "el dompe" because they drop off their useless vinyl couches and urine-stained mattresses into the nearby ravine.

The whistling and hissing of the dust storm outside disrupt his concentration so he sits without a word in his throat, slurping the Campbell's soup as loudly as possible to convince himself that the silence the wind has forced on him has not upset his late-evening meal. Mirinda remains expressionless, staring across the table at the way his large hand holds the tin spoon too delicately, as if she knows he's scooping properly to please her. Even with the dim light she's beautiful, her features as sharp and smooth as mariposa lily petals. The shadows make her face thin out, grow distant as a portrait; but the flickering flame dancing gracefully in the deep ebony of her eyes keeps her within reach. She is tangible and touchable like before. She has reappeared again to disregard the shadows as they flutter wildly like moths above her head. If the shadows flee they will take her with them. But until then the play of light against dark soothes him giving him this gift, this light, this woman who said she was going to leave him but who hasn't left completely. Forgotten are the elbow cramp, the stiff neck and the aching of shoulder blades. He has the urge to find the pretty marigolds he promised her when she agreed to follow him here to this desolate place, far from the run-down trailer camps and low-income housing projects where beauty like hers withers and dies. No, instead they are closer to the ground they left behind in the deserts of Chihuahua, a space so large it is like living inside breath itself. The peaceful evenings are long and familiar, blooming with stars. Stars love Mirinda so much they confuse her for the moon and crown her head. Suddenly the wind breaks in and snuffs the candle out. Mirinda disappears. He wants to kneel and ask her to forgive him for those pretty marigolds. The wind roars. He keeps quiet knowing that his plea is weak in such a wind and will remain unheard.

What is night, Rolando?
Night is the sky keeping its mouth closed.
And the moon?
The moon is the dreams of the dead pressed against the thoughts of the living.
Is that how we will stay together if I should die?
You will not die, Mirinda. The earth always brings its flowers back because it doesn't want to see them gone forever.
And you will love me forever also?
I will love you as if I were the marrow in your bones, and like the blood caressing every inch of you from within. I'm the center of everything—your heart, this bed, the shack, the desert. Without me your world will collapse.
But what if it's you who leaves me first?

I will never leave you because I'm the center of everything. Without me your world will collapse.

Then let's keep the world intact. And if—

There is no if.

And when . . .

When is out of reach, like those shadows and the stars.

And the wind.

No, not the wind. The wind is the grief of both the living and the dead. It's always pushing us back though we can't push it away. Do you want to sleep now, Mirinda?

Not yet. I want to memorize your poetry and recite it over and over again the next day, while you're gone, while I wait, while the sun burns holes into the earth like graves.

The sun is sky spilling the secrets of the living.

And the dead?

The dead get to keep theirs and at night they show them proudly like tattoos. We call them stars.

The wind grows stronger when he rises at four in the morning to pack his lunch and set off on his forty-minute trek back to the road where the bus picks him up to deliver him to the lettuce fields. When he opens the door the moonlight bursts in, lighting the wooden table, the tiny unmade bed with the yellow faded sheets, the gas-tank stove, and Mirinda's white dresser. The looking glass Rolando gave her stares out the door, confronting the moon with its own light. He squints at the glare, grabs his denim jacket, and tries to find the stone silhouette of his wife standing near the darkest corner. He shuffles out swiftly and doesn't catch a glimpse of her. At dawn the desert is cold. He shivers at the thought of the weary march home after work. Red flashlight in hand, he walks behind the shack, bends over the broken-down Pinto to check for damage on the windshield. The green paint looks clean, smooth as skin, so he rubs his hand across it then draws back quickly when a nettle on the surface stings his thumb. Suddenly he's alarmed to be outside. The landscape of desert rocks and manzanita patches appears shrunken, pulled in toward the shack, which becomes its dead center. He feels trapped, like the snowman in the glass bubble Mirinda enjoys shaking at the swap meet to watch the tiny white particles drop. For him the particles strike sideways, strike hard. He moves quickly back around inside, exchanges the jacket for a thicker coat and grabs the brown paper sack, tightening the grip to remind himself how many flour tacos he will have for lunch. He steps out and shuts the door. The padlock snaps. He wishes to retreat, crawl beneath the yellow faded sheets, which will always smell of Mirinda's nape, of a strong sunlight filtered in through the dampness of her long black hair. He walks a few paces forward, hesitating because there's something he forgot. He's afraid to turn around, afraid that when he looks the shack will have vanished and he will find himself alone and vulnerable as the snowman or the palo verde that looks twice as solitary at night. He keeps on walking, sensing his distance from his home, a length that doubles when he thinks that Mirinda's no longer inside rubbing delicate perfume into her earlobes so that any sound she hears is savory and sweet. Mirinda, savory and sweet, desires no other earring over her lobe than the pressure of his mouth and lips nibbling nibbling nibbling on the flower-scented skin above her jaw. He dares to grin; he's compelled to whistle. He remembers that he didn't eat the lettuce.

Why do we laugh?
To wallpaper the rooms we will leave behind for others.

Rolando doesn't wait long for the bus. It's an old school bus painted over in white with the agricultural company's name on both sides. He doesn't have to see it to know it's coming: the muffler backfiring all the way down the road. In the early mornings the sloppy paint job looks clean until the bus stops in front of him and the old yellow coat shows through the wild strokes of white. The doors squeak open and the fat driver in a red plaid shirt greets him with a nod of the head, shifting into gear before Rolando finds a seat. Rolando paces reluctantly toward the space next to Sarita Mendoza, who wears a sweatshirt with words in English that neither of them can read. She likes to save a place for him near the front. Before he takes a seat, Rolando nods at the other lettuce pickers. He wants to relax for the next twenty minutes until he arrives at the fields. He wants to tilt his head back and listen to the small transistor radio don Carlos behind him is holding. But Sarita Mendoza wants to talk. She likes asking questions. She asks about his wife because she suspects Mirinda doesn't really exist. She accuses him of lying to keep her from making a match for him with one of her daughters. Today she invites Rolando and his wife to a family bautismo. He politely refuses. She asks why. The glassy look of her eye makes him nervous. The bus hits a bump on the road and he hears the blades of the short-handle hoes rattle in the back. He wants to look down at the oval blister beginning to callus on his right palm. He wants to pick at it but doesn't, imagining a more intense pain against his hand as he thrusts the hoe into the ground. Instead he traces Sarita Mendoza's chapped lips, smiles, and tells her he'll be celebrating his third-year anniversary this weekend. She jokingly says he's a liar. Rolando laughs with her, trying to think up an answer in case she asks where he's taking his wife to celebrate. She asks. He still hasn't thought of anything so he simply says it's up to Mirinda. Can Mirinda travel to México? Sarita Mendoza leaves her mouth open; the dry lips are cracked at the corners. He answers no, though he should have said yes because now Sarita Mendoza says he should have married a woman with papers. All of her daughters have their documents in order and they can all work in the fields, cook in the kitchen, and perform both chores in bed. Rolando shakes his head. He should try to stop by the bautismo anyway, she suggests, since she's never met this mysterious woman he keeps hidden away in "el dompe." She's heard so much about Mirinda she's willing to wear out her old huaraches on a trip to the middle of the desert just to meet her. And if there isn't anyone there it won't matter because she'll bring one of her daughters along just in case. Rolando looks away, embarrassed. He watches his cut lip grin on the dirty window. He didn't comb his hair. He forgot his baseball cap to protect his head. The red bandanna in his back pocket has been used on his nose all week.

He wants to correct Sarita Mendoza and tell her she's heard very little about Mirinda, that woman, that goddess, that light. Mirinda, passion and appetite, can eat a whole coconut by herself, using up an entire afternoon with a dozen limes and a bowl of rock salt by her side while his heartbeat races to compete with that fervor she has for breaking the shell with her hands— a fever that finally peaks with him taking her fingers in his mouth and pressing his tongue beneath her nails to suck at the salty juice. Mirinda, fury and fire, becomes as silky as her sleeping gown when he braids his limbs into hers, sweating off the humidity from their skins, surrendering themselves like cactus owls on that tiny bed that prompts them toward one another no matter what direction they stretch. Mirinda can touch every place on him at once and make each place jump twice. Mirinda is more than a woman, more than a wife—she took his body in her fleshy arms exactly three years ago and she still holds him there, playing that question-and-answer game that's but another way for them to dance.

What's an echo, Rolando?
An echo is the shadow of the voice. It reveals the truth beneath the lies that people tell.
What are lies?
The black wasps of the throat.

And then that time she didn't ask, she said. She said she was going to leave him, she said she was going to let their world collapse. So he didn't let her leave, not entirely, taking her neck in his hands and widening her mouth until she burst into the air like a puff of dandelion seeds, an explosion of stars in the sky, an outbreak of marigolds. Such beautiful flowers.

He's dizzy. Sarita Mendoza gazes at him and he blushes. When the bus finally stops she leaps up and hurries to the back, her gray sweatshirt coming up on her stomach. She wants to get a good hoe, one with a clean sharp blade that won't give her trouble when she's digging into the ground. The rest of the workers scurry right behind her. Everyone hops off through the emergency exit door.

Rolando looks past the window and at the lettuce fields, the heads looking cool and bright. Beyond the lettuce fields are the grape fields, and next to them sit the onion fields, and the orchards rise just behind them, all of them blossoming so majestically in the desert. He works this land year after year, intimate with its furrows and soils, yet he despises it for breaking his body down, for keeping him alive and slowly draining all that strength. He imagines returning the following season when the fields are lush and ripe again, displaying no evidence that he ever touched them. He imagines Mirinda, buried beneath the broken-down Pinto, unable to comb her long black hair or darken her plucked eyebrows slim as marigold stems or redden those fleshy points in the middle of her upper lip. She left her reflection behind in the looking glass. She returns to the desert to reclaim it and be whole again, and then she thins out into air to become that void he sees when he holds up her mirror. When the white-haired foreman taps on the window, Rolando slowly rises from the seat, unashamed to be the last off the bus. The air is chilly and smells of soil freshly watered: the scent of cool lettuce lifts from the ground.

On the other side of the road lies the barren desert. At the other end of the desert Mirinda's ghost waits patiently inside the tiny shack. In the afternoon he will step inside and breathe her scent of dusty wood. Mirinda will respond with the excitement of the rusty hinges of her tomb.

Plums

Nadie me quiere . . . Nadie me quiere . . . Nadie me quiere . . .

"Is that from a song?" Abi wonders out loud, and the sound of his voice makes an echo because there's nothing much inside the motel bathroom except for the tub, the lukewarm water, his body dumped inside, a thawed iceman, naked, dark and skin-and-bones repulsive. The radio plays a slow tune in the next unit but the memory of the verse isn't triggered by the music. Then it must be from one of his mother's Portuguese soap operas dubbed into Spanish—a sentimental line he overheard while doing his homework on the kitchen table as his mother snuck a peek at the TV. Since they've been seized by religious fervor, his parents have given up on guilty pleasures, including sex perhaps, since no sound save the murmur of prayer emanated from their room at night. But Abi suspects that while his mother stays behind to snatch a glimpse of a soap, his father catches up with his drinking buddies at the other end of the housing project, nursing cans of Coors out of brown paper bags.

Abi runs his fingers over his wet torso while floating stiffly in the water. His lanky arms reach his shoulder blades without effort. His shins knock against the faucet because he's too tall for the tub. To submerge his head he has to let his knees rise like a pair of broken masts on a sinking ship. As he blows out his breath to release a stream of bubbles he imagines sailors drowning, their beautiful, muscular bodies washing ashore weeks later, and eyes on the beach looking on with that sadness that comes to a face when it sees such loss—or waste. He has caught his own mother staring at him that way while she's ironing in the corner of the room and he's flipping through magazines, pausing to gaze at the men.

The muffled noise of the radio in the next unit encroaches on the quiet he anticipated renting a motel room for the night while his parents attend a Baptist retreat in Cherry Valley where, despite the name, the hills grow almond trees. The bathtub at home isn't quite like this: cold and anonymous, yet public somehow, the basin collecting imprints of bodies, layers of impressions betraying no single occupant but holding an orgy of a history, enough to arouse him.

Abi feels an odd sense of safety knowing he's within other bodies as he escapes to the Palm Tree Motel. The first time, he checked in two units down. The rooms are identical: towels worn thin, carpet stained, and a mattress too large for the bed frame.

When Abi stands in the tub, the water sloshes louder than he expected. The radio next door goes off, pushed out by the unapologetic moaning that sounds like two women. Anything goes in the Palm Tree Motel. Usually inhibitions.

Now relaxed, he dries himself and slips into the bed. The covers feel cool and cozy. And as he surrenders to the flatness of the mattress, he starts to get sleepy.

Outside, the occasional car pulls into the parking lot. Most of the guests arrive on foot to the Palm Tree Motel, walked over by the prostitutes from the bar down the road. The rates come cheap enough that even the farmworkers can splurge on a bed to fuck intoxicated and then sleep it off. Abi prefers the rooms that face the road. The rooms in the back, the ones the prostitutes like to use, have windows that look toward the housing project where Abi lives with his parents. Everybody knows about the shadows showing through the curtains of the Palm Tree Motel.

Right now his parents are eighty miles away, making lemonade and talking about the Lord over yellow paperback Bibles. When they got their prayer meeting started in the living room, Abi snuck into their bedroom to pick a few twenties from his mother's purse before they left. If she has noticed the missing bills she has never mentioned it. Abi likes to believe she's letting him get away with it on purpose, a passive defiance to this lifestyle she recently adopted to keep his father appeased.

Why is it that the worst of sinners flip their coin over to become the most self-righteous of preachers? Only once did his father convince him to come down to the tent and listen to the witnessing for God. One after another they confessed their sordid pasts—junkies, prostitutes, drug dealers, adulterers, homosexuals—and then they proclaimed their new mission in life: to keep anyone from making the same mistakes they made. How unfair, Abi thinks, to criticize the fun once they've had theirs.

Since his parents are gone during his escape to the other side of the boulevard, Abi doesn't have to hear the sermon about skipping school and staying out late. His father will be spared having to scold his only child, and also the exasperation of not beating him the way he used to, before the Baptists. Abi can take his time yearning for Gilberto, his make-believe lover, fantasy boyfriend, and the conquest of the decade he would throw his hands into the fire for. Indeed, his god. He imagines his head against Gilberto's tight torso, his warm breath drying the wet hairs on Gilberto's sternum. And when Abi tries to give him a hickey on that muscle-swollen chest, Gilberto will nudge him away with a heavy hand and a sleepy warning: "No plums."

Plums. Such a sweet disguise for a love bite.

A knock at the door startles Abi out of daydream. He jumps up and looks through the cloudy peephole and sees a pair of thick black frames in front of two large, round eyes—the new motel clerk. Abi opens the door a few inches.

"Is there a problem?" Abi asks. He conceals his naked body behind it. He should have spoken through the thin door.

"I'm sorry to bother you, sir," the clerk says. Abi feels awkward being addressed as "sir" by someone he went to high school with. The clerk's nametag reads Tony. Abi's sure his name's Raúl, though in high school everyone called him Toadface. There's no mistaking those thick black frames or the way they made Toadface's pupils bubble out like the plastic eyes on a cheap doll.

"I thought you might need something?" the clerk says, hesitantly.

Abi blushes. The clerk has caught on to the strange new boarder who locks himself in the room without company. Bottle-bottom glasses or not, he apparently notices plenty.

"No," Abi answers softly. "I'm all right." He begins to shut the door, but the clerk blocks the opening with his hand. Against the side of the door, the clerk's fingers are just inches away from Abi's face. The clerk wears too much cologne.

"Because I can help if you have a problem," the clerk offers.

Abi sizes up the clerk from the dirty mat of hair to the worn hiking shoes. Tony-Raúl will never be cute in that charming way high school geeks grow into geeky men. But he likes Abi. Abi can sense it, sense the watering beneath the tongue. This instinct is what allows Abi to pick the man out of a crowd who will follow him, flirt with him, and court him. Many will look, even tease or antagonize, but a select few will make the effort to keep an eye out and find the right moment to proposition him.

"Can we meet at the motel," Abi will say, and he doesn't need to explain which one or when they should meet. "It's more private," Abi will add, so that they know he means pleasure, not business like the prostitutes. And once they say yes, everything else is detail.

"Aren't you afraid of leaving that front desk all alone?" Abi asks the clerk, coyly.

The clerk turns and mumbles under his breath. Behind him the road looks pitch black and empty.

Abi feels sorry for him suddenly, or perhaps ashamed at how easy it is to have the upper hand. The clerk is no match for him, and no fun. "If I ever need help," Abi says, "I'll remember you." He winks.

Abi shuts the door and climbs into bed again. The cool air has chilled him and cleared his lungs of the stale scent of cigarettes that infuses the carpet. For the rest of the night no one'll come knock on the motel room door. Yet Abi imagines Gilberto's touch with one hand pressing firmly against his skin, the other stroking him to orgasm. Once sated, he falls asleep easily beneath the sheets.

When Abi comes home the next morning he's shocked to see his bedroom window broken. He rushes to the entrance.

"Nobody took anything," a croupy voice says softly. Don Jorge balances himself on a cane whose tip pierces the lawn. "It wasn't a robbery. Some kids threw a brick in there out of mischief. They must have seen the apartment empty all night."

Abi winces at the indirect accusation and walks inside without responding. What worries him is how to explain the damage to his parents. Lying is out of the question with that old owl next door that will limp over and gladly repeat his theory.

The apartment's cold. In the bedroom Abi discovers that a brick has indeed been thrown through the window. Don Jorge has already investigated, probably shoving the curtains aside with his cane for a better look. The shards of glass are scattered across his bed and sparkle on the carpet. A vacuum isn't going to suck up all the miniscule grains of glass. Abi imagines himself getting pricked months from now as he steps down drowsily from bed in the morning.

He drops the larger pieces of glass into the trashcan, and then searches for the duct tape in his father's toolbox. A piece of cardboard will have to do for a weather seal. He's about to explore the dumpster at the corner when don Jorge appears with a collapsed cardboard box in his hand.

"You have to make sure it's big and thick enough," he says. "Or else the crickets will crawl in and they'll keep your parents up all night."

Abi stares at the old man in disbelief. He takes the cardboard. "Thank you. I'll make sure this holds back the crickets," he says with a smirk on his face.

"Kids nowadays," don Jorge begins to preach from behind the pulpit of his cane. "No respect. They stay out all hours of the night and behave like criminals."

Abi covers up the old man's voice with the ripping and tearing of the duct tape. He calculates the size neatly, and as he fits the cardboard over the window, don Jorge uses the tip of his cane to hold it in place as Abi applies more tape.

"Thank you," Abi says sheepishly when he completes the task. Don Jorge walks away.

"Don Jorge," Abi calls. Don Jorge turns around with a concerned look on his wrinkled face. "Could you not tell my parents I wasn't here last night?" Abi regrets the question the moment it leaves his mouth. He imagines don Jorge pinning it to the earth with the sharp end of his cane.

Don Jorge stands up straight and glares at Abi. After a moment of self-righteous silence, the old man walks away, clearing his throat and spitting a thick body of phlegm onto the grass. The gesture is obscene, as if it was meant for Abi's face.

Abi walks into the apartment with the roll of duct tape tight around his fist. Hungry, he throws a few bananas and milk into the blender. He doesn't bother to measure the vitamin powder.

As he presses the blend button, Abi pictures Gilberto's mousy wife sweeping the corners of their living room. He has only seen her a few times hanging the laundry out on the clothesline, and she can't be any younger than his mother. Even so he felt slightly jealous as he walked by while she was pinning up a pair of faded jeans that Gilberto wore to work.

As he downs the vitamin milkshake directly from the blender's glass jar, the silver blades at the bottom ascend into view as he drinks the last ounces of the thick liquid.

Gilberto showers at five-thirty and eats his dinner promptly at six o'clock. Afterwards he zones off, shirtless and stunning as a centerfold, watching television on that awful green couch that's visible from the payphone. Abi knows his facts; he's been observing diligently for weeks.

In the phone booth, Abi turns his back to the building so that no one suspects he's there to spy on the residents of apartment 344. There's always too much traffic on this street since it leads to the west exit of the housing project, and the phone booth sits next to the dumpster at the corner of the largest patch of grass, which the neighborhood kids use as a park. When a game of soccer gets going, the old men pour out because now they've got something to look at while they drink their beers in the afternoon.

There's not much activity going on today, except for the Jehovah's Witnesses making their usual rounds. Not one of the men is worth staring at, so Abi turns back to his surveillance. Movement. The wife walks out through the kitchen door, a trash bag in one hand. Abi holds the receiver, following the woman's path from the building to the dumpster. When she comes near enough for Abi to detect the smell of her body lotion, he's stunned to discover a bruise on her chin. For a brief second he feels for her because her father must beat her also, but then he realizes that she doesn't live with her father. She lives with Gilberto. She flings the trash bag into the dumpster, her eyes looking downcast and sullen. As she walks away, a sense of shame comes over Abi. All this time he never noticed any confrontation or even a gesture of violence. He must not have been looking closely enough.

A knock on the glass startles him. A man in a blue shirt with the buttons undone nods as if to ask him how long he's going to hold up the phone. Abi lifts a finger, and that appeases the man. He lights a cigarette and looks out the opposite direction. Abi considers the shape of the man—wide hips, wide shoulders, the neck sunburned, a few long back hairs poking up above the collar. He gauges the man to be in his late thirties, maybe early forties, though it's difficult to tell in men who work in the fields. Their skins wear out so quickly.

"All yours," Abi announces to the man as he steps out of the phone booth.

The man looks curiously at Abi. Abi knows that look of recognition, so he decides to be a little coy. He smiles at the man, brings up one hand as if he's brushing his hair behind his ears.

"It's a nice afternoon, isn't it?" Abi says. He knows he's risking an ass-kicking if this man becomes insulted or outraged at the bold flirtation. But he's also gambling for that rendezvous he's always wanted to have with one of these men at the housing project.

The man ignores Abi's solicitation and steps into the phone booth, digging into his pockets for change. Abi feels strangely unfulfilled, as if he has been cheated out of something. Maybe the man will come around once he's done with his phone call. Maybe this is just the first step, the initial exchange, which is always too subtle. He was still waiting for Gilberto to take the next step, ever since he bumped into him at the convenience store down the road. Gilberto, gorgeous inside his beige work shirt with a nametag stitched to the pocket, accidentally backed into him in line.

"Excuse me," Gilberto had said, though Abi had been trailing him all along. And Gilberto had finally made contact, after Abi stepped forward to catch a whiff of his scent. Their eyes had met, and one of these days Gilberto would notice him at the phone booth at the corner and remember him.

Abi walks away. The curtains of apartment 344 have been drawn and the man on the phone has completely forgotten that there's a young man outside waiting to give him discreet instructions to the Palm Tree Motel.

Abi decides to head for the motel again anyway. At worst, he will spend another peaceful night in a room with no television, only a clock radio with bad reception bolted down to a nightstand. A brisk walk through an empty lot brings Abi to the booth that passes for a registration desk. Tony-Raúl stands frozen inside as usual as Abi makes his way toward him.

"Good evening," Abi says.

Tony-Raúl stutters a "Good evening, sir" back. Since Abi qualifies as a regular client now, he has only to fill out his name and pay the fee. "Miguel Santos," he signs at the bottom. His father's name. When Abi looks up again, the clerk meets his eyes with a fixed gaze and he pushes the room key automatically through the small opening above the counter. As Abi begins to move away, he feels a sudden urge to address the clerk.

"You used to go to Indio High, right?"

The clerk stares at Abi through his thick glasses and gives no response. "A few years back?" Abi adds. At this point he regrets having said anything. A HELP WANTED sign is taped to the inside of the glass.

"Yes," Tony-Raúl finally mumbles.

Abi smiles uneasily. "I thought I remembered you from somewhere." He pretends to strain to read the nametag.

The clerk covers it up. "Raúl. We're not allowed to use our real names here," he explains.

"Neither are we," Abi says in a feeble attempt at a joke.

"Math class," Tony-Raúl says in a flat tone.

Abi is suddenly annoyed by the clerk, who is cold, inanimate, and without passion. Abi grants him permission to speak to him on more familiar terms, and now the clerk has stopped calling him "sir."

"Yes, math class," Abi agrees.

The long silence that follows only confirms for Abi that they have nothing in common. Thankfully, a prostitute and her drunken john stumble through the empty lot, giggling like a pair of girls.

"Well, have a good night," Abi says as he rushes off with the key in his hand. He waves behind him only as an afterthought.

After about an hour of pacing to and from the bathroom mirror to pick at the pimple on his cheek, Abi admits to himself that he actually came back for Tony-Raúl, who hasn't even bothered to come knocking. So he decides on another long bath. He can make a habit of it. He catalogues in his mind the supplies he'll need: bubble soap, bath beads, a variety of candles, scented oil. A bath wouldn't be the same at home. He imagines a cold draft sneaking in through the patched-up window of his bedroom and engulfing the votive candles, the large crucifix in the living room, and the chalk statues of saints. His mother hadn't given up on the Catholic relics when she became a Baptist.

The water in the bath isn't coming out hot, only tepid. The tub is chipped and rusty on the edge of the basin.

Abi removes his clothes and looks at himself in the cloudy mirror. He's dark-skinned, and plums will be difficult to find on his body. The area around his nipples is slightly sore from his pinching. Was it ever possible that his mother once knew the gratifying evidence of his father's hungry mouth on her? There certainly used to be an animal in his father before he found religion. He used to be a voracious eater and drinker and disciplinarian. He must have been a voracious lover as well. Did his mother miss that animal as much as Abi did? Listening to their sex used to make him feel grounded, safe. Feeling pain used to make him feel alive. Since both these activities have ceased altogether, Abi has the strange sensation that he's sleeping among the dead.

Once the water turns cold in the tub, Abi moves to the bed. He feels freedom there as well. Perhaps it's the size—a king, not a twin like his bed at home. He slips under the covers in the nude. Each time his penis rubs against the sheet it grows semi-erect. How he longs for Gilberto. How he longs for the man at the phone booth.

When the weak knock on the door finally comes, Abi jumps out of bed, unable to contain his excitement. This time he pulls on his boxer shorts and opens the door so that the clerk has a full view of his body.

"Abismael?" Tony-Raúl says.

At first Abi is flattered that the clerk remembers his name, though maybe the guy merely combed through an old yearbook to stumble upon the portrait of Abi in a suit that made him look as respectable as a Jehovah's Witness. This had pleased his father to no end. A framed 8x10 stares out in the living room, like a prop for his parents' church cronies to look at with approval when they come over for a prayer meeting.

"I'm off for the night," the clerk stammers, his backpack dangling off his shoulder. "I came to check in on you before I drove home."

Abi chuckles. "Would you like to come in?" he asks.

Of course geekos like Tony-R come prepared. You couldn't surprise them with a snowstorm in the middle of summer because they'd pull a down jacket out of their backpacks. When Abi decides to take stock of the backpack's contents Tony-R doesn't even flinch. Abi pulls out a small bottle of cheap vodka, a traveling chess board, a couple of Japanimé graphic novels, a CD walkman, a pack of cigarettes, a lighter, five burned CDs (none of them labeled), mints, batteries (both triple A and double A), a black notebook with doodles and scribbles, a pocketknife, a computer disk, a dog-eared copy of *Zen and the Art of Motorcycle Maintenance*, a pair of argyle socks, a condom, three packs of gum, an orange and a pen labeled Palm Tree Motel.

"How come there are no pens in the rooms?" Abi asks as he tosses the orange to Tony-R. He opens the vodka and takes a swig, grimacing as he swallows. "I mean, TVs, sure. No one comes here to watch television. But no fucking pens? People need to write shit down, you know."

Tony-R sets the orange down on the lamp table. They are both sitting on the floor with the backpack between them

"And relax," Abi says. "Take your shoes off. Unbutton your shirt."

When Tony-R removes his white dress shirt his gut comes popping out and settles on his lap. Abi appreciates that he doesn't suck it in. They take turns passing the vodka. When Tony-R brushes Abi's fingers during one of the exchanges he shudders and swallows hard.

"I don't know how to play chess," Abi says. "But I bet we can play checkers with these."

Tony-R pushes his glasses back into his face and sets up the board. They drink and play, splitting the orange between them, using the pages of the notebook to keep score: three to three so far. The evening is an odd interaction, but Abi's grateful for the company. Tomorrow morning his parents will return to find the cardboard sloppily taped against the window. Mrs. García, the secretary at the high school, will eventually call in to ask why Abi hasn't been to school in the last few days. Abi doesn't like how she pronounces his name—Abby—all gringofied, just as she pronounces her own, the first syllable soft and rhyming with "scar."

"So tell me, Tony-R," Abi says. The cheap booze has begun to set in. "Why the fuck are you still sticking around in this dead-end Caliente Valley?"

"I'm taking care of my parents," Tony-R says flatly.

Abi feels the blood rush to his cheeks. He recovers quickly, responding: "What a coincidence. So am I. My mother's an invalid, you know. Diabetes. And my father's pretty old. By the time I graduate next year, I'll have to look for a job so that he can retire and rest. Ideally I'd like to take them back to the homeland. Querétaro."

Tony-R rubs a drop of liquor off his chin.

"I'm just shitting you," Abi says. "I have no idea why I said that. My parents are perfectly healthy, and they'll both have long lives and that pisses me off because that means that all three of us will grow old together. Do you know how much that sucks? I'll never be free of them. And I'll be much more of a burden to them because all of their friends will look at them with pity for having had one child—a faggot at that—who will never marry or have kids or a profession. They might as well have been barren. I might as well have been born handicapped."

Abi picks up the pack of cigarettes and the lighter.

"You're in a non-smoking room," Tony-R says.

Abi's jaw drops. "What are you, a retard? Are you going to turn me in? Kick me out?" He lights the cigarette and takes a long drag. "Sonofabitch, I needed that," he adds.

"There's no ashtray—"

Abi doesn't let him finish the sentence; he flicks the ashes on the carpet. "Can't even notice," he says. Tony-R stares back, fish-eyed.

"Fucking relax," says Abi. "Take your pants off."

Tony-R complies and isn't offended when Abi laughs at his white briefs.

"What are you, ten? Here, take a drag."

Tony-R complies. When he takes off his dress shirt completely, Abi is quick to notice the long hair in the armpits, the deep stretch marks along the fat of the upper arms, and a tattoo that wraps around the curve of his shoulder.

"See? Doesn't it feel good to break the rules? I bet you never once broke the rules during your four years in high school. I bet you never skipped school or flipped the teachers off behind their backs. Did you ever ask for a bathroom break just so you could light up? Did you ever copy someone's homework? Jesus, Tony-R, what a fucking vanilla life you've had." Abi takes another drag of his cigarette. "And what's this suppose to be anyway, a row of suppositories?" he adds, indicating the tattoo.

"A bullet belt," Tony-R says.

"You're kidding?" Abi says. "So are you like a gangsta or something."

"Revolutionary, like Emiliano Zapata and Che Guevara."

"Who?" Abi says. Tony-R stares back at him intently.

The silence that follows is broken by the rough sounds of a squeaking bed coming from the next room. Abi smiles, gets up, grabs Tony-R by the hand and leads him up on the bed.

"Let's listen in," Abi says, his voice low. He presses his ear to the wall and motions to Tony-R to do the same. They face each other as the wall vibrates with the knocking of the bed against it.

The woman's screams intensify, as do the grunts spilling out of the man.

"She's definitely faking," Abi whispers. As the couple reaches climax, Abi begins to rock back on the bed and pierces into Tony-R's eyes, which sends Tony-R scrambling away from the wall and back to the floor.

Abi laughs. "What's the matter, boyfriend? You shamed? There's nothing to be afraid of." He walks on the bed, toward the end. Towering over Tony-R, Abi imagines he can crush him simply by taking one step forward. He drops himself on the bed and lands sitting down with his legs over the edge. He bounces a few times, mimicking the sounds of sexual passion and then breaking out into laughter.

"I swear," Abi says. "That was the most unoriginal fucking I've ever heard. Cheap whore, cheap performance. What sounds do you make when you fuck?"

Tony-R looks down at his scattered belongings and begins to collect them.

"Don't leave!" Abi says in alarm. "You're not leaving me are you?"

"No, I won't leave if you don't want me to," Tony-R responds softly.

Abi grins. "No, I don't want you to go."

"Would you like to come with me instead?" Tony-R says.

The inside of Tony-R's car is just like his backpack—cluttered. Abi doesn't bother to push aside any of the objects on the floor and simply plants his feet on top of them.

"So where are you taking me?" Abi asks. His nose flinches from the smell of stale cigarette. "Los Angeles? Phoenix?"

Tony-R doesn't answer. He shifts into drive and they disappear into the dark avenues. When they cross the tracks, Abi knows they're headed up to the summit of the canyon overlooking the valley. All through high school he heard stories about the summit—Caliente Valley's own version of make-out point, except that there's probably nothing romantic about a scenic view of dry vineyards and pockets of housing projects. But as soon as they reach the top, Abi quickly changes his mind: it's still not a romantic spot but the desert landscape at night is breathtaking.

"It's like we're on another planet," Abi says, taking in the valley looking like the felt display case at the jewelry store, the gems splayed out and glimmering.

"I come here almost every night," Tony-R says. "Except on weekends. It gets too crowded."

"I'm sure," Abi says. Tony-R searches for the vodka in his backpack, takes a drink and then passes the bottle.

In the small space of the car, even a sniffle is amplified.

"So tell me, Tony-R," Abi says. He rolls down the window to let the cool air in. "Are you a virgin?"

They exchange the bottle once more in the silence that follows. When Abi takes a drink, Tony-R speaks up.

"I sucked Mr. Hartnett's dick," Tony-R says. "Does that count?"

Abi breaks into a coughing fit. Once he regains his composure he manages to ask, "What the fuck did you just say?"

"I sucked Mr. Hartnett's dick," Tony-R says. "The social studies teacher."

"I know it's the social studies teacher," Abi says. "But I had no fucking idea—"

Abi flashes back to the year before. Social studies. Mr. Hartnett is tall, pepper-hair, hairy-chest. He pins pictures of his seven-year-old daughter's artwork on the wall, right beneath the laminated Bill of Rights. Abi had heard the rumors and had winked at Mr. Hartnett from the back row to let him know it was okay to approach him. Abi waited for him in the library during lunch and after school for months, but Mr. Hartnett never came.

Abi had it all figured out in his head. Mr. Hartnett comes in and stares from the stacks. Eventually he makes his way to the same table, to a seat next to Abi. He stretches out his leg so that it touches Abi's. And that's when Abi goes in for the kill. He'll turn to look at Mr. Hartnett and tell him: "I'll let you fuck me if you give me your watch."

No Mr. Hartnett. No watch.

Tony-R takes another swig of the vodka. He takes off his glasses, revealing small pools of sweat along the creases where the frames rested. "They weigh a ton," Tony-R explains.

Without his glasses, Tony-R doesn't look half bad. Abi feels tipsy. He takes Tony-R's glasses and puts them over his eyes. The sharp lights glaring from the valley flatten into smudges.

"Goddamn, Tony-R, I bet you can see to the friggin' moon with these," Abi says, taking them off.

"I used to burn ants with them when I was younger," Tony-R says.

"Shit, you could roast a chicken," Abi says and laughs. "Why don't you laugh, you? That was funny. Are you offended?"

Tony-R, eyes squinted, moves in closer. "No, I'm not offended."

Abi jerks back. "You weren't trying to kiss me, right? Because that's not why I let you take me out on a ride. In fact, I could get your ass fired." He folds his legs and presses his feet against the dashboard.

"Then why *did* you come?" Tony-R asks.

"What?" Abi responds, surprised.

"Why are you here, then? With me."

Abi draws back. "Why you little prick," he says. "How dare you suggest that I—haven't you been watching the stud who comes to see me? A *real* fucking man. All fucking muscle and cock, if you want to know. Shit, when he enters me I feel like a goddamn cathedral. And that's something you or that pencil-dick social studies teacher will never do for me. You got me? I mean look at you. No wonder Mr. Hartnett came after you. He saw what a dumb little unattractive fag you were, and he didn't have to finish his sentence when you were probably already on your knees with gratitude. Who else's dick are you going to suck around here?"

Tony-R looks out into the canyon.

Abi shakes his head. "Look," he says. "That was a little rough, I didn't mean everything I just said. I'm fucking drunk, you know. The booze got to me."

"I didn't tell him where you were," Tony-R says.

Abi feels light-headed. "What?" he asks, the wind knocked out of him. "What did you just say?"

"Your friend," Tony-R continues. "Your lover. The stud. I told him you weren't staying at the motel. I told him the same thing last night."

Abi feels dizzy. Tony-R looks back at him. His eyes are dark and the eyelids are light, just like the rest of him.

"What?" Abi says. "Come again?"

"The man you meet at the Palm Tree," Tony-R says. "I turned him away."

Abi's jaw drops. He can feel the crease between his eyebrows deepen.

"I've been watching," Tony-R says. "I know everything, Miguel Santos."

After letting the game sink in, Abi slaps Tony-R across the face and yells, "What the fuck is your problem, Toadface? What the fuck business is it of yours who comes to see me?"

Tony-R's face flushes.

"Answer me, you dumb fuck! Are you some kind of idiot?"

"I was trying to protect you," Tony-R says, dramatically.

"Protect me?" Abi says, matching Tony-R's urgent tone. And then quickly adds: "So you know about his wife?"

"Yes. She's a vindictive bitch and she'll come after you if she finds out."

"Yes," Abi says. "Yes, she is one vindictive bitch."

They settle into the seats, exhausted. Tony-R's disposition changes, taking on the look of a proud little boy, his eyes huge and bright. His comic expression makes Abi want to laugh. It's useless to be angry at someone whose job is working the night shift at a cheap motel, a place for desperate fantasy and people who enter its walls for escape. And Tony-R has caught on quickly, fueling the story that Abi has been swirling inside his head all week.

"So what do we do now?" Abi asks, looking out at the vast spread of lights ice-picked into the darkness.

"We can listen to some tunes," Tony-R says. He reaches into the back seat for the burned CDs.

"Let's do that," Abi says. "Let's listen to some tunes."

When the music starts playing, Abi rests his head against the tattooed cushion of Tony-R's shoulder, and breathes in the musk of a cologne that probably didn't cost very much, but for Abi, it's quite valuable and deliciously real.

Good Boys

Doña Gregoria

This season her boys are working the onion, which means quitting time will vary, depending on the heat, which means their clothes, permeated with the stench, will make her cry when she stands over the washing machine. Since today the temperature is only moderately hot, the laborers will pick into the afternoon. Whenever her sons are late coming back from the fields the three names collide into a single sound inside her head, like a pulse pushing out against one of her temples, aggressive and headache-inducing. She tries to distract herself with the television, squinting through her glasses as she pushes the remote control button back and forth between the two Spanish stations until the boredom of implausible soap opera plots and vitriolic dialogue sends her back to abandoned tasks.

First she finishes mending the holes in her sons' clothing with green thread—not because she doesn't know any better, but because she doesn't want them to overlook the small gestures of attention she pays to their needs. Afterward she picks through the costume jewelry cluttered in a box one of her sons made for her in grade school using Popsicle sticks and pasta shells spray-painted gold. She digs her fingers inside and is pleased to discover her imitation amethyst bracelet. And then she pauses abruptly to face her reflection on the television screen. The white cotton of her hair shows transparent and precariously glued to her scalp. A faint tingling on her skin is all she can muster to show her excitement. Today is Lotto day—the day she wears the purple stone bracelet for luck.

Catching a glimpse of her late husband's enlarged photograph from the corner of her eye triggers another reminder: that she had been weeding the purple morning glories on the day Paulo finally passed away. His breath had ceased, and those flowers never blossomed again. Well, that's not exactly true. Or, rather, it was made truth by the rage that had sent her back to the garden that evening to till the soil until even the roots of the morning glories had been unearthed. His death wasn't the cause of her breakdown. It was his debt, what he left behind for her sons to pay.

Doña Gregoria rummages through the stack of paper on the lamp table for the Lotto ticket. Old bills and letters piled high on the table make any search difficult, but Gaspar always manages to find what needs to be found. Even though he urges her to start throwing papers away, tired of sorting through the same material each month, doña Gregoria resists, afraid to lose an important record, like a receipt or an old Lotto ticket. Each postmark, each stub is a sad testament to the passing months in which her family lives hand-to-mouth on a cruel budget. Their only savings account, a slim roll of cash she keeps inside the tea jar in the kitchen. It fattens steadily as a precaution for emergencies. Too many times she has seen families in the neighborhood, none of them with health coverage, collapse under the anxiety of dwindling funds as they're thrown into an unforeseen event, such as an extended illness or death in the family. She wants to spare her sons such a burden twice—having gone through it once with their father was enough. And to give that safety net an added insurance, she gambles on the miracle of the Lotto.

"Play it like the cycles of the moon," Anastasia, the old witch back in Nuevo León, had advised her once. Doña Gregoria chose a set of numbers for each week of the year. The combination of numbers she plays each week will not be played again until the following year. So far no win, but doña Gregoria waits patiently. Luck will eventually come walking in. She senses it in the silver sheen of the moon by night, and in the golden blaze of the sun by day. And though Paulo might have tittered at her superstitious ways, looking to the skies for direction, listening for the messages of her body—an ear buzzing, a muscle pulsing—as signs of things to come, she still makes sure luck does not overlook their home by leaving a spare key beneath the doormat.

Doña Gregoria also regrets that her husband didn't share her notions of the hereafter. For her, any unexplainable breeze or sound is evidence of a restless soul roaming the purgatory of the earth. On those occasions when she senses the presence of a lost creature of God, she offers a silent prayer.

"Dead is dead," Paulo used to say. "I'll simply go out like a light bulb." But she doesn't buy into that. She knows he's at peace now, and that he sends her messages to confirm this fact. She reads the signs. The moods of the living and the dead are always about. Paulo may have been fighting to the last softened bone of his body, but she knew his death was near by the way the trees dropped their branches over the house like a shroud. The birds, struck numb in the face of impending grief, buried their heads in their feathers. And the stubborn morning glories, useless jewels from the ground, mocked her.

She makes one final effort to look for the Lotto ticket and becomes dismayed that there isn't more urgency in her search, as if she knows deep down inside that it won't make a difference whether or not she finds it. What matters is that the pork chops are thawing in the sink, that the clothes are drying on the line, that the picture of Paulo remains stretched across the wall, big as the head of a god, to remind her sons why they get up every dawn to work in the fields, why they go to bed in the evenings with their emotions wound as tightly as the layers of onion they've been picking all season.

Everything's in place so perfectly, like the set on a stage, that it begins to make her anxious. This is the same play, awaiting the same actors to speak the same dialogue. Nothing changes. Nothing big anyway. Doña Gregoria begins to move from room to room like a creature trapped in a cage. Her sons are late coming home from the fields. They're late coming home from the fields. The statement rattles in her head as she feels her way along the walls of the tiny two-bedroom apartment with her eyes closed—an exercise in luck. If any of the bedroom doors have been left open, she will fall in. She makes it around one time, and then once more, until she exhausts herself and drops her body on the couch. Suddenly the door swings open.

"We're home!" Melchor yells out. Doña Gregoria jumps. "Where's my beautiful azucena?" He peeks around the corner of the kitchen and points with his dark chubby finger at doña Gregoria. "There she is! La Doña, flattering her jewels like a princess." Doña Gregoria laughs in relief.

Gaspar comes in after Melchor, dusting the flannel sleeves around his long, slim hands. "Just once I'd like to see you walk in like a normal human being," he complains. "At least keep your voice down."

The two men bend down to kiss doña Gregoria on opposite cheeks. Melchor turns to his brother and quips, "If the onion doesn't bring me to tears, you will, maricón."

"Shut up already!" Gaspar says, swatting him with his cap. Doña Gregoria frowns at how his mane of black hair has been flattened down.

"Don't start," doña Gregoria warns.

"Tell him that," Melchor and Gaspar say in unison. They look at each other in surprise, and then quickly look away before walking into their room.

Baltazar comes in scratching at the dust caught in his long wavy hair. He pauses directly in front of the photograph of his dead father. Baltazar is the only one who resembles Paulo, inheriting the square face and the long nose plunging down between two high cheekbones. Baltazar did not, however, inherit his father's loquaciousness. Melchor and Gaspar on the other hand can carry on a lengthy conversation, and more frequently—especially when they're both in the room—lengthy arguments. Doña Gregoria stands up and kisses him on the cheek, touched that even his way of floating into a room reminds her of her late husband.

"How was your day, hijo?" she asks. Her son's shoulder-length hair makes her think of her own hair, which has had trouble growing in the recent years. She loves that he's the tallest, and when she looks up at his face she sees an unfamiliar angle to her husband's face.

Baltazar shrugs. "Always the same, Doña. Half the day I hear Melchor's awful singing and the other half I hear Gaspar complaining."

"Just ignore them, hijo," doña Gregoria suggests, without much conviction.

"How can I?" Baltazar answers.

Doña Gregoria grins. Her eyes follow him to the room he shares with his brothers. She's pleasantly aware of how the temperature rises with the addition of their heat-suffused bodies. The room smells of sweaty feet; the boys have remembered to remove their soiled shoes before coming in. And though it stinks, doña Gregoria can't help but take a deep, deep breath.

She takes her place in front of the stove and turns on the burners: one for the pork chops, one for the beans, and one for the griddle. The small theater of her sons' homecoming came so fast and with so much force, she never reached the point in her angst in which she wishes she could drop lifeless in the living room like an anchor, sinking the entire apartment along with her, and setting her sons free.

Baltazar

"What's your problem?" Gaspar asks when Baltazar enters the room. With Melchor in the shower, Gaspar kills time by brushing his hair. He has two combs. One he uses before a shower, the other after. But he strokes both through his wavy hair with the same meticulousness and rhythm.

"Nothing. I'm just not feeling well." Baltazar sits down on the small couch with his chin to his chest, one hand pressed against the side of his head.

"If it's nothing, you're sure as hell making us notice," Gaspar says.

Baltazar glances at his older brother. Even as a boy Gaspar has been a hateful person. He has always been vain about his good looks and trim body, admiring himself in front of any reflection he comes across. Years of flattery and compliments from friends and strangers have made him self-righteous and resentful of his plain-faced brothers. People's eyes open wide to take in the perfection of Gaspar's features. Little do they know about his heavy, spiteful heart and cruel tongue.

"My head has been hurting again," Baltazar says. "You could be a little more compassionate."

"It's always hurting," Gaspar says. "Tell me something new and I'll listen."

Gaspar puts the comb down on the dresser, his domain. Only he can place his things there. The two combs lie parallel to each other with the teeth pointing the same direction. He turns suddenly. "Don't you think I get headaches? Even fatso gets them. Do you see us coming home *in tears?*" Gaspar says the last two words in a mocking voice. He shakes his head. "Mama's boy," he adds.

Melchor bursts into the room with a towel wrapped around his head, turban style. His dark flabby stomach spills out above his baggy shorts. A small tattoo of a masked Mexican bandit rests above his right nipple but it's barely visible against his dark skin. "Next!" he yells.

"It's about time, whale skin," Gaspar says. "I hope you didn't leave your dirty clothes all over the bathroom floor. What am I saying? Of course you did."

"You love me so much, Gasparín. Why don't you get behind me and fuck me in the hole?" Melchor drops the towel on the floor on top of Gaspar's good shoes. Gaspar leaves the room with his clean towel across his arm.

"Pinche maricón," says Melchor. "If it wasn't for Doña I'd have kicked his puto ass years ago. I hate guys like him." He turns to Baltazar. "What's up with you?"

"Nothing," Baltazar responds. "Well, my head hurts again."

"Oh that," Melchor says, casually. "Hmm, do you smell that? I bet la Doña's making pork chops. Chingado! She must have drowned them in pepper. Makes me want to sneeze!" He walks out of the room, biting down on a fingernail. He rubs his wet hair with his free hand, and drops of water splash against the door.

With his brothers out of the way, Baltazar relaxes on the long couch, where he sleeps. He doesn't mind sleeping with his legs over the armrest. When he tires of the couch, he sleeps on the living room floor. Actually he doesn't have a choice. Melchor and Gaspar will never give up the bunk beds crammed in the corner of the room. Doña has asked him repeatedly to move into her room, but Baltazar has enough problems fighting off the mama's boy image already.

The pain in his head is concentrated on his left side as if that was the most exposed spot on his head while the sun strikes for hours in the open fields. He avoids telling Doña every time he has it. She doesn't have to know. And although the pain intensifies as time passes, only once or twice a week does he let her take out the bag of herbs to make a hot tea to take with aspirin.

He pushes against the side of his head, which feels impaled on a fiery poker. He remembers reaching for a flattened penny on a rail just after the train rode over it. The hot metal burned his fingers to a blister.

Steadily, the pain in his head fades, leaving only the numbness of a fat bruise. He will rest and eventually doze for a brief moment, until Gaspar comes out of the shower to rattle the objects on top of the dresser, or until his mother shakes his shoulder to wake him up for dinner, or until Death steps in to claim this shriveled body stripped down to a t-shirt and undershorts. In the meantime he boils inside his fever.

And through the fever he detects Gaspar's body enter and exit the bedroom, his mother's body come in to guide him to the table, his own body work mechanically to lift the knife and fork, shoving the food inside his mouth, which he imagines dispels heat like an oven. He can barely make out Melchor's babbling with his mouth full and Gaspar's scowls across the table, asking for silence. Baltazar too would like silence. Only doña Gregoria looks at peace, passively observing the three men, and easily detecting his state of distress.

After dinner their gathering shatters immediately and everyone flees in different directions because this semblance of unity is a farce. Always has been. Only doña Gregoria pretends it's not as she snuggles up next to him on the living room couch to wait for the Lotto numbers to be called.

"I've got a good feeling about tonight," she says, and neither of them believes it. As Gaspar passes by on his way out, she calls out to him, "And don't forget to look for my ticket when you get back, hijo!"

Gaspar waves back, not to say good-bye, but to say fuck off. Baltazar has seen that gesture too many times. It's the last thing he sees when his eyes finally close, though he isn't asleep, and he isn't dead. Not on the outside anyway. It's the first thing he thinks about as he sleepwalks to the shower after his mother unbuttons his shirt and unbuckles his belt. *Fuck off!* he wants to tell her, but he doesn't because at the moment he doesn't even have the strength to wish her away.

Melchor

Melchor stands next to the dusty white Chevy, watching Gaspar pull out in the old blue Mustang he refuses to dirty by driving it to the fields. Instead they take the Chevy, which gives Gaspar one more chore on the weekends as he rises early to wash it out with laundry detergent and a rag. Otherwise he won't ride comfortably to work on Monday morning. Gaspar's obsession with cleanliness, organization and punctuality irritates Melchor, but not as much, Melchor thinks with satisfaction, as his own sloppy habits bother Gaspar.

Doña's pork chops with a side of refried beans and raw jalapeños lightly warmed on the griddle has been a fulfilling meal. He loves her homemade flour tortillas. Not one looks quite circular but that doesn't matter since, despite their shape, they're all equally tasty, especially in the way they stick to the roof of the mouth— doughy, but flavorful. He enjoys prying the soft clumps off his palate with the famished muscle of his tongue. Dinner, at least, has made him forget the smell of green onions buried deep under the fingernails. He once tried to dig it out with a nail file, but he only managed to stink up the metal tip, which angered Gaspar.

Melchor breathes in the warm dusk as he looks out across the parking lot full of pot holes. The air lifts an odor like rotting fruit. The conditions in the housing project are worsening, but they can't leave. Not yet. Not while they work seasonal jobs in the Caliente Valley without migrating north like other farm workers. His father's death and unpaid hospital bills anchor them here as firmly as the headstone in the cemetery grounds.

That debt's the reason Melchor keeps at his second job. Today is Wednesday, the day Mauro comes to tell him where the next weekend will take them. They hit La Quinta too often this month and that only prompted the creation of a militia-minded neighborhood watch that made any brown or black face suspect. He'd be crazy to suggest going there again. Palm Springs is always out of the question because of the high-tech security systems. It's like trying to break into a bank vault with a lockpick and a string of firecrackers. Maybe Indian Wells. They haven't hunted there in a while, and they have it coming with their damn snobbery on the highways, speeding up or slowing down to avoid looking at the Mexicans who drive beside them in beat-up cars. Often he fantasizes that those Cadillacs getting all panicky on the streets find their way to the driveways of homes they've just burglarized.

Mauro pulls up in his black Camaro. Despite the tinted windows and the darkening sky, his small straw hat with the feather on the side still shows through.

"Bandit," Mauro says, climbing out with a paper bag in his hand. He never goes anywhere without his black leather vest. "I've got your share: four hundred and thirty."

"That's it?" says Melchor, opening the bag to count the money on the Chevy's hood.

"Don't count the money out here, pendejo! People will think we're dealing drugs or something."

"Around here that's nothing strange," says Melchor.

"Still," Mauro says.

Melchor scowls. "You're the fucker that brings it over in a paper bag. Are you fucking me over, or what? Why so little?"

"That gold shit Felipe said was twenty-four k's?" Melchor nods as Mauro takes his hat off to blow into the feather. "It wasn't worth the toilet paper we wrapped it in. Fake."

"Chingado!" Melchor says. "I thought you said he knew his shit. I bet my mother can do better. At least she can tell you right away what's fake. Shit, she's been looking at it all her life."

"Is she available this weekend? We're desperate. Shit," Mauro says, grinning.

"So what's next?"

"Palm Desert. We found a house on vacation. Saturday. One." Mauro glances over his shoulder before pulling out a joint from his shirt picket. He offers it to Melchor, who refuses it.

"It's the good stuff, Bandit. Not this fucking oregano the kids around here make in the kitchens."

"That's why Felipe can't tell gold from his boogers," Melchor says.

Mauro's thin mustache twitches with his lip as he lights the joint. He doesn't wear any jewelry or flashy accessories except for a pocket watch, which he pulls out of the vest pocket with ceremony each time.

"Hey, so, when are you getting rid of this refrigerator on wheels and buying yourself a decent ride?" Mauro bangs one fist on the Chevy.

"Like what? That piece of shit over there the looks like a flattened beer can."

"Easy, man, the ladies like that ride. Makes them look classy," Mauro says.

"Lily Munster classy?" Melchor retorts.

"Chale, Bandit," Mauro says. "You're in a mood tonight."

"No hard feelings, man," Melchor says. He holds out a hand. Mauro takes it; they shake.

"It's getting late, man. I still need to give Felipe his share," Mauro says. He flips open the pocket watch.

"His share," Melchor mutters.

"Take easy, Bandit. It'll get better. See you Saturday?"

"Yes, whatever. But we better hit something big soon. I'm tired of risking my neck for some chingados pennies."

With the joint still going, Mauro climbs back into the low car seat and drives off, honking once at the kids playing soccer on the road before he turns the corner. The kids jeer at him and flash him the middle finger. Mauro sticks his middle finger out the car window in response.

Melchor rolls up the money in the bag. The truth is, he looks forward to his second job—his night shift, Mauro once joked. The first time Mauro invited him to come along, Melchor nearly struck him, outraged. But after his father's death and with all those bills growing strong and Doña working overtime at the packinghouse in the winters, he knew he had to make some easy cash. That was then, when even Gaspar, that cold-hearted sissy, had pawned what little strips of jewelry he had saved up for his future girlfriend. That was then. At this point it's also about the risk. Every hit becomes a challenge. He can't imagine how trite his life would be without that weekly venture into the homes of the rich citizens of the Caliente Valley. Gaspar has his string of female admirers, Baltazar has Doña pampering him like an invalid. What does he have without the local fame, stumping the authorities with the ingenious ways he maneuvers himself in and out of a house, undetected? The Invisible Bandit, one paper had christened him; Bandit, his fellow thieves. He saved an article about it from *Noticias del Valle*, the local Spanish newspaper. In it the white leaders of the white citizenry blame the rising crime rate on the influx of illegal immigrants—a bigoted remark that had pumped some blood into the fading brown activism. It made him feel heroic somehow that his burglary had inadvertently been the cause of all the ruckus at one of the Caliente Valley town meetings.

"Was that Mauro, hijo?" Doña Gregoria's soft voice creeps up from behind.

Melchor takes the bag and faces his mother. "He was in a hurry, Doña."

"A person can never be in too much of a hurry to say hello," she says.

"He left this for you. An old debt he paid back. Buy yourself some Lotto tickets."

Doña Gregoria takes the bag. She makes the sign of the cross with the money and kisses Melchor on the shoulder.

They walk back into the apartment, doña Gregoria with her arm stretched across half Melchor's back and Melchor with his heavy hand on her shoulder.

"I couldn't find today's ticket," she says when they reach the doormat. "But I wrote down the winning numbers they announced on the television. Gaspar will find the ticket later, he said."

"Sure he will," Melchor says, bending down to kiss his mother's head. Her hair smells of a flower he doesn't recall the name of at the moment. Perhaps he has come across it during one of his forays through those fancy houses. Maybe it had been sprayed into the expensive drapes. Maybe it had settled into the carpet after the incense stick burned out. Maybe he found the scent in one of the immaculate gardens, better taken care of than any of the people in his neighborhood. Or maybe it's simply a common flower he doesn't remember. One of those flowers not valuable enough to be plucked.

Gaspar

Driving through the back streets at night relaxes Gaspar. The sky's black, the road's black, and there are no street lights. He feels like the only beating heart in a body of silence that stretches from Avenue Forty-Eight to Avenue Fifty-Six. It's good to be alone, without Melchor snoring on one side of the room and Baltazar talking in his sleep on the other. Out in the endless back street, with the windows down and the air blowing into his hair, there's too much open space to feel claustrophobic.

He watches the front lights swerve with the road, momentarily lighting up the grape fields, the carrot fields, the orchards—even the dreaded onion stalks flash by swiftly, harmlessly, with no time to cast individual shadows. The night drive zips by in one quick blur, the way he wishes the days to be—not long enough to trigger his anger, an anger that begins with the first signs of heat, and that ends with the stick shift moving into third gear as soon as he leaves his family behind in the project.

Finally, after reaching the last dark avenue, before the first streetlights, he pulls over. He turns off the engine and headlights, and then inhales deeply. At that point in his journey he feels the urge to cry but can't, even though his eyes are ready to tear. Tiny spasms force his lids to pound as if they can't keep open any longer. His throat becomes raspy, choked up with bitter bile that crawls up from his stomach. But he can't cry. Just as he's about to release a pent up wail—the kind he imagines only women are capable of—the grief deflates in his chest. The courage to burst open is lost. Why can't he cry now that there's no one near enough to hear him? Even that's become trapped.

He doesn't smoke, but he has a craving for a cigarette. Everyone who's depressed, he notices, smokes. Like at Los Arcos, a nightclub full of men and women pretending to have a good time, making believe they aren't the same people who, just hours before, have been kneeling on dirt, fated to return to that same filthy earth day after day after day. That's why he doesn't smoke at the club. Every Friday the women eye him through a thick layer of make-up and beckon him to the hazy dance floor with their short skirts and tight blouses. Who do they think they're fooling with their coy mousy voices and delicate steps on boot-blistered feet hidden inside those high-heeled shoes? Come Monday they'll be back at work, leaving behind those caked masks in exchange for those tired, ugly faces, sunburned and chapped.

He only started going back to Los Arcos after his brothers told him Lorena isn't seen there anymore. They had been inseparable since that night he spotted her sipping a daiquiri at the bar, but her proposal made the beads of sweat leap out of his pores faster than the hottest minute in the fields.

"Get married?"

How could he explain to her the impossibility of her proposition without having to detail the suffocating life he had, still living at home and sharing a room with his two brothers? Their father had long since pointed out the direction of their fates. First by taking them out of Nuevo León and out of school, and raising them in California to be farmworkers. Then by getting swallowed up by a prolonged and costly sickness. Gaspar has been picking vegetables so long he doesn't know what else he can do, though he's sure he will someday break out of this snare in the Caliente Valley. He imagines himself moving south, into Mexico City, where they say a person can reinvent himself, forget his past, and create his own future. The city is so huge, any worry dwarfs into insignificance. Any loud headache disappears into the din of the noisy streets. But until then he's stuck just like everyone else. Marrying Lorena will certainly bind him closer to this vicious penance he knows has to come to an end.

"I can't," he whispered his response to Lorena without further explanation. The words struck their chemistry bluntly, like a dull hammer. Lorena squinted as if he had backed away far from her.

"What?" he asked, uncomfortable with the way she was leering at him.

"It's not true is it? What your brother always says about you."

The blood ran up to Gaspar's face. "You stupid bitch," he said, and walked away.

After that night he lost the aromatic skin that snuffed out all memory of the stink from the onion fields. And if he happened to see her, they crossed paths like strangers despite the intimacy with which they had known each other's touch.

Gaspar leans his head on his arms wrapped around the steering wheel. A car passes by. The flash of light fools him into thinking he moves in reverse. His body jumps. The fright doesn't leave him until he's able to get the ignition started. He turns the car around and heads for home. The ride back is short. In fact he gets there sooner than he expected, which makes him realize that he didn't drive that far after all.

Doña Gregoria and Baltazar

The kettle steams on the stove. The heat makes the kitchen uncomfortable to be in. In this heat, it's hard to wrap her brain around the fact that she turns the oven on to warm the house in the winter. Doña Gregoria stirs in the right amount of brown sugar for each pinch of manzanilla in the tea bag. Baltazar watches from the living room, holding up a warm compress of tomatoes and alcohol against his head.

"I'm going to ask doña Martina to bring back some more of that medicine she buys across the border. I forget what it's called but it comes in a green box. Magnopirol, I think," doña Gregoria mumbles from the kitchen. "How's your head, hijo?" she asks.

Baltazar turns his head as red juice runs down his temple. "I'm feeling better. Really, Doña, I'll be fine."

"My poor Baltazar." Doña Gregoria shakes her head. "Your father used to worry about you so much when you were small." Doña Gregoria cools the tea by pouring it back and forth between two cups. She removes her glasses to keep them from fogging up. "He used to joke that I had used up all my strong milk on Melchor and Gaspar. Especially Melchor."

Baltazar looks down at his swollen hands, ashamed that not even his mother can see him out of the role of family runt. Melchor is the happy one, Gaspar the feisty one, and he the sickly one, the weakling of the litter who stays home from school half the year to soak up Doña's plants and herbs. Even though he has never missed work on account of his headaches, his brothers still make him feel he's holding them back. Their cruelty hints at their fear that he'll have to see a doctor soon and bring up the household debt. But he refuses to see the expensive American specialists their father went to. Back then it seemed so easy to make the choice of financial sacrifice over pain and suffering. Things are different now that they have recovered some. If there's an expense imminent it will have to be saved to cover Doña's healthcare or her funeral, not his. He has to endure the pain, help the family pretend everything's all right and let Doña believe her teas help ease his misery.

"I'm well enough to go to school," he remembers pleading one of many mornings in Nuevo León. "I'm going to fail the fourth grade again."

"Melchor failed the sixth grade and he went all year," Gaspar yelled from the kitchen. Melchor threw an apricot pit in reply. It missed Gaspar and flew between Baltazar and Doña.

Doña shook her head. "You can't go to school today because it's too hot. You'll get another nosebleed."

"A nosebleed," Melchor and Gaspar mocked.

Over sixteen years later and Baltazar is still locked inside his ten-year-old body. They live in a different country now, and his mother still goes out to collect home remedies. It embarrasses him how much she blesses everything from money to medicines, as if faith has any power in this house. There is no God here, no protector, only that grim reminder on the wall, the enlarged photograph of his dead father, the fallen authority.

"Here's your tea," doña Gregoria says, walking up to him with the hot cup trembling in her hand. "And don't forget the aspirin."

Gaspar walks in as Baltazar takes the cup from doña Gregoria's hands. "And don't forget the pacifier," he snaps as he passes by, jingling the car keys in his hand.

Baltazar decides to sleep in the living room tonight and let the monotone song of the swamp cooler soothe him into sleep, though it's not exactly sleep what comes over him as soon as his mother turns off the light. It's more like a coma, because he goes motionless and still manages to suck in the sounds from the two bedrooms. The doors need to stay open to allow the air to circulate.

In one room, Melchor and Gaspar argue about taking Baltazar to see a doctor. Neither of them wants to, but Melchor is the more sympathetic one tonight.

"I'd rather he get better to work than get worse and stay home," he says.

"I'd rather he just stop pretending," Gaspar says.

"Asshole."

"Pig shit."

"Cocksucker."

"Pussy fart."

And after a brief pause between insults, Melchor asks, "Do you really think he's faking it?"

On the other room, doña Gregoria lies wondering the same thing. She's unable to light a candle because the force of the cooler puts it out every time. But she keeps the votive candle out anyway. She reaches for it in the dark and lifts it to feel its weight. The glass jar is still heavy with wax. It's more like a stone. She lifts and brings it down repeatedly, the sound of the glass knocking on the nightstand until her strength is spent, until there's only numbness in the small apartment.

Early the following morning, after having prepared three work lunches for her sons, and after waving to them as they backed up the old Chevy from the parking space, doña Gregoria tightens the yellow shawl around her and rushes back inside. She remembers the Lotto ticket.

She listens to the radio at dawn while she wraps the lunches in aluminum foil, but she prefers the din of the television for the morning background noise. Buying a large screen television on lay-away had been the family's greatest luxury, so she takes pleasure in it, especially now that she isn't working anymore. She reaches for the top of the lamp table and finds the scrap of paper with the winning numbers. Written in thick pencil, the numbers look long and flattened, like those letters painted in the middle of the streets at school zones. She tilts the paper outward and pushes her head back. The numbers are still difficult to read.

Looking around the room, trying to remember where she last left her glasses, doña Gregoria hums the tune to an old Mexican ballad just like Paulo used to do when he sat out in the back by himself. He wanted to be left undisturbed when he soothed the pain in his head. Paulo's photograph stares down at her from the wall. His lips are shut tight, the line between them almost perfectly horizontal, as if he were grinning when the picture was taken. But he wasn't grinning, doña Gregoria likes to believe. In her eyes he was humming.

"It's because you can't sing," she told him. The phrase jumped out of her mouth unexpectedly. Paulo turned around in his chair, *Noticias del Valle* flat on his lap.

"Are you talking to me?" he asked. His anger rose so quickly. But suddenly doña Gregoria didn't feel like backing down.

"I said you hum because you don't have a singing voice."

Paulo rolled up the newspaper. "Come closer," he commanded. And when she was near enough he swung at her, but she moved back swiftly to avoid the blow.

"You're lucky I'm close to dead," he said. "Otherwise I'd get up to kick you."

"If you're close to dead, I'm indeed lucky," she said.

Paulo made an effort to get off the chair but was unable. "What has gotten into you? Where's Melchor? Ask him to come take away this crazy woman before I hurt her! You'll never be rid of me, woman. Not even after I'm dead. I curse you, you and your goddamn worthless boys, those other two. Where's my Melchor? Bring me my boy!"

Doña Gregoria left her husband there, ranting until he succumbed to sleep, and then locked herself in her room to mull over why she had said what she did. But she knew. Paulo's sickness made him forget recent memory, or at least it convinced him that it had just been a dream or a hallucination induced by the fires in his brain. When he woke up that afternoon he was a bit grumpy, but he didn't remember. And doña Gregoria's guilt intensified, not because of what she had done, but because she felt like doing it again. But she never did.

When she finally locates her glasses, a search ensues for the Lotto ticket, which Gaspar never looked for as he had promised. But it didn't matter; it gave her something else to spend a few hours on as one more day went by. It wasn't here, or here, or over there. Not here either. No, not there. Or there. Thursdays were particularly boring. At least when Fridays came around, she had the trip to the gas station to look forward to. The walk to Sameer's was slow, but it was her only venture out of the apartment during summers because the packinghouses were closed down until the fall.

"I think this is the winning ticket, Gloria," Sameer would always proclaim as he handed the peach-colored paper over the counter. He could not pronounce her name, and after so many years, doña Gregoria didn't mind it.

"I think so too, Sameer," she'd answer, and then she'd look around for his two sons, who were usually chasing each other around the aisles after school.

"Isn't it wonderful to have sons?" she'd say to Sameer once she spotted the boys struggling over the same toy, and Sameer would beam in that way that reminded her of Paulo when he used to walk down to the plaza with his three children, his strides long and proud because he knew he was the envy of those who had no sons, or less than three.

At last she comes across the ticket. She sits on the couch and places both the ticket and the winning numbers she wrote down the night before side by side on her lap. As she carefully goes through each number she feels her heart flutter. After finding a match for the first three prized numbers her palpitations grow stronger. She has never achieved this much. Already the ticket is prized. And just as she prepares herself for certain disappointment, the fourth number matches, and then the fifth. Her hands shake. The room spins around her. She feels dazed, still incredulous. She has all six prize-winning numbers in her ticket, and there's no one around to help her up from the couch, let alone take her to the onion fields to tell her sons.

Baltazar

The workers kneel on the fine hot dirt to pull out the green onions by the slender stalks. They're easier to yank out than the year before when the bulbs had grown too heavy. That season the workers had to dig into the fiery ground with their fingers before they could uproot the onion or else they risked pulling out the stalk without the head. Gloves are useless in the job because they're too bulky. They expect to work in a field without shade, but last year the crew had threatened to walk out if they had to poke through the top layer of hot soil all season. A promise had been made that the crop would not be overwatered again at the height of the summer season.

Melchor, Gaspar, and Baltazar take turns collecting the harvest as they pick, tie blue rubber bands around each handful, and then toss each bunch into the cardboard boxes they drag alongside the rows. This hour Gaspar's the collector. Whenever his brothers begin to slow down with the burning sun, he speeds up to force them to keep up with the rest of the crew. At the moment there's no need for that tactic. The walk on the loose sand to the scales at the end of the field is long and taxing, but they're working at a steady pace.

"I don't know how some people can bend down," says Melchor as he pulls up his hat to wipe his forehead. He breaks out into a sweat with little effort. "I'd rather put up with the heat on my knees than with the pain on my back. It's not like we're picking asparagus, chingado. I wouldn't want to end up a hunchback."

"Then what do you call that hump over your shoulder?" Gaspar says.

Melchor looks at him and smiles. "Fuck off, maricón."

The two have been at it since the morning, and Baltazar's patience is running thin, but it's Thursday, which means today the buildup of rage will reach its height. They agree on a truce on Friday, because it precedes the two-day break they will have from each other. And on Saturday they will both vanish from the apartment, leaving Doña and Baltazar to entertain themselves because the older brothers take the cars. On paydays every other week, all three drive up to Los Arcos together—Gaspar because he wants to drink and can't drive intoxicated like Melchor, and Mechor because he needs Baltazar.

"Oh, look at that girl over there, the one in the blue dress!" Melchor will elbow Baltazar and Baltazar will spill the drink he has been nursing all evening. "God, I love girls with hair like that. Did you see that? I think she looked over here. Go pass by and see if you can hear anything. I think they're talking about me."

Baltazar will roll his eyes but play his part, giving Melchor hope that there's a young beautiful woman in the room who's interested. He weaves through the crowd and stands near the target, all the while receiving pantomimed instructions from Melchor across the room. And each time, as he's driving them home, Gaspar passed out in the back seat, Melchor will replay the night's events, trying to figure out what went wrong and what he will do differently the next time.

He himself has no aspirations for a girlfriend, let alone a wife. That's Gaspar's domain and Melchor's, in his own twisted way. Baltazar, still a virgin at twenty-six, feels as asexual as a doormat. He has no curiosity about it, either. And if a woman ever dares approach him at Los Arcos, she sees immediately the distance in his look, a look that says, *Keep walking, stranger, there's no one home.* The woman's face melts away, and then she leaves.

"Wake up, stupid!" Gaspar screams. Baltazar is rattled out of his daydream.

"Stop bullying him, man," Melchor says.

"You just keep your hump low," Gaspar replies.

"I'm warning you."

"You, buffalo, work!"

Melchor finds a small clod of dirt and throws it at Gaspar. Gaspar's about to throw the box of onions at Melchor when Baltazar reaches up to hold him back. Angered by the interference, Gaspar jerks his arm and swings back, elbowing Baltazar on the nose and knocking him to the ground.

"You keep out of it," Gaspar says. Melchor laughs and continues picking.

"You made my nose bleed," Baltazar complains, pinching his nostrils shut with two fingers.

A few workers in the neighboring rows turn to stare and chuckle. As Baltazar rises, others goad him to defend himself. Melchor quickly diverts attention by bursting into song. One man trills his tongue, another whistles, and the incident goes forgotten by the time Melchor makes it to the second chorus.

Melchor knows how to distract the onion pickers from the heat, the smell, and the hot earth radiating only two feet away from their faces. Every worker within earshot appreciates those sudden outbursts of humor—everyone except for Gaspar and Baltazar, who hate that they're called the Three Stooges, not the Three Wise Men as prescribed by their names.

Gaspar shakes his head and mumbles, "Shut up already," as he walks to the portable toilet. He turns his head on the inevitable applause and Melchor's theatrical bow.

Baltazar reaches into his pocket to pull out a small wad of toilet paper. He rolls it into a ball and shoves it into his nose to stop the flow of blood. Confident that this will work, he brings his chin down to his knee and tugs softly at an onion stalk. The pounding in his head grows. He tilts his head to the left as if his pain has materialized, adding weight to that side. He remembers his father displaying a similar gesture. The tumor on his father's brain had been on the right side, not the left. By the time his father's body collapsed under the pressure of lack of medical attention there was very little the doctors could do to treat him. One unsuccessful surgery and months of therapeutic treatments for the paralysis came to an end with Baltazar holding his father's frail hand, light and bone-thin as a pair of grape cutting scissors.

"Do you want me to call Doña?" Baltazar remembers asking his father nervously as his father descended into unconsciousness. So full of foolish hope he had been that he actually believed his father would wait for the rest of the family to come into the room before expiring. It would have been a symbolic gesture, his father's dying in the presence of all of those who cared for him. But death wasn't patient. Baltazar suspected his brothers held that against him as well. Somehow he thinks that all would be different had Melchor and Gaspar seen what he had at the moment of their father's death: a peace so costly, so agonizing, that in his desperate eyes glared the wish to transfer that pain from father to son. Maybe it had been.

"It can't happen to me," Baltazar says under his breath as he presses his hand against his head. The pain's like a drilling from the inside as if the pair of scissors in his thoughts has materialized, the blades pushing seamlessly through the brain and now anxious to puncture through the skull.

Gaspar

Gaspar steps out of the portable toilet and walks to the water tanks on the back of the foreman's truck. A woman stands there pouring herself a cup of water. He waits behind her, looking out at the opposite side of the field. He left his baseball cap in the car. He'll have to get it during the lunch break. All vehicles, with the exception of the foreman's truck, are parked at the road's narrow shoulder. There isn't any traffic until the end of the workday, when the crew scrambles out of the heat and into the protection of their cars. Until quitting time the road lies quiet, deserted, and the only dust that kicks up is what the workers cough back into the air.

"You're brother's funny," the young woman says suddenly. She gives Gaspar a paper cup.

"Yes," Gaspar agrees. He pours water from the spigot and gulps it down quickly. "He doesn't have to try very hard."

The woman giggles at his remark. She giggles again when Gaspar aims the crinkled cup at the empty carton near the truck wheel and misses. "You're funny, too," she says.

Gaspar looks at the woman more carefully. She's attractive in a way. Not too fat, not too thin. Her hair's pulled back and tucked beneath a baseball cap. He guesses it's probably braided. Hair is the most beautiful feature of a woman's body, but he can't see this woman taking care of it the way Lorena does. Lorena's is dazzling as a streak of lightning striking down the road at night. His fingers used to slide freely through the entire length of her hair. She said she never braided it. That kept it from knotting.

"I've seen you at Los Arcos," the woman says. "You go there with your brothers."

"Yes, we do. But they can't help it. I'm the one with the nicer car," Gaspar says. The woman giggles for the third time.

No, Gaspar thinks, this one won't do. She's quick to please, too easily amused and satisfied. She's one of those lovebirds who hangs all over her boyfriend like a monkey, who sits too close to him in the car while he's trying to drive. She's one of those who likes to cuddle in the most public of places, while he yawns at the unemployment line or while he browses through a restaurant menu. No, she's not going to do at all. She's the marrying type.

"Thank you for the cup," Gaspar says. He leaves the woman behind with the water tanks, a silly smile plastered across her face.

The field evens out as the workers crawl their way to the east. By noon the clothing blends with the dirt and the people disappear.

Gaspar can't help but recall the horrifying day he realized this was his lot in life.

"Stop complaining, boy," his father had yelled at him when they headed back home from the grape fields, Melchor dozing in the back seat. His father drove with one hand on the steering wheel while holding the other against the right side of his head. "You've got to learn to do a man's job. Next year you start getting paid like Melchor."

The young Gaspar, pressed to the car seat and pouting as the guitar and accordion band played in the car stereo, felt a tear running down his cheek. He wasn't crying because he had cut himself six times with the scissor blades; he was angry that this was only the first day and that his father had promised to take him back the next morning, and a thousand mornings after that.

In the midst of his failing health, his father had become an ogre, bitter and intolerable. Only once did he try to hurt Doña, striking her with a soiled bedpan. The bedpan was plastic, otherwise he wouldn't have been able to lift it. The act had been more comical than alarming. But somehow, embedded deep in the recesses of his memory, Gaspar feels the urge to claim that his father had always been hurting them. Gaspar knows, because he does the same thing: allow the resentment to turn to hostility, and then direct that rage against his brothers.

Lorena was going to solve that. She was the only person who could keep him from turning into a monster at the smallest provocation. Gaspar suspects that his brothers miss her even more than he, because without her he's back to his old self with the current in his blood always ready to spark and shock. But there would not be another Lorena, not for a while. Not until this was all over, this prison sentence he and his brothers were serving.

Gaspar bends down to pick up the cardboard box and takes his place between Melchor and Baltazar. When they first crossed into the U.S., their father had informed them that fieldwork was their future. He had been right. They work the onion and then the grape in summer, then whatever they can find in the winter—sometimes citrus, sometimes asparagus. Always they feed a little of it into their father's hospital debts. The creditors have warned them about leaving the country. There's no escape. What's there to go back to anyway in Nuevo León, or México for that matter? They've been managing well enough between the three of them. But until that debt's paid out completely and until Doña passes away, whichever comes last, Gaspar concludes as he pulls out another handful of blue rubber bands from his pocket, there's only this.

Melchor

As he keeps a steady yanking rhythm, Melchor shifts his eyes sideways to glance at Gaspar. Gaspar grooms himself too much, but Melchor has to admit he looks attractive even knee-high in dirt. Baltazar meanwhile wears the face of an ailing rabbit, the kind everyone wants to nurse and feel sorry for. Melchor coughs, letting out an awkward noise that sounds like a raspy three-syllable hiccup. He hears a few people laugh at that.

"What the fuck?" he says, looking around for the culprits. It's always like that. People look forward to his antics. They want something funny even when there's nothing to laugh at. They turn to him when they need to relieve some nervous tension building up inside their bowels—they need him to shit out their stress. Even his father had looked forward to his little fat clown when he was tossed into bed by his headaches.

"Come here, panzón," his father called as usual. "Come talk to me."

Melchor, always a large boy, walked over to his father with a smile that pushed against his pudgy cheeks, shaping his eyes into almonds. "Papi?"

His father grabbed Melchor's arms to squeeze the fat with his long, thin fingers. "You're going to be a strong, healthy man, panzón. The hardest working of my boys." After a pause he asked, "What did you learn in school today?"

"In school?" Melchor looked around as if to find the answer written somewhere on the walls, like in a classroom chalkboard. "What did I learn in school?" He scratched his head. Suddenly the epiphany. "Ah," he said finally, "I don't learn anything today, Papi. Today's a Saturday."

His father had laughed to the point of tears, rolling over on the bed in a coughing fit as his knobby knees pushed against the blanket. In the end, as his coughing subsided, he was able to say in a dry voice, "Panzón, you're also the brightest one."

Melchor stands up from the hot ground and arcs his back, making it crack. Sweat scurries down his temples. It *had* been a funny response. Melchor chuckles at first but the more he thinks about it the funnier it becomes.

"I'm using my head on Saturdays now," Melchor declares out loud. Gaspar and Baltazar look at each other, shrug their shoulders and continue picking. Melchor goes back to the task as well.

Melchor figures that his luck will eventually run out, that Mauro or one of the knuckleheads that come along to do some heavy lifting will slip up, get sloppy, or simply turn them all in for the reward money. Melchor, especially, the Invisible Bandit, has a decent price on his head. Yes, it's all a matter of time. He can hear the clock ticking on that one, for sure.

Doña will be upset of course. Gaspar will get so angry his head will explode. Baltazar, well, he'll have to snap out of his little fantasy that he's got the same thing their father had and step up to the plate.

Melchor stops and gets up on his feet again.

"Now what the fuck is the matter with you?" Gaspar says. "If you take one more break the foreman's going to throw all three of us out."

Melchor ignores him. He senses something out of place. He's not as quick as Doña to believe in signs or intuition, but something's wrong. Most definitely. Maybe it's Doña herself, maybe it's something else in the air, heavy and toxic. Maybe it's Mauro or one of the knuckleheads. Something's up. The end of something is at hand.

"Get to work, you bitch!" Gaspar says. "The foreman saw you."

Melchor gets back on his knees and starts pulling on the onion with renewed urgency. The faster they get through this crop, the faster whatever it is that's coming, will get here.

"Are you okay?" Baltazar asks. "Are you okay, Melchor?"

Melchor simply moves forward, his brothers trailing behind him like they have been doing all of their lives.

Paulo

Doña Gregoria can do nothing but sit on the couch and wait for her sons as if this day were like any other unlucky one. If she has been this fortunate, why can't she also sprout wings and fly her message across the acres of fields in one breath? This is the day she has been waiting for ever since she started using the number cycles, just as Anastasia had instructed her to. And just when she thought that another year was going to slip through her fingers here are the winning numbers clasped tightly in her hand.

"Paulo," she says, waving the ticket at the photograph. "What do you think about your little curse now?"

Paulo takes the news with indifference, biting down on his lips and gazing out across the room in his frozen expression. Doña Gregoria decides then to mock him even more by doing a dance in front of him. She even lifts her blouse up to expose her sunless flesh, the sagging cups of her brassiere.

Finally after years of working with her sons in the grape, then spending winters by herself in the packinghouses; after years of mending clothing repeatedly, always at the knees during onion season, and at the side seams for her oldest son's shirts—that growing boy; after watching her sons slowly dissolve their brotherly bonds to the point of clawing at each other like caged cats; after all that and every cup of manzanilla she has stirred for Baltazar and herself . . . finally, finally she'll have her reprieve from worry.

Putting her feet up on the couch, she looks around at the small living room like an old friend she's about to leave. She wants to remember what it looks like with its thrift-shop oil paintings of green forests of trees and rivers sweeping through bright flower beds—all the nature she can never have in the Southern California desert. Perhaps now with this money she can climb into one of those paintings and take her sons with her.

Doña Gregoria shuts her eyes. They'll pay off the debts and return to their beloved Nuevo León, run back through Anáhuac, Rodríguez, Villa Aldama, Allende, and all of those other cities they left behind when they first traveled north on the ties of the railroad track. All those years ago Paulo's dream took them away from their land, where the sun comes up like an opaque flame in a slow-burning stove, not like a crazed fire on a smelly garbage heap. Yes, she romanticizes the past, but what's there to look forward to if not the better days that used to be? Her family will be a family again and that's all that matters.

Perhaps, if generosity strikes her, she'll also do something for Martina and Anastasia. And Sameer of course. All of them have served her well.

Doña Gregoria blushes at her phrasing, but that's the privilege of the lucky, the privileged, and the free. She imagines herself dumping every item in this house, throwing it out into the street where the less fortunate can take their pick like pigeons. She'll take a gallon of gasoline and a match to whatever's left—just a useless heap of garbage. What a scandal she'll cause, exiting the project in a fancy car. What a thrill to be able to fantasize and squander an entire day like this, she thinks. She hasn't even bothered to cook a meal for her sons. But why should she? They will go out and celebrate in style in one of those fancy restaurants where people just sit down and call out orders. She might even indulge in a beer.

"What do you think of *that*?" she asks Paulo. Up until now she has never dared to speak to him. She can't help but break out into tears every few minutes, swept up in the moment of bliss.

"I knew it would all get better," she says to him. "I knew God's grace would be with us." And then the sobbing comes to an abrupt stop when she hears the Chevy pulling in.

Doña Gregoria rushes to the door. Watching her sons walk sluggishly out of the car makes her heart race once again. She forgot how she has rehearsed the announcement, what words she has picked carefully during those restless hours to tell them that everything's going to be fine. When Melchor opens the door, bending down to kiss her on the cheek, she pushes him back violently with all her weight and simply stutters, "We won."

"Won what?" Melchor says, his brows wet with sweat.

Gaspar tries to pass by next but doña Gregoria blocks his way and grabs him tightly by the arm. Behind him Baltazar beats his work shoes against each other to dust them off.

"The Lotto!" she says out of breath, showing them the two pieces of paper. Melchor takes them from her hand and scrutinizes them suspiciously.

Gaspar leans against the door. "Can we go in now, Doña? Even if we're millionaires we're still hot and annoyed."

"Sonofabitch!" Melchor yells out. He lifts doña Gregoria off the ground and carries her inside. "We won, we won?" he keeps repeating.

Walking in after Melchor, Gaspar and Baltazar eye each other.

"See?" Melchor shows them the numbers. "All six of them match! I knew I sensed something. I knew something grand was going down today!"

Gaspar snatches the numbers. "Let me see that," he says. His hands begin to tremble. Baltazar joins doña Gregoria and Melchor at the center of the living room. Melchor reaches out to pull Gaspar into the circle but Gaspar resists, looking closely at the slips of paper.

"These are last night's winning numbers?" Gaspar asks.

"Yes," doña Gregoria answers excitedly. "I know they're last night's numbers because I had to write them down in the only piece of paper I could find and I used that little piece right there. You see that?"

"We're going to get the fuck out of California, out of the U.S.!" Melchor declares.

"We're rich?" Baltazar asks in disbelief. "Brother, are we really rich?"

"The richest!" Melchor says. He reaches over and pulls down Baltazar's head to kiss it. Doña Gregoria begins to cry.

"Oh, don't cry, my beloved azucena," Melchor says. "Don't ever cry again."

"But I'm so happy," she replies.

"I can't believe it," Baltazar says. "I can't fucking believe it."

Melchor leads the three of them in a circular jog up and down on the floor as they scream out, "Rich! Rich!" each time their bodies jerk up in unison. They then break out into another pattern with Melchor yelling out, "What are we?" and Doña and Baltazar answering back, "Rich!"

"What are we?"

"Rich!"

"What are we?"

"Rich!"

"Wait!" Gaspar yells out suddenly. The dance in the living room comes to a halt.

"What? What's the matter?" Melchor asks in alarm.

"We're not rich," Gaspar says flatly.

Melchor snatches the ticket. "Of course we are, Gaspar. It says so right here. What are you talking about, brother? All these numbers, they match." Doña Gregoria nods her head in agreement.

"You stupid pig," Gaspar says. "Stupid, stupid pig. Look at the date on the ticket. Look at the date on the ticket!"

Melchor checks the ticket while Baltazar looks on mortified, his arms wrapped loosely around doña Gregoria.

"What? What's the matter?" doña Gregoria asks softly.

"The ticket's no good, Doña," Melchor pronounces with an exhausted tone in his voice. "It's an old ticket."

Doña Gregoria puts her hands over her mouth. "Are you sure? But it's this week's ticket, isn't it?"

Gaspar falls back on the couch. He bursts out laughing, though hot tears are streaming down his cheeks. "It's so goddamn unfair," he says.

"Gaspar?" doña Gregoria says. Baltazar stops her from moving toward him.

"Leave him alone," Baltazar warns. He relaxes his body against doña Gregoria, who responds by letting the weight of her head fall on his shoulders.

"We must be cursed," Gaspar keeps saying.

"I'm going to take a shower," Melchor announces. Before walking away from the living room he looks up at the photograph of their dead father and instinctively mirrors the grin of the tight resignation locked on the mouth.

In the bathroom, he quickly strips and sets the shower running. When he steps into the bathtub, he lets the hot water wash it all away, this temporary reprieve from their tragedy. And when a car pulls up at the driveway, he turns toward the window instinctively.

It's a black and white. Even from this distance he detects the squad car radio let out the static of the voice at the other end. Melchor watches closely as the officers step out of the car and head toward the apartment. He reaches for the soap and makes sure he scrubs abrasively beneath his armpits and into the hair of his groin. When the knock on the door comes, Melchor is already ahead of the game, lathering shampoo into his hair. For another brief moment he is somewhere else, clean and liberated from the smell, from the repetitive days of the work week, from the lonely nights without a female companion, from the godforsaken household of apartment 421, where an old stupid woman believes in hope and who will spend the rest of her days trying to convince her stupid sons to do the same: believe that there's such a thing.

After the shower, his body relaxes, as if he has rinsed off every last weight on his body. It's enough to make him sing. And then he hears his own singing. Through the knocking of the bathroom door, he hears his own singing. Through the shrill of his elderly mother, he hears his own singing. Through the voices of the officers, through the angry screaming of his brothers, he hears his own singing. Through the memory of his accursed father, he hears his own accursed singing.

The Call

Friday afternoon comes as humid and oppressive as every other afternoon this week, so quitting time for Tom is once again the hour of anxiety. He can feel the angst creep out through his fingers, making him clumsy. He fumbled with the car keys at the school lot and at the supermarket, and now he's stalled outside his apartment with his knee pressed against the door to keep the bags of groceries from slipping through his arms. He struggles to find the right key. There are six on the ring, color coded, but the system fails when he can't see the tabs. On the second wrong guess his frustration grows. In the one hundred degree heat, his jeans tighten around his thighs. The neighbor's kids splash noisily in the pool behind him. Sweat continues to slide down the middle of his chest. Each time a bead runs it feels as if his necklace unclasped.

When the door finally bursts open he tumbles in, spilling the groceries on the carpet. The tomato cans roll to the linoleum as he throws the door shut. He'll consider leaving a note on his neighbor's car—a friendly reminder that children are not allowed to swim without supervision.

The AC is on automatic. All day it has been going off and on in the empty rooms. Next to the car payment, the electric bill will be Tom's biggest expense, but it's worth coming home to a cool place after eight hours at the high school counseling center. The offices are comfortable, but he's still doing clerical work, filing and updating student files in the back, a cramped prison for dusty cabinets. Any day now the retiring counselor will call it quits, pack it in, and leave, vacating the head counselor's office. Any day now Tom's knowledge about adolescent psychology will go into practice.

Peeling off his jeans is like skinning an eel, but standing in front of the vent feels good. His calves welcome the touch of air. The long black hairs come unstuck from his flesh. Tom reaches down and pulls his briefs away from his genitals, lets his privates breathe. He can do those things out in the open now that he lives alone.

During his college years he had to share a living space with fellow students, but now that he has finished his undergraduate degree, and with this lucky break thanks to his diploma from Redlands, he has complete control over the wall décor. No Malcolm X posters, no bloodred American Farm Workers Union flags, no Madonna clad in chains and leather, and none of those tacky paintings his last roommate said were part of his soon-to-be critically acclaimed art thesis—charcoal nudes with oversized asymmetrical breasts. Tom never felt comfortable asking a girl over without giving this lengthy disclaimer about his roommate's project. No matter how he phrased it, there they were, large odd shapes waiting obscenely for the next pair of eyes. No, he doesn't have that problem anymore. The most explicit piece he owns is a bamboo scroll from a former girlfriend: three Chinese women bathing in a lake. The women's bodies are discreetly submerged underwater, exposing only their round faces and shoulders, the lake dissolving their nudity. And in this similar state of bliss, cool and thoroughly relaxed in front of the AC, Tom's eye wanders to the answering machine. The small red light flashes twice. Two messages.

He presses the play button, feeling somewhat vulnerable inviting voices into the room while he stands there with his jeans around the ankles. After the first beep his father's voice comes on. In spite of himself, he bends down to pull his pants up.

Patricio Villanueva has a commanding tone that made him a shoe-in for union president at the local truck drivers chapter, which he leads when he's not driving across the country. He prefers to use Spanish though he speaks perfect English, but with Tom he does that mix-and-match linguistic thing that is the street speech of the Caliente Valley and beyond.

"Hey, wassup, mijo?" says his father. "Giving you a late-night llamada from Blythe. Wanted to know how the new chamba's working out. I'll be in Arizonaztlán for a week before getting back to Califas. Te llamo después, okay? Let's grab some tacos down at Pete's when I'm back in town. I hear he's upgrading to pitbull. Te cuidas, vato. Glad you're back."

Tom winces. The pitbull reference is an inside joke. The first time his father took him to Pete's, a week after the funeral, Tom ate voraciously. It was the baby step out of the grief of having lost his mother in a car accident on the day he turned fourteen. It was also the day he realized how emotionally disconnected his father was to him. There they were, sharing a moment of true intimacy at the taco stand on Van Buren, and his father decides to turn it into a male bonding ritual.

"You know what kind of meat this is?" his father asked.

Tom shook his head.

"Dog," his father said. Tom gagged. The only other image he recalls from that night is Pete's toothless laughter. Since then, every awkward invite to dinner from his father comes with a mention of that joke about Pete's. Since then, every awkward invite is made from the road—an indirect apology from his father for never being around.

After the second beep, Tom expects a message from Clara, the old neighbor woman who watched over him during his high school years while his father was away, and the only other person in the Caliente Valley who has his new home number. He gave it to her out of respect.

"If there's anything you need, Clara," he told her, "call me. You're like a mother to me." He didn't mean either of those statements, but it made Clara feel good. He owed her that much. Besides, he didn't offer her—or his father—his cell number.

But when a stranger's voice comes on, this makes Tom pause.

"Tommy," the stranger says. "You got an answering machine, how thoughtful of you. This will definitely keep you from missing any interview requests. How's the job search going, anyway? I don't mean to pry or anything, but you know, I worry about you plenty. So give me a call, all right, son. I love you."

"How odd," Tom says, but he doesn't dwell on it any further. It's almost six o'clock and reservations at Las Cazuelas are at seven. On his first date in a year, he can't keep Connie waiting.

He quickly shelves the groceries, strips naked, and is about to run the shower when his cell phone rings a muffled tune from inside the pocket of his jeans.

"Connie?" he says into the phone.

"Tomás, this is Margarita Blake."

Tom nearly drops the phone by the surprise of talking in the buff to the school principal.

"Oh, hello, Principal Blake, what's the occasion?"

"I'm sorry to be calling you with such late notice but there's a special meeting on Sunday regarding the district sex education initiative and you need to be part of the project since you'll be replacing Raymond. I just found out he neglected to keep you informed about the meeting, but never mind that, I'll deal with him later. Anyway, make it a point to be there. McCandless Memorial Library. Noon. See you then."

"Yes, of course," Tom says, nervously. "Thank you."

He drops the cell phone on the couch and shuffles into the bathroom, annoyed at everyone. At the principal, at the reluctant retiree, at his father, and even at the stupid white man who can't tell the difference between his son and this Chicano kid. Good grief. Tom's got less than an hour to jerk off in the shower, press a shirt and then drive over to the restaurant to meet up with his high school girlfriend, senior year.

Connie's late, which doesn't surprise Tom. She always said this was the most Mexican part about her, the concept of time. In México, time doesn't fly. It walks. But Tom would argue that the most Mexican part about her was her traditionalist view of pre-marital sex. And since Tom has no intention of marrying her any time soon, he isn't expecting to get more than a good-night kiss tonight.

Las Cazuelas hasn't changed much either, except that the menus are more presentable, having been upgraded from Xeroxed color paper to laminated sheets. The waitresses still wear the same green skirts. And Lola's still around, burgundy-haired and bug-eyed. This used to be the hangout after the MEChA meetings. The restaurant continues to play folklórico music and the occasional brass band, which suited the nationalistic mentality of the group back then.

Tom is toying with a red chip when Connie makes her entrance, wearing a brown flower print dress that hides her curves but flattens against her stomach, showing off her slim physique. Her hair now drops well past her hips, smooth and shiny as he remembers it.

"Connie!" Tom says, springing up to greet her.

"Tom!" she says, kissing his cheek. Tom notices she still refuses to wear perfume.

"You're keeping fit," she says, "a little thin, maybe. Are you feeding yourself back at the bachelor pad?"

Tom pictures the early morning rush, the peanut butter jar left open with the knife sticking out. "I try," he says. He pulls out the wooden chair for her. "You look great. What have you been up to without me?"

"Plenty, actually," she says. Tom reddens.

"I'm the community-appointed liaison between the Hispanic Chamber of Commerce and the Spanish-speaking PTA," Connie says. She pushes the menu away to place her arms on the table. "And," she continues, "I also do some translation for the counseling center at another high school. In fact, we're rivals now."

"What?" Tom says, puzzled.

"You work for Indio and I work for Coachella. Rival schools, remember?"

Tom raises his eyebrows, wondering if Connie understands this is a date.

"Anyway, that's why I was ecstatic that you got in touch with me so quickly. Now that we have one of ours in that school you can help us network into the mexicano community. They're in desperate need of a link to better resources and information in Spanish. I mean, do you realize what the mexicano drop-out rate is in the Caliente Valley?"

No, Tom concludes, she doesn't know this is a date.

After a pause for a drink of ice water, Connie goes on. "Principal Blake isn't making too many waves because she's up for that district position, so we need to pressure her even before she becomes a bigwig. Show her we mean business. And now's the best time for a preemptive attack against the prejudicial policies that Howard Blake has imposed on the school district and which Mrs. Blake plans to keep in place if she takes over his position next Spring. Their idea of a minority is a brown person who knows English. This is Caliente Valley, for crying out loud. Howard Blake can't run again, but his wife can, which is like keeping him in office. And what with all these attacks on bilingual education nowadays—well, we need all the help we can get. God, this is perfect! What do you say?"

Tom stares at Connie in disbelief. She hasn't seen him in four years and she starts talking to him as if they have just come back from picketing Safeway for selling grapes.

"Connie," he says.

"Call me Consuelo," she says, smiling as she reaches for a tortilla chip.

"Consuelo?" Tom chuckles. "Connie, I really didn't want to discuss that sort of stuff I mean . . . there's a time and a place for everything and frankly this is not the time."

Connie lets her jaw drop. "Oh, Tom, I'm so sorry. I didn't mean to overwhelm you like that, I feel so awful."

Tom smiles. He has the urge to reach across the table and take her hand but as soon as Connie opens her mouth again, he's glad he didn't.

"But I'm sure you understand the urgency of these issues," Connie says, becoming excited again. "It's not like we're back in high school when the extent of community involvement was a food drive for Thanksgiving or a weekend car wash to benefit the Mexican American Scholarship Fund. This is real life, Tom. We have to be aggressive. Muscle is what gets the job done, not petitions."

Tom leans back, embarrassed.

When the waitress comes to take their order, Connie dismisses her, asking for a few more minutes. "Well, Tom?" she asks.

"I'm thinking about the chiles rellenos," he says. "I hope they're still homemade."

Connie pulls down the menu from his hands. "Tom, I'm serious."

"Jesus, Connie, let up some," Tom says. "I just started that job and you want me to go busting in with pamphlets or something? Give me a fucking break."

"There's no need to get hostile," Connie says.

"Hostile? You're the one who walks in here with some 'plan of attack' and calling yourself Comrade Consuelo. I mean, fuck, I thought I came here tonight to have a good time, not to plot an insurrection."

"Wow," Connie says, after a pregnant pause. "I guess college has changed you."

"And for the better, I'd like to believe," Tom says. "Now let's shut the hell up and order."

Tom barely manages to finish the sentence when Connie jumps up from her chair and heads for the exit. Just then the waitress returns. Before she begins to say something, Tom chimes in: "I'll be dining alone. I'll have the chile relleno plate."

When he walks back into his apartment, his eye immediately catches the glow of the answering machine light. He expects to hear his father's voice again, but after the beep, it's the same stranger as before. Tom's body stiffens. He leans over rigidly to listen more carefully.

"Tommy," the man said. "It's Dad, again. Why haven't you called back? I really need . . . we really need to talk, son. Please, Tommy. Call me back. We have to talk about it. Please?"

Tom is overcome with goose bumps, awed by the coincidence: twice a man dials his son's number and accidentally reaches another person by the same name. *Hello, this is Tom speaking. Leave a message.* Twice the same mistake. In any case there's nothing Tom can do. Tommy's shit out of luck. And so's his father.

Now that the evening's events have settled, he sits on the couch and dials Connie on his cell phone. Predictably, she doesn't answer.

"Hey, Connie," he says. "I'm calling to apologize. I didn't mean to be such an asshole tonight. Listen, I'll make it all up to you, I promise. I have a meeting with Principal Blake and company this Sunday at noon at McCandless. I'll put in a word about this whole bilingualism issue, okay? Anyway, hope to talk to you soon. And I'm sorry."

Tom belches the aftertaste of refried beans. Suddenly this new apartment of his is not equipped for dateless living. He still has no television, no Internet, and the stereo got damaged in the move. It's like Clara's all over again. Madre Clara. He will have to drop in on her tomorrow. If he's going to kill a perfectly good Saturday, he might as well get fed doing it.

Driving into the old housing project the next day gives him chills. The church house is gone, replaced by what looks like a prison cell. Back then the crazy street preachers came on weekends to do their witnessing over a microphone so that everyone could hear them testify to the handful of misguided farmworkers who turned up for the religious antics. The loud speakers were obnoxious, but not any more than the deafening hip hop blaring out of customized cars cruising through the grounds.

He drives into the parking lot no one uses because everyone here knows it's best to keep a close watch on your vehicle, so they park on their front yards. This early in the morning there will be no theft attempts. No cruising Impalas either.

Clara lives in apartment 234, right next to apartment 233, where he lived alone most of his high school years while his father worked out his widowhood on the road. Since he left for college, his father gave up the place and moved all the way next door, into Clara's living room. The widow and the widower, knitting their webs together.

"Muchacho!" Clara cries out as soon as she opens her front door. "You should have called. But that's fine. I'm so glad you're here. Come in, come in."

"Thank you, Clara. I thought I'd surprise you."

"Well, this is a nice surprise. And you're just in time for breakfast. Chorizo y todo. Siéntate. How have you been? Your pops is on the road again."

"Yes, I know," Tom says. "He left me a message last night." Tom notices a few of his father's things here and there. A second pair of work boots in the corner, an old family photograph, slightly invasive among Clara's porcelain knickknacks. He doesn't want to wonder if they're sleeping together, what with Clara about fifteen years his father's senior.

"I was just thinking about you this morning, because I want to come measure your windows for curtains," Clara says.

"Curtains? Oh, really, Clara, there's no need. I've got blinds."

"But they're so impersonal. Curtains are more like home."

The sound of the chorizo frying on the pan drowns out her next statement, but Tom's too distracted by the thought of flowery cloth in his new apartment. Clara's sewing machine sits at the corner, mocking him. But since he doesn't want to piss off everyone he knows in town within a week of moving back, he lets it go. He'll figure out a way to weasel himself out of that one later.

"You know, Clara," Tom says.

"Tell me, mijo."

"I had the strangest phone calls recently."

"Oh. Is it those telemarketing gente? I used to tell them I didn't speak English, but now it turns out they're all bilingual." Clara serves Tom a modest serving of chorizo with egg, and then goes back to the stove to warm up tortillas. She pours coffee for both of them.

"No, not that. It's difficult to explain, but I had the same man dial my number twice while I was out. And it so happens he's trying to reach someone who's also named Tom. That's why he doesn't know he's calling the wrong person when he hears my name in the answering machine. He's leaving distressing messages."

"Well, that *is* odd. Maybe you can call him back or something if it happens again. Clear it all up."

"I could," Tom says, but without conviction. Within minutes he cleans off his plate with a last bit of tortilla.

"Would you like another serving?" Clara asks. "There's still some left in the pan."

"Thank you, no. I'll just have more coffee."

"Tom," Clara says, after she pours. "I'm glad you're back."

"It's good to be back," Tom says, but he doesn't mean it the same way.

"I know your pops will probably kill me for telling you this, but I'm afraid he's not going to phrase it correctly when he finally comes around to telling you."

Tom feels a prickling on his neck. So this is why they were waiting for him to become independent.

"Let me guess," Tom says. "You're getting married."

Clara laughs. "Cielos, no! I'm too old to get married again. Mijo, we're not even novios or anything. My, you thought all this time that your pops and I—qué risa!"

Tom blushes. "Then what is it he wants to tell me?"

"Pues, I'm only telling you this because I want to soften the blow, not because I'm being a chismosa or anything."

"Go on," Tom says.

"Your pops is leaving the Caliente Valley."

"Okay . . . " Tom says, cautiously. "There has to be more than that. Where's he going?"

"That's the tricky part," Clara says, more uncomfortably now. "You see, mijo, when your moms died, may she rest in peace, she left behind a small piece of property in Arizona. That's where her people are from."

"Her people?"

"Ay, mijo, surely after all these years you've figure out you aren't one hundred per cent Mexican."

"I'm not?" Tom tries to compile a close-up memory of his mother's face. Nothing's coming to him.

"She was part Chicana, yes, but also part some tribe or other from that area. Pima, Navajo, qué se yo. Anyway, he was waiting for you to come of age so that he could sell that property and go back to *his* people."

"What do you mean, *his* people? My father isn't Mexican either?"

"Pues, knock me over with a feather, huerco. The only Mexican you ever had in you was from your mother's mother's side. Your pops is Filipino."

Tom feels his world spin out of its orbit. All this time he was only a quarter Mexican, and there he was, living like he was a full-blooded, César Chávez–loving farmworker from the Caliente Valley?

"I think I'm going to throw up," Tom says.

"Ay, mijo," Clara says, "not on the rug. I just cleaned it!"

When he opens the door to his apartment, still reeling from all the revelations, his eye catches the flashing red light of the answering machine. Now he wishes he had given his father his cell number. He presses the play button.

"Hello, Thomas," the voice says. "It's Dad." A pause follows. "I don't want to keep pestering you so please just return my call. I'm not calling again, ok?"

A second beep. No message.

A third beep. "Tommy, it's Dad again. I'm not sure if I'm making myself clear here. I'm your father and you're not a little boy anymore, and we need to speak like one adult to another. No yelling, no arguing, just plain and decent English. Is that acceptable? Fine, then you know how to reach me. Good-bye!"

Tom sighs. There's something sad in the way this man, Tommy's father, knows his messages are being heard and ignored. Tom listens to the messages a second time. He recognizes the desperation of facing the wide chasm of non-communication between a father and son. It's a terrible feeling that not knowing what is going on in the other person's head, and why that person did what they did, and why there are always more questions than answers with every minute of silence.

"Tommy, it's Dad again . . . "

The next morning, arriving at the McCandless Memorial Library, Tom notices Principal Blake and Raymond standing outside the entrance, arguing. Raymond is an impish man with a small bald head that makes his shoulders look even wider. Tom decides to wait it out in the car, since it's clear she's reprimanding him for not letting Tom know about the meeting. Besides, Tom needs to get all the yawning out of his system. He spent half the night waiting for his father to call, and the other half in a state of restless sleep, searching for clues for his mother's Native Americanness or for his father's Filipinoness, but finding nothing. His entire family had been passing for Mexican all this time. And for what? To fit in? He can't even see it in his own face. What's he looking for anyway? He can't see himself as anything but Chicano.

As Principal Blake's voice shrills, Tom can't help but think if this new information will affect his attitude toward all the Mexican kids. It has certainly tainted his memories of his nationalistic adolescence.

He checks his watch. Almost noon. He doesn't want his new boss to think he isn't showing up so he climbs out of the car and walks toward the library, hoping to approach without surprising them. He resolves to clear his throat once he's within earshot to give them ample warning that he's near. But just as he's about to do that, Principal Blake shifts her weight and suddenly Tom realizes that they're not arguing with each other but with a third party: Connie.

Fuck. Beads of sweat break out on his forehead and along his neck. His body temperature rises even faster when Connie catches sight of him and calls out: "Tom!"

Principal Blake and Raymond turn around to look, their faces twisted into menacing scowls. Connie pushes through them and runs up to Tom.

"Tell them you know me, Tom," Connie says, out of breath. "Tell them about how you're going to be working with us." She then looks at Principal Blake and points at her with a fierce finger. "We're onto you, Blake. We've got one of ours through the door and you can't get rid of him without exposing your plan. He knows all about you and your husband's scheme to retain the status quo of the flawed district policies. Things are going to have to change! Tell them, Tom."

Tom feels dizzy, betrayed. Principal Blake stares down at Connie as if wanting to pounce on her. Then suddenly her body relaxes, her face lets go of its tension. She turns to Tom and calmly asks, "Is this true, Tomás? Are you collaborating with this irrational young woman?"

Tom's heart pounds, his body on the verge of spasms.

"I warned you about hiring one of these upstarts from around here, Margarita," Raymond interjects. "I told you we should have gotten someone from the outside, but no, you wanted one of these local do-gooders to make peace with the PTA. Well, here are the consequences. These radical Chicanos with their know-it-all attitudes—"

"Quiet, Raymond," Margarita Blake says as she holds up her hand. Slowly the hand comes down. "Tomás, I'm going to ask you again: are you collaborating with this individual and the organization she represents?"

"Tom?" Connie pleads, softly.

Tom feels himself falling out of a picture as if they were all flat figures on a TV screen just turned off. Everything around him looks gray and he's floating through it with nothing to help him keep his balance. Perhaps his parents found themselves in a similar predicament, having to make a split-second decision with irreversible consequences. Perhaps when they were filling out an application at the housing project, which caters exclusively to Mexican immigrants, to the farmworkers and the factory workers, not the Filipino truck drivers and their Native American wives who worked the cosmetic counter at the mall. And since they looked the way they did, blending in so perfectly even though neither of them was Mexican or immigrant, what was the harm in simply going with the flow, in assimilating for the sake of a better life?

"No, I'm not," he hears himself say in monotone. "I'm not part of anything."

A long silence follows.

He thinks for a moment that perhaps no one heard. He considers repeating it. Or maybe it's not too late for him to reconsider his response. Maybe he can still save face with Connie and tell them that he *is* part of her group. That he always was. And that there isn't anything or anyone that can change that. But they *had* heard the first time.

"I think you better leave, young lady," Raymond says. "This is a private meeting." Connie speeds away in tears. Tom watches her shrink from the corner of his eye.

Principal Blake claps her hands twice. "Well, we have a meeting to attend to, gentlemen. Raymond? Tomás?"

Raymond shakes his head and mouths a threat that Tom can't decipher. "I told you," he mutters to Principal Blake, who doesn't respond.

The library doors open automatically. Tom walks in after them. He knows that no matter what happens next the damage has already been done, though he wants so desperately to believe that he can still make things right. There's so much he wants to believe. He wants to go home to hear the phone ring, to pick up the receiver and tell Tommy's father that this is not Tommy, not his apartment, not his life. And that that's a good thing, see, because he has a second chance to say the right thing to his son. "My name is Tomás, not Thomas," he will say to the man, and they will have a polite laugh about the whole matter and Tom will wish him luck in contacting his son.

Or better yet, he wants to hear the phone ring, pick up the receiver and tell his own father that it's all right, that he understands that sometimes what should come out right comes out wrong, and that we're only human and will continue to make bad calls, and that that doesn't mean it has to sting forever.

But Tom suspects that if indeed he speaks to the man, the man will hang up abruptly, embarrassed but relieved that he can rethink what he says to Tommy. And if he indeed speaks to his own father, his father will babble his way into another unforgivable comment.

And Tom also suspects that come Monday morning he will be informed that Raymond has decided to postpone his retirement for a few more months, maybe until the end of the school year. Yes, Tom will be kept on the payroll, same salary, but he has proven such a valuable resource in that back room, that he's going to be asked to work there indefinitely.

Confessions of a Drowning Man

I'm drunk and driving down the back roads to avoid the cops when I spot a squad car making a left turn at the next intersection and head my direction. I make a left turn myself into the landfill on the dirt path that leads to the old canal. When I was younger, my cousins and I used to hide out here from our parents to smoke dope. It'll be wise to hide out again so I follow the path clear to the end. The soil's softer than I remember and I know damn well as I drive those last few yards that the car's going to get stuck. When I shift into reverse the wheels spin around without moving me back onto solid ground. I laugh it off at first. This'll be one more adventure to tell my cousins about as I enlist them to help me pull the car out. I know this area well. My cousins used to live here. The projects down the road have payphones because many of the residents don't have their own lines. And tonight I don't either since my company canceled my cell because I missed a few payments. Well, maybe more than a few, but blame my girlfriend Valeria for that. She yap-yap-yaps in my ear so much that I set the cell phone down for minutes at a time and come back to it periodically without her even noticing. So getting my cell cut off is actually a blessing in disguise, though not a very lucky thing tonight.

Since I'm still too tipsy to walk out to the projects, I decide to sleep it off some. And as my eyes are set to close, my head against my arm against the steering wheel, the howling coyote startles me. In all my years living in the desert I have never seen one, but suddenly I don't want to either. I make a mental note of the crowbar beneath the seat.

The second time the coyote howls the animal sounds farther off so I relax, knowing it's moving away from where I'm sitting. And that's when I notice it, the glowing body floating on the water's surface. I don't believe in ghosts, but there's nothing like being alone in a deserted landfill at night to bring out the superstitious Mexican in me. My heart speeds up its beating. I lock the car door and immediately I feel pretty stupid about it. So to make myself brave again I unlock the door and roll the window down to stick my head out for a better look.

The apparition's a body all right. A woman's body, white as a bathtub. I can't see her face, only part of her torso, which is turned inward, the leg jutting out and bent at the knee. I can tell it's a woman's body by the leg because it looks smooth and hairless. Valeria comes to mind, but I let go of this thought right away, afraid that it might just be my girlfriend's body sticking out of the canal. The more I try not to think about it the more I do, so I have to make sure once and for all that this isn't the woman who's probably waiting for me at home, ready to bitch my ear off for staying out drinking with the guys. And all I can do is sit there and take it like a dumbshit because I can't tell her I go out to forget I promised to marry her. Blame the alcohol for that one, also. I step out of the car.

As soon as I near the edge of the canal I get a better view of the body. She doesn't look so graceful from this angle. She isn't yet bloated, but the skin glares in the moonlight like she's wearing those plastic bodysuits I've seen in the winter Olympic games on TV. Her head's completely submerged in the water, but the hair floats up like brown seaweed. Valeria's hair is black.

I try to imagine how this woman ended up here. The canal isn't deep enough to drown in on purpose, so I rule out suicide. If she had accidentally stumbled in, perhaps while drunk, she would've had to walk quite a distance from the road to find the canal. And there's no other car sitting around except for mine. That's when it hits me. She's been murdered. Either she was brought here and then murdered or murdered somewhere else and then brought here. In any case the evidence'll be in the tire tracks, the footprints left behind, maybe even in the vehicle that might have transported her here. Like that one over there, still stuck in the soil.

Panicked, I jump back into my car and press the gas pedal until I drown the engine. Stupid luck! Stupid luck! Stupid luck! I walk out a few times to bounce on the trunk. I even gather some stones and shove them into the hole that the wheel's digging up but nothing works. The car's stuck. My only hope then is my cousins. I rush back down the dirt path. My body wearies after a few steps since I exhausted myself in the desperate effort to release my car from the sand trap. To pass the time in my slower pace, I rehearse what I'll say to my cousins. *Hey, it's me, Mac. Get me out of here, guys, I'm parked in front of a dead woman.* Too dramatic to be believed. *Hey, guys, it's Mac. I'm in a little bit of trouble here.* Too self-accusatory. *I was trying to avoid the police so I drove into the landfill. In the middle of the night. Drunk. And there's a dead woman flung into the canal.* Never mind. I'll simply tell them to come pick me up. *Don't ask any questions.* The mystery of it'll reel them in.

When I finally reach the road I'm dizzy and thirsty. The road's empty. At a distance, a few lights are on at the projects, and I envy these people suddenly, phoneless but safe inside the comfort of their beds or couches. I'm about to cross the road when I step into a piece of wood. It's just what I need to roll the car out of the dirt so I pick it up and head back to the canal. This'll save me all the trouble of giving explanations to my cousins. They're like my brothers, and like my brothers they know I'm not exactly kind to women. I imagine they'll pretend to believe whatever I say, but in the back of their minds they'll let the doubt buzz about until the fuckers wise up and turn me in, hoping for reward money.

My mouth goes dry. When my cousins and I took trips into the desert as kids, before any of us had cars or girlfriends, we did so during the day. The heat was intense in the summers, but we knew that the canal was at the end of the path, its water fresh and cool. In the winters we would pull our pocket money together and hold a contest: whoever kept both hands inside the cold water the longest got to take the winnings home. I was never that desperate but I did my best not to be the first to take my hands out and push them into my armpits. I can't imagine drinking out of the canal with the corpse in it, but I'm getting weaker with each passing minute and I feel a headache coming on.

The car looks like a junked shell. I always wondered how cars ended up at the landfill. If they were useless to begin with, how did they make it? It seems a waste to tow them here when the junkyards pay decent money for them. I used to go with my father to pick out parts at these junkyards, and the fat white guys who ran them charged by the pound. After that seat-belt law passed with a vengeance in California, everyone who owned old clunkers went in to unscrew them off the dead cars, and we all respected the fat white guys for not jacking up the price for seat belts when they could have.

When I bend down to shove the wooden plank under the wheel I hear a splashing that stops my heart. I freeze, shuddering at the thought of the woman come back to life. I stand up slowly to check.

The woman's still in the canal, same position, but the coyote has come around sniffing. It pushes its snout against the woman's torso and the hand moves in the water, startling the coyote back. I get angry all of a sudden and disgusted by the sight of the coyote come to scavenge so I let out a roar that frightens the wild animal off like a common house cat. That release sobers me up completely, but now I'm more exhausted than ever. Like it or not, corpse and all, I'm going to have to take a drink from the canal.

I walk to the canal as far away from the body as I can, against the current. I face away as I drop my hand down to scoop the water. I force my brain to think about anything but the body: I think about Valeria and how I'll be nicer to her, how I'll never hit her again when she pisses me off, though there are certain things that will still merit an ass-kicking, like when she overspends on clothes and I have to ask my parents to help pay the rent so that this idiot and I don't end up on the street. I think about how I'll try to do right by my parents, lay off the pot, the booze, and marry Valeria and give them a grandchild finally since my sister ended up a spinster with a nose ring that makes her look like a granola-crunching dyke and my pretty little wide-eyed brother who went off to college is most certainly a homo. Botanist, my foot. He studies flowers. Enough said. I think about my job down at the pizzeria and I promise to wash my hands more often when I do the dough. I'm careless on purpose because I resent making pizza for all those losers who come in with their clipped coupons. If they come in with their girlfriends I get even more pissed off because they're taking their girls out on a cheap date. In my book a girl has to be treated right, you know what I'm saying?

I'm about to take my second drink when I catch a glimpse of a white high-heeled shoe in the water and that tosses me back on my ass. When I strike the ground, a few stones dig into my tail-bone and I cry out like a girl. I'm glad no one's around to hear me or to watch me rub my butt. I get up and splash some water on my face. I use a stick to fish the shoe out by the mouth. The water in the toe end makes it heavy and the stick breaks, dropping the shoe back into the canal. I grab it firmly with my bare hand and crush the water out of it. When the shoe caves in I feel like a brute. I look over the canal to spot the second shoe but I don't find it. And then a thought occurs to me.

I walk closer to the body and sure enough I'm right: the second shoe's on its foot. I want to show some respect by putting on the shoe she lost so I walk into the canal and toward the body. I've never touched a dead body before, but I know it can't be any different from touching a living one, except the dead body's probably stiff and unresponsive. As my hand nears the body I pretend I'm sneaking up on Valeria as she sleeps, but I shake that image off—this isn't my woman. My woman is as loud at night as she is in the daytime, and it won't matter if I record her sleeping she'll still deny she snores.

The leg's stiff, but I don't have to lift it much since the water helps me ease it to the surface. The skin's clammy, but I slip the shoe into place without trouble. Now the body looks more complete and I congratulate myself for my courage. I guide the foot back into the water until the shoe rests nicely at the bottom. This is my good-bye.

I go back to the car and kick the plank in to secure it beneath the wheel. I give it one more kick for effect, miscalculating my own strength and hurting my toe. I limp to the driver's seat, and as soon as I reach toward the ignition I somehow sense I'll grasp at nothing because the keys are gone. Retracing my journeys back and forth I conclude that they're either somewhere on the edge of the canal or in the dirt path anywhere from the canal to the road. Regardless, only luck'll help me find them in the dark, and luck has been bitch-slapping me from the moment I made that left turn. The thought of calling my cousins seems obscene now because I have let so much time pass. My sneakers are muddy and my fingerprints are all over the dead woman's shoe. By my watch it's a little past midnight. By the moon and the dark and the cold it seems much later than that. At this point I have no choice but to spend the night in the car, but I won't be able to sleep, knowing the body'll still be there in the morning. I make another decision I know I'll regret: to bury the body in the landfill.

My father always said to never get caught without tools in an emergency. I have the crowbar beneath the seat in case some sonofabitch tries to give me lip on the road; I have my kick-ass jack and spare tire in the trunk; I have a canvas in case I have to park the car in the hot sun; and I have my heavy-duty tool set. Of course, none of these things did me any good in trying to free the car from the sand or in helping me hotwire the engine now that my keys are missing. My cousin Lalo said he'd teach me how but I always thought that was the first step to becoming a no-good car thief, which he was, and I want to keep myself honest. At least now I can use the canvas to wrap and drag the body to the landfill. If entire cars can vanish in the rubble, a body'll be no problem.

Before I move the body onto the canvas, I wrap the face with my bandanna. I don't want to know if the eyes are opened or closed, or if this body looks like anyone I know. There's a story here I don't want to find out, namely, why this woman has been killed.

There might be a dozen reasons why she ended up here, lifeless in the desert. Some of them might even be her fault. Who am I to tamper with her fate? She's been dumped here to disappear.

I use the crowbar to roll the body on the canvas, and then I secure the canvas around it with the rope that goes through the metal loops. It doesn't look much like a body anymore as I drag it off. The sound grates against my ears so I whistle. I was going to sing a tune but that seemed too disrespectful.

The landfill's actually a ravine piled with garbage. When I was younger I used to search for hidden treasures with my cousins. Mostly we looked for discarded porn magazines, which we found without fail. Once I found an old textbook and when I flipped through it, out came a twenty-dollar bill that had been used as a bookmark. My cousin Lalo once found a check for seventy-five dollars inside a Bible. The check was no good my uncle claimed, but my cousin swore it was, otherwise why would his father have kept it. Lalo held it against his father for many months after, but he said he got every dollar back eventually as he picked his father's wallet the mornings after payday when his father slept in after a night out drinking.

When I reach a nice cluttered part of the dump, I shove the garbage out with my feet and the crowbar. I don't have anything to dig a hole with, but I don't really want to bury the body. I just want to get it out of the way.

I drag the body into the shallow grave and start piling the garbage over it. I even come across a porn magazine and it falls over the pile, exposing a naked woman holding up her breasts. It's too tacky to leave on top of the body, so I grab the magazine and fling it across the ravine. It flutters like a wounded bird. Satisfied, I sit down to rest. Now that the body's out of the water I can go back and safely have a drink.

More than an hour passes by, almost two. By the time I make my way back to the canal it's a quarter past three. I splash water on my face again, breathing easier. And I know my luck has changed because there, shining like gold nuggets in the water, are my keys. I snatch them right away and use whatever energy

I have left to run back to the car. My breathing slows though as soon as I sit down and push the key in the ignition. If there's a moment to reflect, it's right then and there as I'm about to drive away from this night and this place. What does it all mean?

Ma always said there'll be obstacles to overcome in life. Perhaps this is the one for me. I've been given a chance to get back on track and do things differently. I rack my brains about what I'll do differently from now on. I decide to go back to that old high school slogan: "Don't drink and drive." Yes, if I hadn't been drinking in the first place I wouldn't have gotten myself into this mess. Had I been sober, I'd've crossed paths with that police car without incident. He might've taken note of my driving behavior in passing and concluded there was nothing there to bother with: *There goes another good citizen of Caliente, California, on his way home after a late night of honest work.*

I turn the key and the reliable engine wakes up with a roar. I shift into reverse and press-ease the clutch out, the gas pedal in. I can feel the car moving back but just as I apply more pressure I hear the plank snap and the car locks down in place again. I get out to check under the wheel. One of the broken halves is lodged in there, so I hope it'll still give the wheel enough friction to guide it out. But I have to do this swiftly. Driving skills, don't fail me now.

Back at the wheel, I work the clutch and gas pedals. I shift into first this time to see if I can move forward. No dice. I shift into reverse. It's working. Now I'll simply have to shift back into first to move out of the soft spot entirely. The car jerks back, then forward, skidding as I shift, and I know I have to shift quickly into reverse before the motor dies on me again. The adrenaline makes me sweat profusely, and as I grit my teeth I bite my tongue, which gets me worked up even more.

It takes seconds for the car to slide out of the soft soil, and before I know what's happening it skids toward the canal. I try to turn the wheel and push in the clutch in time, but this only locks the breaks and the sudden force sends the car reeling over the edge. I hear the roof of the car crack with the pressure and the windshield pops into spider webs. My shoulders feel crushed in, and that's when I realize I'm upside down in the canal. I don't feel as if I'm upside down because my head's twisted to one side as if I'm lying on my side. The smell of gasoline and motor oil makes me dizzy. I become disoriented quickly because I can't move. Matters worsen when the water starts filling up the tight cabin, and I feel the cool fluid brush against my scalp. And then the water starts to rise up to my cheek. I think I see a stream of blood grow out into my line of sight, and when I spit I confirm it's coming out of my mouth.

My body starts to shiver and this sends vibrations of ripples on the surface of the water. I know then I'll drown if I don't freeze to death first. Either way this is the end of me. As my eyes shut themselves I imagine how I'll be found sooner or later, perhaps by some crazy kids who come over from the projects to smoke out. They'll start talking about how a car happened to jump over the edge like this and killed its dumbshit driver. They'll say that the driver was probably drunk or high or wired—a tecato because of the old English lettering of my tattoo. "Maclovio," "Mac" to everyone else, the only cholo fool to ink his first name on his back and not his last because there were tons of López motherfuckers running around the old neighborhood. What a dork, they'll say, what a waste. They might say other things, but in any case they'll have a story to tell. And Valeria will wear black for all of one week and move on, and my mother will wear black for the rest of her life and light candles in front of the only photograph in the album that makes me look innocent—my high school portrait, senior year. All my acne scars have been airbrushed, and I've yet to get that scar above my left eyebrow, the injury that got me expelled for the rest of the year for breaking this gringo's nose with my head. He got a new nose and I got no diploma.

My teeth stop chattering, which means I'm a beat away from death. And if there's a God he must be removing me like an ugly mole on the skin of the Caliente Valley. Well, at least my mother will miss me.

Then suddenly the light. My abuelita always said that'll be the first sign that la pelona has climbed off her parlor chair to come get you: the circle of light coming into focus like the big yellow eye of an approaching train. That eye is coming all right, swiftly without a shimmy or a twitch and zeroing in on my face.

I must have blacked out at that moment, because the next thing I remember is getting strapped into a gurney while hearing the grinding of boots in the sand. Even in my fucked-up state I can put this simple math together. And when I hear the cop say, "I wonder what the jackass was doing out here in the first place? Lucky for him I was parked out on the side of the road." I know it must have been the splash of the car going into the canal in the dead of night that brought him here.

The brace around my neck keeps me from dismissing the whole thing as a bad dream. And as the ambulance pulls out of the landfill, I conclude that the best thing I did was get rid of the body. The cop would have been asking a very different question if I hadn't. I figure if she's meant to be found, she'll be found. Fate has a clever way of aligning the stars, Ma always said. I pity the dead woman. I wonder what she did to get herself into this mess. And as the ambulance turns the corner at that intersection where my whole adventure got its start, I wonder if the dead woman misread the signs that could've saved her soul.

Men without Bliss

for Richard Yañez

At the "good-bye and good luck" party, Andrés looks at the faces of his coworkers and tries to remember when he has had an intimate conversation with any of them, but he can't recall a single exchange that warrants their theatrical display of last-minute friendship. In the corner, the silver helium balloon has begun to flatten, and Andrés knows that the blue corn tortilla chips, staples at every function, come from a garbage-sized bag in the storage room. He takes pleasure, however, in watching the people parade up to him to say their good-byes, one after the other.

"You'll be missed," declares a tall, hefty redhead Andrés has never been introduced to until that afternoon. Her lipstick matches her bloodred nails. She retraces her steps to the center table for a second slice of chocolate cake. Andrés wants to watch her eat it, but his view is blocked by another well-wisher.

"You'll be missed," he tells him.

Andrés doesn't recognize the overweight white guy dressed in a white shirt and polka-dot tie. "Why?" he asks him. The white guy titters uncertainly as he walks toward the punch bowl.

Thirty minutes after ushering everyone into the conference room, Mary Ann, the supervisor, announces that it's time to get back to work. The French, Spanish, German, and Italian tutors shuffle obediently out the door. Only a few of them walk up to Andrés to shake his hand or to give him a European kiss on both cheeks. The hefty redhead sways forward again and tilts her head to the left. Teary-eyed, she declares: "What's the Italian group going to do without you?" She's out the door before Andrés can tell her he tutored Spanish.

Only the ill-humored secretary—Program Associate according to the nameplate on her desk—stays behind to clean up. She mumbles under her breath as she wipes the conference tables clean and drops the uneaten chips into a trash bin.

Mary Ann returns with an envelope in her hand. "You'll need this," she says. "A letter of rec. Accrued sick days will be included in the final paycheck."

Andrés takes the envelope.

"I'm sure you'll do better in your next place of employment," Mary Ann says. She's shorter than Andrés, but in her high heels and with the tone of reprehension in her voice she seems taller.

"I'll certainly try," Andrés says.

"Professionalism cannot be compromised," Mary Ann adds as she shakes her head. "I'm sure you've learned your lesson here." Andrés taught individual and group tutoring sessions for a year at the language center, never once canceling an appointment or showing up late. And then they fired him.

"I don't think I've done anything wrong," Andrés mumbles. In the background, he sees the Program Associate roll her eyes. His teaching evaluations were generally noncommittal, but every other month one or another of his female students launched a harassment complaint. Not even Mary Ann, who was a stickler for policy and procedure, could articulate clearly what he was doing wrong.

"We've discussed this, Andrés," Mary Ann says. "With you we're risking a lawsuit that we can't afford." She said the same thing when she gave him his notice two weeks ago.

"But I've never done or said anything that was inappropriate."

"The complaints read the same: you make them feel uncomfortable when you look at them. That's enough for us to take action," she says.

None of the male students had complained, though it was true that he sometimes looked at them in a way someone might call funny. But they preferred to make their appointments with the female Spanish tutors anyway, so he hardly saw them. "Maybe that's their problem," Andrés says.

Mary Ann shakes her head in disbelief. "If you want to file an unlawful termination of employment form, you can speak with someone in resources." She storms off to her office.

The Program Associate closes the cake box and wipes the knife with a paper towel. "I'd appreciate it if you emptied your desk out before four o'clock," she says. "I don't want to put in overtime setting up your cubicle for the new Spanish tutor. Do you want to take the rest of this cake home?"

Andrés walks out of the building with the cake box and the helium balloon. The bag over his shoulder holds a few blank pages of good cream-colored paper he'll need for his résumé, three used Agatha Christie paperbacks, and a recycled manila folder to seal the damaged screen in his father's bedroom window. He's well aware that he's been dragging the deflated balloon behind him like an empty dog collar, but he has no choice because the string is tightly bound to the cake box and he didn't want to ask the edgy Program Associate for the scissors. He throws everything into the back seat and drives off, taking one last look at the language tutorial center. He can't recall why he ended up tutoring Spanish in the first place. His training that one semester at the community college was in psychology.

When he gets home he finds his father slumped on the couch. A janitor at the elementary school, he hasn't changed out of his dark blue work shirt. The name stitched above the left hand pocket reads "Rapael."

"They tried to spell "Rafael" the gringo way," his father explained when he first brought home the three regulation shirts he had been issued. "And then they left out the *h*. I don't really give a shit. They never call me by any name anyhow."

Andrés sets the cake box and newspaper on the table; the deflated balloon hangs over the edge like a silver placenta trailing its umbilical cord.

"Rapael," he says to his father. "Do you want a piece of cake?"

"With my diabetes and high blood pressure?" his father answers. "I'll take two pieces. Is it my birthday or yours?"

"I lost my job," Andrés says. He rummages through the cupboards for a plate.

"Oh," his father says, disinterested. "What kind of cake is it?"

Andrés cuts a large piece for his father. "The store-bought kind," he says.

"I like those," his father says, twisting his pinky into his ear. "Don't skimp on the frosting."

As Andrés looks over the classifieds in the newspaper later that same evening, his father watches television on the couch. He hasn't changed out of his work shirt. In fact he hasn't changed position all afternoon.

Andrés is fascinated by the exotic items in the "for sale" listings. "Do you want to buy a ferret, Rapael?" Andrés calls out.

"A parrot? No, they stink," his father says.

"A ferret," Andrés says. "It's like a weasel."

"They stink," his father says. "How about another piece of that cake?"

After giving his father another helping of cake, Andrés circles potential jobs. Delivery Driver. Dental Assistant. Healthcare Provider. Housekeeper. Teacher's Aide. All of them minimum wage, but that didn't matter. Healthcare doesn't require any previous experience, so he makes a note of the address.

"You know what this cake reminds me of?" his father says. He waves the fork in the air, dropping a few crumbs on his lap. "The day you were born."

"You had cake on the day I was born?" says Andrés.

"It's a birthday cake, ain't it?" his father says, exasperated.

Andrés circles an ad for proofreader, though he isn't a good speller. But he figures he can run the documents through the computer's spell check.

"So what about the day I was born, Rapael?" Andrés says.

"On the day you were born I went to see a movie," his father says. "Since you took your damn time popping out of your mother's oven. The hospital waiting room was making me sick." He laughs at his own joke and coughs a few times.

"Don't choke on your funny," Andrés says.

"Fuck you," his father says. He continues talking with cake in his mouth, spitting out crumbs. "Anyway, so I took a long walk and ended up at this movie theater. A few hours of distraction is what I needed so I bought a ticket. You were born halfway through the movie. I could feel it in the way my body relaxed. But I decided to stay and watch the other half. Your mother was pissed, God rest her soul."

Andrés suddenly looks up from the newspaper. He turns to look at his father.

"What movie did you see?" he asks.

"I don't remember," his father says.

"You don't remember the movie you were watching while I was being born?"

"That was like forty years ago," his father says.

"Thirty-eight," Andrés corrects him.

"Whatever, it's still a lifetime ago. Last millennium as a matter of fact."

"Don't you even remember what it was about?"

"Nope," his father says.

Andrés turns to the sheets of newspaper again.

That night Andrés tosses in bed. He can hear his father wheezing in his sleep in the next bedroom. He tries to guess what sort of movie his father had been watching and how it could have marked his own fate. Knowing his father, he'd probably walked into a porn theater, which is why he didn't want to say what he watched. Andrés tries not to think of his father sitting in a smelly dark room as the projector tosses out images of a naked woman taking it from behind, her breasts knocking into each other and jiggling like water balloons.

Andrés overdresses for the visit to the group home in nearby Palm Desert, though he's only going in to drop off his résumé. On the porch, a cluster of old guys in faded clothes blow smoke into each other's faces. Cigarette butts are scattered on the porch, and Andrés recalls the shreds of paper after a string of firecrackers explodes.

As he walks in, a musty odor invades his nose. His father's room smells the same.

"The title is residential counselor," the young female administrator says. She's wearing an ankle-length dress with a slit going down the side that exposes her calf when she crosses her legs. She looks closely over his résumé.

"Looks like you've got plenty of work experience," she says.

Andrés counts the piercings on her face: one nose stud, one eyebrow ring, two lip rings, six earrings on the left ear.

"We only have graveyard shift available at the moment," she says. "The hours are eleven P.M. to nine A.M."

"I'm interested," Andrés says. "What are the duties required?"

"Primarily that you be awake and aware at all hours in case of an emergency. You'll need to get your first-aid and CPR certification. Secondly, you'll need to fetch anyone for meds if they haven't taken their bedtime pills."

Andrés pictures himself whistling from the front porch and the residents running up to him like trained dogs.

"And thirdly," she says. "Make them breakfast at seven A.M., plus start handing out the morning meds to anyone who's awake. Usually only half of them are. You need to log into the record book for each resident as you dispense meds. But it's super easy."

"How many residents?" Andrés asks.

"Twenty-five. Twenty of them are males. These are all developmentally disabled adults. Most of them have families here in the Caliente Valley, but rarely do any of them get visitors," she adds. "Pretty low maintenance. They do everything for themselves, except they can't cook and they can't manage their own meds. They're very low-key. Nice people."

Andrés is suddenly aware that she's trying to sell him the position.

"So you'll let me know if I need to come in for an interview?" he asks.

"Oh, I thought this was it," she says, flustered. "I mean, you seem very capable and you're our strongest candidate. It's yours if you want it."

Andrés is suspicious but just as desperate as she. So he accepts the position: full-time graveyard shift Sunday through Wednesday. Health and dental included. He will start the next day. They give him thirty days to get his CPR certificate. He hopes no one needs CPR before then.

At home, Andrés opens up a can of minestrone soup for dinner. When his father arrives from the school, he carries a bag of toilet paper, the partially dispensed rolls varying thicknesses, and a stack of paper towels from a bathroom dispenser.

"Soup's on, Rapael," Andrés says.

"What kind of soup is it?"

"Vegetable," Andrés says.

"Any more of that cake left?"

Later that evening Andrés stares at his father dozing off on the couch. At his feet, the untouched bowl of soup. On his lap, a small dish with crumbs. The fork dangles loosely from his left hand.

"I found a new job," Andrés says.

"What?" his father responds in a sleepy tone.

"I found a new job. I'll be working nights Sunday through Wednesday."

"That's good, son," his father says and then falls asleep again.

In the morning Andrés fries eggs and sausages for breakfast. He also makes toast, oatmeal, and fresh juice, which pleases his father.

"Smells good," his father says.

"I'm practicing for my new job at the group home," Andrés says. "I'll be making breakfast for a dozen people every morning at work. Try the sausages."

"What kind of people are these, retards?"

"They're developmentally disabled adults."

"Retards," his father says.

The young female administrator, Cassie was her name, said that most of the residents were paranoid schizophrenics. "But they're harmless," she was quick to add.

"You know I think I remember a little more about that theater I went to the day you were born," his father says.

Andrés' ears perk up. "What do you remember?"

"A woman in a red hat," his father says.

"There was a woman in a red hat in the movie?"

"I didn't say anything about the movie," his father corrects him. "I said I remembered something about the theater."

"You met a woman with a red hat in the theater?"

"No, stupid, let me finish," his father snaps. He takes a long gulp of his orange juice and then continues. "There was a movie poster at the theater showing a woman in a red hat. That's why I bought a ticket in the first place. The poster looked interesting. You couldn't see the woman's face because the hat was tilted forward. You could catch a glimpse of her chin. And I think her fingers were resting on the brim of the hat like she was pulling it down to hide her face. Her nails were as red as the hat. That's it. Draw your own conclusions."

"And you're sure there was no woman in a red hat in the movie?"

"I don't remember," his father says. "The orange juice could use a little sugar."

Andrés tries to nap during the day, but ends up reading through the pages of *The Body in the Library* without much interest. He finishes the murder mystery by the time his father returns from work but he can't remember who done it. He resolves to reread the ending at work since there will be nothing else to do in the predawn hours.

At ten P.M. he decides to drive off to work early. His father is already wheezing away in his room.

Every light in the group home is on when he pulls into the driveway. The same cluster of residents smokes on the porch and a new cluster has gathered in the garden to smoke as well. They puff away without talking, like a row of strangers smoking at a bus stop.

"Are you the new guy?" one of the residents asks. He has a long beard and wide blue eyes that look as if they're being crushed open by his glasses.

"I sure am," Andrés says. "I'm Andy. Good to meet you." The old guy shakes his hand.

"That's disgusting, man," another resident says. He has a large tattoo of a bird on his forearm. "He was picking his nose all afternoon." The other residents laugh.

Andrés walks into the hall, wiping his hand on his pants, and then steps into the small office where he was interviewed. The swing-shift person is surprised to see him. She's sitting on the chair with her feet up on the desk, a bag of yarn on her lap.

"Hello, there," she says, setting her knitting needles down. "Welcome. I'm Louise. You're Andy?"

"Yes," he says. "The graveyard shift."

"That's nice," she says. "The rest of us were taking turns with that shift. I told Cassie she better hire someone quick or she'd have a group of disgruntled employees in her hands."

"Well, I'm here to relieve you," he says, attempting a smile.

"You sure are," Louise says. She stuffs her knitting in a plastic bag and rushes out of the office before Andrés can remind her that his shift doesn't start for another twenty minutes. He had been hoping to chat with her.

Andrés follows the instructions Cassie provided: he checks the record book—all of the residents have received their evening meds; he goes down to the storage room to bring up breakfast supplies—milk, coffee, eggs, sausage; he makes sure any lights not in use are off; he makes his rounds through the top floor, where residents watch televisions in their private rooms; he sweeps the dining area where a few residents watch television at no volume.

"It doesn't work," one of the residents says to him when he suggests turning up the sound. He leaves them staring into the screen.

He sits down at the desk with his book in his hand and by midnight he falls asleep. He's awakened numerous times during the night by the shuffling of bodies around the halls. Each time he thinks it's his father sneaking into the kitchen for a midnight snack.

"Hey," one of the residents walks into the office. "You got any smokes, buddy?"

"I don't smoke," Andrés answers with a yawn.

"Then you're not going to be very popular around here," the resident warns. He's a large man in suspenders that stretch precariously across his belly. He's about to leave when he suddenly turns around and adds, "Well I hope you last longer than the other guy."

"What happened to the other guy?" Andrés asks, curiously.

"Heart attack," the resident says. "I dialed 911 myself, but they didn't get here in time."

"Oh," Andrés says.

"I kept dialing the wrong number," he says, breaking into chuckles as he walks off.

Before dawn Andrés drags himself into the kitchen and gets the stove going to prepare breakfast. A few residents knock on the kitchen door demanding their morning meds and Andrés maneuvers between the two tasks.

"What's your name?" he asks each of them as he runs his finger across the row of Medikits.

"Brunswick," one the resident answers, annoyed. "Haven't you learned my name yet?"

"I'm sorry, sir," Andrés says. "But this is my first day."

"It is?" Mr. Brunswick says in surprise. "Aren't you the guy who had the heart attack?"

Andrés finishes cooking and logs in Mr. Brunswick, Mr. Shepley, Ms. Calloway, Mr. Newman, and Mr. Harrison-Boyd. All of them have helpings of scrambled eggs and toast, spooning jam from a container the size of the coffee can. When it's clear no one else is coming down for breakfast, Andrés helps himself to a plate of eggs. They taste bland.

"Hey, buddy," the large man in suspenders says. Mr. Velasco, Andrés has learned.

"Ready for some breakfast?" Andrés says.

"You got any smokes?" Mr. Velasco asks.

"Sorry, Mr. Velasco," Andrés says. "I don't smoke. Would you like some eggs?"

"Shove the eggs up your ass," Mr. Velasco says before storming off.

When the morning shift comes, Andrés hands over the keys to the office and walks sleepily to his car. Once in bed he sleeps all day until his father gets home from work. The noise from the television wakes Andrés up.

"How was your new job?" his father asks. He has his hand stuffed inside a yellow box of breakfast cereal.

Andrés makes circles with his head, stretching out his neck. "I need to get used to staying awake at night," he says. "How was your day, Rapael?"

"Nothing exciting. Except some kid brought a gun to school."

"Did he threaten to shoot anybody?"

"For show and tell," his father says. "Made one of the girls piss in her panties. I was called in to clean it up. The kid didn't know any better. Say, do any of those retards take Lipitor?"

"They're not retards, Rapael."

"Departmentally handicapped adults or whatever. They take Lipitor?"

"Some do," Andrés says. "Why? You want me to bring you some home?"

"I'm running out," his father says.

"No problem," Andrés says.

He opens another can of soup and serves his father a bowl with crackers he brought back from the kitchen at work.

"Have you given any more thought to that woman in the red hat?" Andrés asks.

"Not as much as you apparently," says his father. He dips each cracker into the soup until it gets soggy before he pops it into his mouth. "I told you I don't remember anything else besides the red hat and that weird writing on the poster."

"What weird writing?" Andrés says.

"I thought I told you about that," his father says. "They had this weird-looking title above the red hat. Like those letters in the Chinese menus. But they were American letters made to look like Chinese letters."

"And?"

"And nothing. That's all I remember," his father says. "I thought that was the movie I was walking into, but nope. The movie had no Chinese letters or woman in a red hat to speak of."

"Interesting," Andrés mumbles.

"I'm sure they're also taking Depakote," says his father.

"Say what?" Andrés says.

"Your people," his father says. "Check if they're also taking Depakote. Big pink pills."

"Oh," says Andrés. "Sure."

That night at work he has to track down Ms. Ryan to give her her meds. She won't open the door to her room.

"I've got keys, Ms. Ryan," Andrés says. "Either you open up or I do."

"Got to hell!" she screams. "I told them I wasn't taking any more meds. Been taking meds for thirty years and I'm losing my eyesight because of it."

"Well, is everything all right in there?" he asks.

"I'm not even decent so you better not open that door!"

He walks back into the office and marks the medication log: R for refusal.

"Hey, buddy," Mr. Velasco says. "You got any smokes?"

Andrés looks up at the old man in suspenders. "I just ran out," he says. "Mr. Shepley took my last one."

"That goddamn Shepley," Mr. Velasco says, and walks away.

Andrés checks the resident records, pulls out the Medikits that have Lipitor in the small plastic compartments and fishes out a few pills. Since the residents take up to half a dozen different pills, one less isn't noticeable. In the shelf marked refills, he finds entire bottles of Depakote. He stuffs the one labeled for Mr. Velasco into his coat and resolves to bring him some cigarettes the following week. For the rest of the night he simply presses his fists to his mouth as he leans on the desk with his elbows and thinks about the woman in the red hat.

"Say," one of the residents interrupts. He holds a large sheet of paper in his hands.

"What is it, sir," says Andrés. "Mr. . . ."

"Gilman," the man says. "Can I show you my drawing?"

"Sure," says Andrés. "What did you draw?"

Mr. Gilman turns the paper over. "A ship."

The drawing has been made exclusively with straight lines.

"Is that the Titanic?" Andrés asks.

Mr. Gilman chuckles. "Not quite. I have many more in my room if you care to see them."

"Why not?" Andrés says, and he follows Mr. Gilman into his room down the hall.

The room is small with an unmade bed on one side, and a chair with an old suitcase on it. The wall opposite the bed displays a small gallery of drawings—ships, helicopters, cars—all of them drawn with ink and a straight edge. Andrés notices a picture of a space ship in the center of the drawings.

"That's interesting," Andrés says as he leans in closer to inspect it. "Is that like the Star Trek Enterprise?"

After a brief silence Mr. Gilman speaks up. "That's the mother ship," he says in a serious tone. "She's hovering up in space looking out for us."

"Well, thank you for sharing, Mr. Gilman," Andrés says as he slowly backs out. "I need to get back into my office."

Mr. Gilman places one hand on Andrés' shoulder. "You do understand, don't you?" he asks.

Andrés nods. "I do," he says.

The rest of the night goes by without incident.

That afternoon after waking up, Andrés goes into the bookstore at the mall. Helen J waits behind the counter.

"Hi, Andrés," she says, waving him over. Andrés makes his way over reluctantly.

She leans over to kiss him on the cheek and Andrés complies, slightly embarrassed. Helen J's hair feels coarse when it rubs against his skin.

"Haven't seen you in a while," she says. "Here to buy some more mysteries?"

"Not exactly," he says. She seems disappointed. "I came to buy a movie guide."

"Are you looking for DVD recommendations?" she asks excitedly. "I've seen some great ones lately."

"No, Helen J," he says. "I'm looking for a book that will tell me about the movies that were out in the sixties."

"Oooh, the classics," Helen J whispers in an attempt to sound impressed. "I love those old movies."

"Well, does such a book exist, Helen J?"

Helen J smirks as she walks around the counter and leads him to the reference section. She pulls out a thick book from the shelf.

Andrés takes it from her hands and leafs through it.

"Is this what you're looking for?" Helen J asks.

Andrés turns his back on her and begins to browse through the glossy reproductions of movie posters. It will be a painstaking process, but he has the time, hours on end of time, at his new job.

"I'll take it," he says when he looks up finally, but Helen J has returned to the counter to ring up another customer.

His father is already on the couch when he walks into the house. The empty cake box sits on the floor beside him.

"Where were you?" his father says. "I had important news."

"About what?" Andrés says. He sets the bookstore bag on the table.

"About the woman in the red hat," his father says.

"Really?" Andrés says, holding back his excitement.

"She was using her left hand to pull down the brim of the hat," he announces.

"Oh," Andrés says, disappointed. "Why is that important?"

"You should know, stupid," his father says. "Left-handed people always notice other left-handed people. You're left-handed. So am I. So was your mother. One houseful of goddamn left-handers."

"My mother was left-handed?" Andrés says.

"Jesus Christ," his father says. "I can't believe you. You only knew her for about eighteen years."

Andrés remembers the day his mother died. His father wasn't home from work yet. His mother was in the bathroom and wouldn't come out. Andrés knocked and knocked but got no response, so he pushed the door open only to find her slumped over on the floor. The zipper on the back of her dress was wide open. He was shocked to see her freckled back and the pink strap of the bra. She'd had a stroke while getting dressed after her afternoon shower. Andrés zipped her up before his father came in through the door.

While his father watches television for the rest of the evening, Andrés sketches a picture of the woman in the red hat with the left hand pulling on the brim.

Andrés decides to hold off on his search for the woman in the red hat until Sunday night. He uses the three days of rest to sleep and clean up the house, which is susceptible to ants. His father's couch floats like a small island surrounded by an atoll of crumbs and spilled food, and Andrés circles it a number of times with the vacuum cleaner.

On Saturday afternoon he and his father take their usual outing to the bar at the end of town. When his mother was still alive she wouldn't allow alcohol in the house, and his father had to drop in at the bar for a beer after work on Friday evenings. When Andrés came of age his father invited him for a drink, and since Andrés' twenty-first birthday fell on a Saturday, his father changed his weekly outings to Saturdays. Andrés was surprised to learn that his father drank alone all those years and had made no friends at the bar, except for Pirata, the one-eyed bartender. But Pirata had died ten years ago. His son, who took over tending bar, had invited them to the funeral, but Andrés' father didn't want to attend. The next time they came by the bar, Pirata's son didn't ask why they didn't go, but after that he never made an effort to be friendly with them. Not even after ten years.

"The usual," his father says to Pirata's son after they hop on the bar stools.

"Right," Pirata's son says, and brings them two bottles of Corona.

They chug their beers in silence while the jukebox plays the same tunes it played the Saturday before.

"What do you think of that new margarita mixing machine?" Pirata's son asks.

Andrés' father glares at it. He takes out his glasses and places them on his face. After taking another swig of beer, he says, "What's the point?"

"Saves time, I guess," says Andrés.

His father looks around at the near-empty bar. "To do what?" he asks.

They chuckle into their beers. Pirata's son throws an annoyed look in their direction.

"Another round?" he asks.

"If you're not too busy," Andrés says, and they burst out into laughter again.

On Sunday, nothing unusual happens at the group home, except that the television has been repaired and now the residents keep it on at full volume. Before she left, Louise warned him, "Good luck trying to get them to turn that down."

The dining room is cold. Andrés turns the television down and leaves. As soon as he's out the door, he hears the volume go up again. The pattern repeats itself twice before Andrés goes to the basement and shuts off the breaker to that part of the house.

"The lights went out," a voice comes to inform him at the office. Andrés flashes the light on his face.

"I'm sorry about that, Mr. Shepley," he says. "We're on it. We'll get them back on as soon as we can."

He then turns the flashlight on his DVD book and slowly makes his way down the columns of photographs as he searches in the semi-darkness for the woman in the red hat.

By the time he turns the switch back on, it's past two in the morning. A few residents are still smoking on the front porch. He looks through the medication record book. Five residents haven't taken their evening meds, so Andrés pulls out their Medikits and drops the pills into the garbage can, logging in each evening dose as if it's been taken.

The next morning he serves the same breakfast as always, eggs and sausage. He stuffs the automatic dishwasher with dirty dishes and then hands the keys over to the morning shift before heading home. As he drives into the neighborhood, he realizes he left his DVD book in the office, but it'll be safe there.

Andrés sleeps seven hours, waking up at five P.M. When he walks out to the living room, his father greets him from the couch.

"I've got some more news for you," his father says.

"About?" Andrés yawns.

"About the woman in the red hat," his father says.

"Do tell," Andrés says. He opens the refrigerator to rummage for a soda. He finds two cans left in the door, both half-consumed and abandoned by his father. He takes one and sips the flat, cool liquid.

"She wasn't Chinese at all," his father says.

"How do you know?" Andrés says. "Her face was covered by the red hat, remember?"

"Yes, I know," his father says. "But her hand wasn't a Chinawoman's hand."

"What's a Chinawoman's hand?"

"You know," his father says. "Yellow."

"That's actually a misconception about Asian people, Rapael. They aren't really yellow. Just like black people aren't really black."

"Well, what I meant was that I remember it was a Latina hand."

"You mean her hand was brown?"

"Oh, so brown people really are brown, are they?" his father snaps.

Andrés takes another sip of soda. "Go on," he says.

"There's nothing more to it. I knew it was a Latina, so I thought maybe I was walking into one of those artsy foreign films."

"That doesn't sound like you, Rapael. I think you're making all this up," Andrés says.

"Why should I make all this up? You're the one who wants to know what goddamn film I watched while you were being born. What the fuck does it matter anyway?"

Andrés pulls out a chair and sits down. He feels a slight tension at the temples.

"You know what, forget I said anything about any movie or any woman in a white fucking hat. I don't remember shit!"

Andrés says softly, "The woman's hat is red."

"Shut up with that," his father demands and turns up the volume on the television.

Andrés' headache worsens. He decides to lie down for a while longer. He still has a few hours before going to work. In bed he presses his fists to his eyes and somehow manages to fall asleep.

When he awakes his heart is pounding. The sound of the television carries into his room. He didn't set his alarm clock because he didn't think he would sleep this long, but it's close to nine o'clock.

On his way to the shower he calls out to his father, "Turn that down, Rapael." When he comes out again, one towel wrapped around his waist, another hanging over his shoulders, the television is just as loud. He's annoyed but decides to leave his father alone. He dresses, thinking he'll show up to work early again so he can make himself something to eat in the kitchen. The Sysco cheese is stocked in bulk, the odor pungent but appetizing.

As he makes his way down the hall he notices his father's left hand dangling over the arm of his chair. Andrés walks around him to turn the television off. He lifts his father's arm to drop it on his lap, the way his father usually falls asleep. His father's arm is cold. He tries to shake him awake, but his father remains unresponsive.

Andrés bites his lip and his foot taps uncontrollably against the floor. Pressing his hands against his mouth he releases a muffled wail. He squats, taking a few deep breaths, calming himself down. The need to cry surges and he grabs his face with both hands as he does this, piecing together the image of his father through the openings between his fingers.

And then suddenly the grief lifts, as if those few moments of panic were all he had to offer. He looks around the room. Nothing seems different. Even his father's body on the couch is a familiar sight. It's as if he's sleeping.

After a few minutes on the floor he checks his watch. There are twenty-five people expecting him at the group home. Someone has to make sure they've taken their bedtime meds. In the morning, half of them will want their eggs and sausage. He turns off the living room lights and walks out to his car.

In his office, there is a woman in a red hat, waiting.

Part Two

Men in Other Places

Nayarita Blues
México

I'm stranded between the agave hills and timber mountains of Nayarit, just short of reaching the Tropic of Cancer. The temperature's hot and humid and the train sits trapped in a storm, sleeping it off like an old bull after it just got its balls cut. If I had a clean thumb to suck on I'd do just that to pass the time. But my fingers are filthy and sticky, so I keep them in my pockets and hum a tune, pissed at myself for being too afraid to travel abroad with an iPod. I keep myself distracted by trying to recall the last playlist: Lila Downs, Los Lobos, Manu Chao, Ozomatli— all the trendy college Chicano standards. I try to recall the order in each CD. It's a useless exercise, but what else is there for me to do after my one-month trek through south central México? Nothing but wait stupidly while the rest of the world spins on without me. I imagine that even the indigenous weavers making their baskets as they squat on the indifferent square of Coyoacán are getting more action than I am. The conductor says that help will arrive as soon as the engine returns to the main station in Guadalajara—six hours back. That means the passenger cars will sit overnight for at least twelve hours, vulnerable to attacks by robbers if the coaches don't first implode with the buildup of body heat and carbon monoxide.

Though we're advised not to leave the cars, many of the younger men jump off to smoke or move around. A group of women pray out loud. The mood grows somber at sundown when the train becomes completely dark. Suddenly the stuffy night comes alive with the legend of La Llorona, shape shifters, man-eating mountain lions, and water devils with the power to wash the flesh right off the bone. The prayer meeting makes me uneasy as well, reminding me of the only Mexican funeral I've ever attended—for my father's first business partner in Los Angeles thirteen years earlier—so I step up to an exit door left wide open to help circulate some oxygen through the train.

The rain subsides but still comes down steadily. The clamor of shifting foliage continues and the thought looms in the back of my mind that someone or something hides, watches, waits, and moves in the forest, its stirrings well disguised. Between the flashes of lightning the only source of light is the partially concealed moon whose weak glow illuminates the muddy earth and a thick wall of trees near the tracks. On one side the train stands parallel to a ravine. At the bottom, a river has been set in motion with the heavy rains. People begin to worry that the soil underneath the tracks will soften, hurling the train over the embankment. I stand with my weight over the open door, careful not to trip into the steeper steps. My face is clammy and my eyes ache from having spent too long inside the coach, trying to adjust to the darkness. I don't have any water. I regret not buying a gallon before boarding the train. I watched passengers make the sign of the cross at the start of the journey, and hope that I too am divinely protected, if only by association.

I wonder if I can sleep standing up, since going back inside will trigger my claustrophobia. I stand, neither on nor off the train, immobilized, paralyzed, fixed to the mountain like a dot on a map. Someone comments on the warm rain. Those smoking protect their cigarettes with a palm cupped above the lit tips. Each time they take a drag their hands glow.

One of the men in a soaked shirt calls to me. "Hey, man," he says. "You might as well get wet."

I acknowledge his suggestion with a nod. I recognize him as the older bearded man who sits in the seat opposite mine. After he heard me speak in my broken Spanish earlier, he wanted to start talking politics: how the U.S. butts in all over the place as if it owned the world, how it's NAFTA's fault the Mexican peso devaluates each day, and how the hell did that idiot end up in the White House? I quickly reminded him that I wasn't an ambassador—I'm just a college kid making a pilgrimage to the motherland. When I inform him that being born in the U.S. doesn't make me a gringo, he says: "Of course not." Then adds: "That makes you a pocho."

I've been defending myself against that word for a month now and I'm tired of it. While visiting the pyramids of Teotihuacán one of the guides offered to give me a tour in English, but when I let him know I spoke some Spanish he laughed and said that pochos didn't know Spanish that wasn't food. In Hidalgo my slicked-back hair, my designer glasses, and jeans also pegged me as a foreigner. Taxi drivers kept stopping beside me to offer a ride up the long trail to the Tolteca ruins. "Come on, pochito, just get in," they insisted. I finally gave up repeating that I *wanted* to hike and simply climbed on.

Maybe I should have worn my hoop to fit in. I'm surprised at how many young Mexican men wear earrings, some even daring to pierce their eyebrows or the cartilage of their ears. But that would have given people a different impression of me altogether. I want to come across as ordinary, not subversive. Subversive is the UFW flag I tattooed on my calf to show solidarity with the striking grape pickers. The trip down to the Caliente Valley excited us UCLA Chicano punks enough to commemorate the march and our first civil disobedience arrest with a black eagle on a red background. But since I was advised not to wear shorts in México, no one got to see it either.

"We're fucked," a voice behind me says.

I turn around but can barely make out the man whose face is too deeply embedded in the shadows. The rain falls quietly; the rosary inside the coach has ended. A sense of finality hovers in the air, borne not out of accomplishment, but out of resignation. Nothing moves except a few buzzing mosquitoes that have taken refuge inside the train.

The voice says, "They say this setback is a plot against the government to protest the shutting down of the railway companies. The train workers want a little publicity before they lose their jobs."

"Do you think that's true?" I ask, keeping my Spanish to a minimum.

He shifts forward and brushes my arm, his gaze fixed away from me. I recognize the aquiline profile that graces the Aztec codices. In Mexico City I spent two rolls of film on the street and market vendors, so beautiful in their needlepoint dresses and braids. The little girls, all eruptions of streamers as their colorful hair ribbons chased them across the square. I want so much to identify my ancestry as Tarasco or Zapotec or Anáhuac, but my bloodline is diluted with Spanish blood, three generations removed from the homeland, that I have no choice but to claim the Aztec as my honorary forefather.

"It's probably true," he says. "We won't know for sure that it was all a setup until we get to Baja California."

Inside the coach a baby cries. The noise floating out of the dark like that reminds me of lying in my hotel bed late at night and hearing a dog bark—suddenly the room splits open to the world and I'm no longer safe beneath the covers. The smell of wet earth fuses into the atmosphere. I open my mouth and breathe in the familiar flavor. Outside of the Basílica la Villa de Guadalupe in the state of México, two old women sold tiny clods of tierra santa. I bought a small piece and put it in my mouth just as they had instructed. It didn't taste holy at all; it tasted like common dirt.

"How long are they going to leave us here like this?" I ask.

"Who knows? Maybe just long enough to get some attention. You know, make headlines."

"They can do that?" I ask, and then I realize I have betrayed myself as an outsider. Of course they can do that. This is México. México loves drama: political assassinations, natural disasters, buses and trains that plunge into the depths of the wilderness from steep cliffs. Mexican history is one huge headline. While traveling through Guerrero I witnessed the takeover of a municipal building. Everyone knew who had done it and why and what would be the outcome of all the fuss and if there would be bloodshed or not—everyone except me. I was too embarrassed to ask any questions about the armed men wearing ponchos or about the men in clean white shirts forced to squat in the middle of the plaza with their hands on their heads. I walked away pretending I had seen it all before, though my heart was pounding so hard that my body jerked with each beat. I hid in my hotel room for the rest of the night, enlightened about what the tour books conveniently omitted. I had wanted to end my visit right then, but didn't because I had no way to explain to my parents back in Brentwood why the one-month itinerary they were paying for had been shortened to a week and a half. I can just hear my mother saying: "I *told* you not to go down there. It's dangerous." My father would have chastised me also, telling me that I should've never planned a trip in an election year. Who knows what's going to happen now that Vicente Fox is out of office? And with the election results as confusing and contested as the ones we had in the U.S., it's bound to be a shaky path toward disappointment for the Mexicans as well.

I press myself against the cool metal of the train's exit. I expect the man with the aquiline nose to ask me, "Where are *you* from?" but he doesn't say anything. Instead he whistles a tune that sounds somewhat familiar. I access the catalog in the back of my brain, but to no avail. I can't name the song. Just when I think I know, the notes blowing out of his lips sound new and unidentifiable.

I exhale deeply. I have spent an entire month in México and haven't experienced any spiritual awakening or discovered any insight into my personal being. Just a few months ago I'm sitting at a college football rally, grieving my unremarkable life: my parents never got divorced, nor have I ever seen them fight, and as the only child in a dual-income household, I've had everything offered to me without effort. I'm a healthy heterosexual with liberal views. My life is empty of scandal and hardship, except for the fact that I grew up as agnostic as my parents, but in the Southern California of the new millennium, who didn't? In other words, I'm relatively normal. About the only true life-altering moment I've ever had happened a few months ago when Susana thought she might be pregnant, which would have ended my plans for this voyage south. But she tested negative, so here I am in México, with its empty promise to fulfill me, to nourish my soul in some exotic, pre-Colombian way. The closest I came to inspiration was when I visited the geyser of Ixtla. Even then I knew I had been awed because I had never seen a geyser. I shudder to think that I would've been just as impressed with Old Faithful in Yellowstone. Nonetheless I can already hear myself telling Susana about having been reborn, about having connected with my indigenous roots, mis antepasados, mi raza, mi Aztlán. Blah, blah, blah, blah. My parents will listen patiently, locking eyes as if to agree with each other that, yes, this is that phase third-generation Chicanos go through in college, like my ethnic studies degree and then my masters studies in secondary education, my noble attempts at political poetry, and my constant questions about our family history. I had been disappointed to learn that my great grandparents hadn't fled persecution during the Mexican Revolution or that my grandfathers hadn't been recruited for farm labor during the bracero program. Way back when, my great grandfather had entered the country on a visiting artist's visa.

"He was a landscape architect," my father pronounced proudly behind a copy of the *Wall Street Journal*.

"You mean like a gardener?" I asked, hopefully.

"No, Jonathan," my father said, noticeably annoyed. "He designed magnificent gardens for the mansions of politicians and millionaires all over the Americas. You should respect that."

I didn't want to offend my father by letting him know that our family's privilege was nothing to be proud of in light of the travesties perpetrated against working-class Mexicans on both sides of the border. Each election year the racist propositions go up for vote on the ballots, and every month the body count of the murdered maquiladoras along the border keep rising. Our activist group on campus keeps tabs on these issues. It's our responsibility, mine especially. My father's an investment banker and my mother's a paralegal. I am the son of the middle class.

"They probably won't feed us again," a low voice says behind me. It's the man with the aquiline nose again. I like the way we remain anonymous in the dark, yet united by our shared experience—the disappearance of this train. With no introductions and no polite ceremonies, a person throws a comment out into the open. Inevitably someone catches it.

"The kitchen staff can give us the same bad chicken we were warned not to eat at dinner," I say.

The man laughs. His hand reaches out to offer me a cigarette. I don't smoke but I take it anyway, careful not to cough when I suck as he holds the lighter. The cigarette doesn't have a filter; I spit out a shred of tobacco.

"Going to the border or across?" he asks.

I become nervous. My answer will determine what comes next. Perhaps questions like: *Is it true that the government gives you pochos money to go to college? Is it true that gabachas like to fuck Mexicans? Is it true that Americans put ketchup on everything they eat?*

The stale air I inhale makes me sick. I turn my head to answer him directly. "Well, I," I say, speaking too slowly, "I'm visiting relatives in Baja Calfornia."

"Mexicali?"

"Yes," I say. "I have an uncle who's a taxi driver there. He'll be waiting for me at the station." I feel my body tingle at how easily those words flow out of my mouth.

"Lucky you," the man says. "Those sonsofbitches suck your blood for a ride out of the station. No offense to your uncle."

"None taken," I say.

"So where are you from?" he asks. "You don't sound like you're from the south. Are you from the border or are you chilango?"

At first I think he says Chicano and my face freezes. In México, Chicano is synonymous with pocho. After regaining my composure I say to him, "Originally from the border."

"Yes, I could tell," he says. "Your Spanish is slow and flat. No offense."

"None taken," I say.

"And you probably went to school on the other side, didn't you?"

I become nervous again, tongue-tied. I know I can't convince this man I'm not a pocho. "On both sides," I answer, and I'm grateful he doesn't ask for any further clarification because even I'm not sure about what I mean.

The longer I stand in front of this man, the more I don't feel like myself anymore because I'm convincing him I'm someone else. I could never pull that off in any other place, not even at the poor folk taco stands where my shyness at squeezing in my order in a crowd of vocal natives kept me edged out and hungry. And I always felt humiliated that the barefoot child beggars saw me coming from miles away and ran over to surround me, turning heads at the plaza. No matter how I dressed down or adjusted my gait, I could never shake off how conspicuous a foreigner I was. But now here I am, playing the part I had been fantasizing about all month and feeling like a jerk doing it. And there's no turning back either. I'm like this train, facing forward and heading one direction. To backtrack would be to lose the ground I've gained.

"So why are you traveling by yourself?" the man asks. "Are there problems at home?"

"Problems?" I say, stupidly.

"You know, kids your age don't usually travel alone unless they're in a bit of trouble," he says.

This year I turn twenty-one and I'm not going to be a daddy. I'm on my own from now on, yet I can't shake the feeling that somehow I've always been alone, taught to be fiercely independent by my fiercely independent parents. I see a vision of my room in adolescence, changing only a little each year as it became equipped with the latest competitive technology. When we sat down at dinner together, conversations with my family were dull, and nothing more alarming than a leak in the garage ever took place. And nothing more inspiring than a reading suggestion from my father. Meanwhile the television and newspaper showed me everything I was missing and wasn't part of—the outside chaos of people struggling. That's why I set off on this trip in the first place: to go outside. Because I was bored. God, what a jerk I am!

"Nothing serious," I finally stammer.

"I didn't mean to offend," the man says, concern in his voice.

"No, of course not," I say, dry-throated. I take a long drag of my cigarette and release the smoke slowly into the air.

"Federico Montes Pérez," the man says as he holds out his hand. I take it and it feels coarse against my palm. I'm sure he can feel how tender and smooth mine is. "Juan," I say simply, and even then the syllable wants to get lodged in my throat although it's been the name I have adopted for the entire trip.

"You remind me of someone, Juan, that's why I'm bothering you," he admits. He keeps up with me, puffing on his cigarette after I do.

"I have a son about your age," he continues. I've witnessed this type of intimacy before. Whoever said Mexican men are too macho to admit to emotion has never been to México where, between men, a stranger can confide in another stranger over a beer, over the newspaper at a bus station, over the shoulder in a taxi, or in situations like these when there is nowhere else to go but into the recesses of the heart. Mexican men do like to talk the blues, as my father once observed at his partner's funeral. He himself felt uncomfortable participating, so we left too quickly, against my mother's wishes. I admit now that I had been secretly glad we left as well. The openly somber tone of the funeral had put me ill at ease.

"He went up north. Haven't heard from him since," he states flatly.

I make a strained effort not to clear my throat so loudly but it doesn't work. Federico takes it as a sign to keep explaining, though at this point I can fill in the blanks myself.

"That's why I'm going up there, you know. To try to find out what happened to him. His mother's going mad with grief. We just want to know is he dead, is he alive? Is he out there driving around that fancy car he always wanted, too busy speeding through the freeways to call? Or is he clawing his way across the desert because la migra threw him out? We just want to find out, that's all. I promised her."

"How long ago did he cross over?" I ask.

"About two years ago," he says. "But I know I can find him. We've got this connection," he says as he presses his fist to his chest. "The truth is worth all the money we saved up for the train ticket."

I can find no words of consolation, nor do I want to sound condescending by offering words of false hope. Of course he's not going to find him. But I suspect he knows that, and that not making an effort anyway is unacceptable. I'm feeling nervous again and small inside my deception. *Confess, confess,* my conscience hounds me. It's the only way to save myself. Maybe he will come at me with his wrath, or maybe he will tell me he knew all along. Either way I will have shattered his trust in me.

I feel I'm back in those tense minutes when Susana and I sat in my bedroom waiting for the home pregnancy test to tell it like it is. We decided that if she was pregnant we would keep the baby, that despite the fact we were both pro-choice we would want to keep this one, even if it was an accident. We would finish graduate school, get teaching jobs in the LA school district, and raise our child. We would live in my parents' house for a few years and save some money for a down payment on a home. A few years ago I would have scoffed at the prospect of this future because it sounded so tame, not the thrill ride of our political aspirations in college. But at least it's a clear direction. And when the test result broke apart that possibility neither of us sighed in relief. We were somehow let down. And then we split, amicably, promising to keep in touch like friends.

"Listen," I say, my lip trembling. "I—"

He turns to me with his eyes wide open and this startles me.

"Look, look!" he says, pointing into the darkness.

The rain has stopped completely. The night has cleared and the moon begins to show through the shifting clouds. People stir inside the coach and outside the train, and we're caught in the middle—Federico Montes Pérez and me—both of us standing stiffly in our own exhaustion, sweat running down our bodies. But tonight the fireflies come to greet us, flashing steadily on and off. Federico claps his hands together, opens his palms just slightly and allows me to see the insect sitting still between his fingers. I imagine the firefly warm against his skin, the glowing dust of its tail cooling off like a blown-out match. I have never seen fireflies this close up before, and I worry that the one he has captured will die inside the cave of his flesh.

I'm suddenly overwhelmed with grief and I can feel a tear run down my cheek. I wonder if Federico can see it catching the light as it trails down to the edge of my lip. Or does he think it's just another common drop of sweat? I'm going back to being the unremarkable Jonathan I've always been, and now this gift from Federico Montes Pérez, the most remarkable person I've come across. And the more I think about it the worse I feel that neither of us has a child at the end of this excursion with whom to share the beautiful things that come to life after a storm on the mountains of Nayarit.

Día de las Madres
Los Angeles

Heriberto sits uncomfortably stiff behind the wheel as if he's riding a roller coaster up the first ascent. I had volunteered to drive but it's he who determines that when it's a choice between him or me. I'm now the passenger to his nervous bitching. He bitches and bitches about how Catarino resents coming back to LA, that people like Catarino would rather keep it high maintenance in New York City, where they can jump into cabs and get car serviced everywhere like Miss Daisy, and talk on the cell in the back seat while the driver talks on his cell in the front.

"The only small space he ever jumped out of was the closet. Know what I mean?" Heriberto says.

And I do know what he means. He means this whole rant is about how Catarino left *him* when he couldn't just up and leave to go to New York City with him because I was still in junior high and our mother was ill and the only way Heriberto could remember not to be like our father, who took off without a second thought, was to break open the family album, a thin book with images of a man I don't recognize anymore. When his cell phone rings, Heriberto picks it up and screams, "We're getting there! Chill!"

Heriberto says that New Yorkers should stay in New York because everywhere else they gripe about how it isn't New York. But for everyone around them it *is* New York because there's a loud New Yorker in the room.

But Catarino has to come. Our mother wished it so when she thought she could do one last thing for Heriberto by coaxing Catarino into coming back for him.

Heriberto doesn't let up. "Like a true spoiled New Yorker," he says, "Cata doesn't drive anymore, bitches about traffic, and expects *me* to weave through the highways to pick his ass up at LAX. We have cabs here, too, I'll have him know." But he won't dare say it to Catarino.

Despite his aversion to the West Coast, Catarino has agreed to make the cross-country flight and help drop our mother's ashes into the LA River. Our mother always said she would have wanted it this way, to help clog the toughest vein of the city, just behind Griffith Park, where all the dispossessed converge: the homeless, the aging tennis players, the horse-riding aficionados, Latino golfers, and the bloated blue bodies with their stories locked inside their swollen mouths. "And the homosexuals," Heriberto added. Ma ignored him. But she couldn't ignore how unhappy he became when Catarino went away, waiting for her to get better or to die. She died first, a race that took seven years to finish.

In those seven years Heriberto aged fifteen. Maybe twenty. His hairline scuttled back too many inches for his vanity, and he developed those permanent frown lines bracketing his mouth, like Ma had, though hers sunk out of view like the rest of her face because of the sickness.

Finally we turn into the airport, and I'm grateful that at least Heriberto's conversation will change. The tone will stay the same.

We snail-pace up to the terminal, and I spot Catarino looking flustered in a black coat while all the other travelers move comfortably in t-shirts and shorts.

"Ahí, ahí," I say, pointing, excited that the search didn't take long.

"Will you look at that? It's eighty-eight degrees, but he won't take off his designer coat because then people might think he's from around here or something," Heriberto says as he wedges in between two cars to get to the curb.

"I thought you'd never get here," Catarino says when we pull over. I step out to let him ride shotgun. I take his bag and throw it in the back with me. Once inside he leans in to give Heriberto a hug. He still wears that gold stud on his left ear. He stretches out an arm to draw me into their space.

"Your coat is itchy," Heriberto says.

"And you are bitchy," Catarino says.

We drive out of LAX and Heriberto turns up the volume on the radio as soon as we merge into the flow of the 105 from Sepulveda Boulevard.

"I miss Mexican music," Catarino says. "In New York it's all about salsa and merengue."

Heriberto throws me a knowing glance through the rearview mirror. I ignore him.

"So what are you up to nowadays, Helio?" Catarino says.

"College," I say. Then add, "I'm a freshman at Cal State, Long Beach."

"All growed up," Catarino says. "Studying what?"

"I'm a women's studies major," I say and he raises his eyebrows.

"It's how he hangs around the girls," Heriberto says, making a gesture with his fingers, like he's playing piano. "They're not all lesbians, you know."

"Well they are where I teach," Catarino says. "If I were a dyke I know exactly where I'd go."

"And if you were a fag?" Heriberto says.

"I'd stay in LA," Catarino says. And they keep talking and laughing like they always have in whatever code they're speaking in. I have stopped trying to crack it long ago, so instead I look out the window and do the only sightseeing that can be done on the highways of LA: I check out cars.

I'm not a car buff exactly, nor do I know much about what goes on under the hood. What I like about a car is its history, outside and in. Outside I look at the dents and scratches, and those funny bumper stickers people like to flaunt to roaming highway eyes. At the flag decals and those telltale traces of body shop fixtures. I like to watch for antennae decorations and customized tire rims. All of these things give a car its individuality. But when I talk about the inside, I don't mean rearview mirror accessories. I mean the people who ride in each distinct vehicle.

There's a story moving around within every single car. Like the one I'm in now, an eggplant Jetta with two former lovers bantering because there isn't a bed nearby they can throw themselves onto. And in the backseat is the killjoy little brother with one foot over the urn that holds his mother's ashes.

On the highways our community of stories grows exponentially. In that forest-green Taurus rides a group of ski bums. They're all excellent skiers except for the chubby college kid in the back who hasn't graduated from the novice slopes. And his buddies poke fun at him but take him along anyway because it's his father's ski rental that supplies the equipment for free.

That horse trailer carries a born loser with a name he can't live up to like Golden Hoof or Mercury's Wind. He's getting transported to a petting zoo, where he'll be called Pinky or Brandy, and he will long for the freedom of the racetrack while some kid cries as soon as he's strapped into the saddle.

"Have you tried out the Velvet Margarita?" Catarino asks. "I hear it's a bit kitschy, but the menu's fabulous."

"Overpriced, like every other trendy establishment in the city," Heriberto says. "A taco's a taco in my book. Know what I mean?"

"So are you seeing anyone, Helio?" Catarino says.

"Mesquite," I say.

"What is she, Native American?" Catarino says.

Heriberto laughs. "Mesquite's his car," Heriberto says. "This boy's strange like that, remember?"

When I see Heriberto's eyes framed inside the rearview mirror, it's as if I'm staring at myself. It's the only feature we share besides our dark skins. We have large black eyes that look as if they're perpetually dilated. In high school, both of us came under suspicion for drug use.

"Don't mind him, Helio," Catarino says. "Your brother doesn't understand this love for material possessions."

"And what's yours, your Paul Smith wallet?" Heriberto snaps back.

My first love was Jiminy. He was a cricket-brown Honda Civic with an embarrassing horn that would confuse rather than startle other drivers. He took me out of LA for the first time, as far south as Tijuana and as far north as Sacramento. He was the best of Heriberto's hand-me-downs, and I would have driven him straight through high school had he not given up on me on that road trip to Las Vegas. Amber broke up with me because we never made it, and because she had to ride to the nearest town next to the smelly tattooed guy in the tow truck. What I lamented most about that failed trip was the loss of the car, and that should have given me a clue that any girlfriend was always going to be my lesser love.

I lost my virginity in Doctor Demented, my beloved ambulance-white station wagon. I was expecting to have the lamest ride in high school when Ma bought this old Chevy from the paralytic neighbor who was letting the car deflate closer to the ground each month. And since I was neither the beggar nor the chooser, I accepted it, and then christened it, the letters reading backwards with red spray paint: Doctor Demented. Suddenly it was the coolest car in the school parking lot. At least Daniela thought so. Enough to let me enter her from behind as she leaned over the hood. I tried to do the same with Serena, but she slapped me across the face and yelled out, "Are you demented?" I tried to explain that it wasn't me. That it was my car. Doctor D also liked getting places fast, even though it couldn't take the highways the way Jiminy could. But a trooper to the end, he collapsed at the exit ramp, after having given it one last go during rush hour.

"Isn't that right, Helio?" Heriberto says.

"Right," I say. And they break out into laughter again.

"You're not even listening," Catarino says. "He doesn't change, does he?"

"Nope," Heriberto says. "The boy likes his trips to outer space. Know what I mean?"

Mesquite is my current ride. He belonged to Ma, who gave the car that name when I was still driving Jiminy around. Mesquite is a honey-colored Corolla whose only excitement has been watching Ma deteriorate over the years. But Mesquite and I share the most secrets, like when Ma cried that she wasn't going to live long enough to meet her grandchildren. She cried to me because Heriberto sure as hell wasn't going to reproduce. She cried about that as well. It was also the only time she spoke about our father, a foreman for an agricultural business down in the Caliente Valley who was also an Elvis nut, apparently. He ran off to an impersonators convention in Vegas and never came back. I sometimes picture him on a stage somewhere, crooning "Hound Dog" in a thick Mexican accent to a startled crowd.

"Probably found a Doña Elvis," Ma said, no irony or sarcasm in her voice.

Ma did most of her grieving in that car, on the trips back and forth to the hospital for those blood tests that didn't reveal anything except that she was going to die. She cried that she was going to leave us all alone in the world. I did the driving while Heriberto did the income earning.

A Corolla passes us by. And then another. They're the most nondescript of cars, but to me they stand out because I'm currently in a relationship with one. I miss him, but I had to leave him parked at home. My brother usually takes control in these situations, like carpooling to the airport en route to drop the remains of our mother into a concrete river.

"Are you kidding me?" Catarino says.

"No, we're going to take care of this today!" Heriberto says.

"At least let's get some lunch first and let me shower for shit's sake!" Catarino says. "I feel absolutely disgusting."

"You're the one who waited to book a goddamn plane ticket until the last minute. It's today or never."

"You know I had to wait for the end of the semester!" Catarino says.

"Go ahead," Heriberto says, "hide behind your fancy job in your fancy town."

"Slow down!" Catarino calls out.

We moved swiftly from the 105 to the 110, but have suddenly slowed down to a near halt close to the Golden State Freeway exit, just before getting on the 5. When we stop altogether, it's a sure sign that there's a bad accident up ahead. In any case we're stuck in traffic, and the cars going the opposite direction mock us with their steady speed.

"I knew I should've stayed in New York," Catarino says.

"I can drive you straight back to the airport if this is too much drama for you," Heriberto says.

"Cut it out, both of you!" I say. "Fuck! I mean, we're doing this for Ma. Can you stop thinking about yourselves for a minute and think about *her?*"

My flare-up is enough to shut them up. For the moment. We sit there quietly, paralyzed with the rest of the cars around us. Heriberto turns the radio down.

After Catarino came Lamont. He worked for the same bank that Heriberto did. And although he was shaped like a football player, Lamont broke down in tears as easily as a girl. I was stunned the first time it happened. But by the fourth or fifth time I became desensitized to it, recognizing it as the same tactic girls used on guys to disarm them with pity. Ma didn't care for Lamont because he was black. I didn't care for him because he was such a wimp.

Kyle was a relief. He was patient, masculine, and polite as hell to Ma, who took a great liking to him. She changed her mind about the black issue, though she qualified it by saying Kyle was a black man from the South and not from Compton. Kyle was the one who taught me to drive, since Heriberto has the patience of a dynamite fuse. On those weekend afternoons when Heriberto balanced the books, Kyle showed me the art of parallel parking—the most important maneuver for survival in the residential streets of LA. And although I love my brother, I couldn't help but let it slip one time to tell Kyle, "You're too good for Heriberto." Kyle laughed it off, but beneath those facial muscles I saw it: he agreed. I have learned to detect such truths within the intimacy of cars. The twitching, the sniffling, the rubbing of the nose with the index knuckle—all of these are signs I can decipher.

When Kyle left, he was replaced by Heriberto's white version, Charlie.

"Stop daydreaming and answer me," Heriberto shouts back at me.

"Quit yelling at him like that," Catarino says.

"Well?" Heriberto says.

"Well, what?" I ask.

"Should we just cancel the ceremony and leave it for tomorrow?"

"It has to be today," I say. "It's Mother's Day."

"You see?" Heriberto says.

"Mother's Day is on Sunday," Catarino says.

"In the U.S.," Heriberto says. "In goddamn México it's always May 10, no matter what fucking day of the week it is."

"Can we cut it out with the expensive words? I'm not sure I can afford to hear them." Catarino looks back at me, sighs, and then says, "Fine, fine. Today it is. Hopefully we'll be up and running soon though. I'm tired and I'm hungry."

Heriberto sits back as if this is some hard-won victory for him. Catarino raises the volume on the radio. Next to us, the couple in the jeep is also fighting. None of these people knows the trick: roll the window down and let the rage escape. Instead they breathe it back in and back out and back in again, each time making it more toxic.

"Now what?" Heriberto says.

I look out to the side. A man is walking down between the rows of cars. Motorists left and right roll up their windows, lock their doors or check to see if their doors are locked.

The man's a Mexican in his early fifties, looking as harmless as the ice cream vendor that pushes a white cart that reads PALETAS MICHOACAN. He's looking discombobulated, stressed out, and he turns to peek through each car window as if he's searching for someone. When he gets to our car, he spots me. It *is* the ice cream vendor who pushes the white cart through our Eagle Rock neighborhood. He taps on the glass. I roll the window down.

"What the fuck are you doing, Helio? This guy could be crazy," Heriberto says.

"I know him," I say.

"He what?" Catarino says to Heriberto.

"¿Algún problema, amigo?" I say.

The man begins to gesture. He's a mute, which makes some twisted sense because the only sound I ever heard coming from his direction was that bell attached to the metal bar. I never purchased anything from him, but Ma did, bringing me back a coconut Popsicle each time. All this time when she was moving her mouth it was a one-way conversation.

"You're not getting out of this car," Heriberto says.

I open the door and follow the ice cream vendor back through the center of the rows of cars. I can hear the police sirens approaching.

"Helio! Get back in here!" Heriberto shouts. I hear him calling my name until I arrive at the accident scene.

The ambulances are sure to follow because it doesn't look good: a cargo truck of ice cream carts has collided with an SUV. The driver of the SUV looks shocked but unharmed. Though injured ice cream vendors sit scattered everywhere, it's the ice cream carts that catch the eye. Some have traveled clear across to the right lane to spill their contents all over the highway. Colorful ice cream bars are tossed about, melting quickly on the hot surface of the highway.

The ice cream vendor takes me to the driver of the cargo truck. I knock on the glass and he doesn't respond.

"Ya viene la policía," I tell the vendor. He shakes his head, insists that I keep at it.

"Sir, sir, are you all right?" I ask. Behind me, other Samaritans have come forward to offer comfort now that the severity of the event has become clear. Mostly they stand over the shell-shocked vendors and speak to them in loud English.

The white man slowly lifts his head and locks his blue eyes on me. I motion to the lock. He lifts it open. And as soon as I open the door, the ice cream vendor rushes forward to attack the driver.

"Whoa, whoa!" I tell him. "Espera."

A cop steps up and pulls the vendor away. The driver slumps back in his seat and sighs. There isn't much guesswork to this story: he's been underpaying the group of undocumented aliens, asking them to work long hours through the streets of LA. The workers must ride in the back like chattel and are willing to put up with all of the job hazards if the driver promises to stop driving while intoxicated. I can smell the liquor in his breath.

"You need to go back to your car, sir," the cop says. "We've got it all under control."

It's not the phrase that makes me shudder; it's the inflection of the cop's words and the uncanny likeness to another voice I've heard before. I look at him closely, my eyes squinting, and he mistakes my response as a hostile gesture.

"Is there a problem?" the cop says, puffing out his chest like a shield.

The cop doesn't remember me. I look at the tag above the badge and confirm it: Diamonds—the unusual and unforgettable last name of the salt-and-pepper-haired breaker of bad news.

"Sir," he insists. "You need to return to your vehicle immediately."

"You were the one who found my mother," I tell him. He's unprepared for my statement.

"I'm sorry?" he says.

"My mother, Angelina Ramos. She passed away in her car on our driveway," I say, my voice a little embarrassed suddenly. "She was trying to drive herself to the hospital and you were patrolling the neighborhood. Eagle Rock. You found her because her foot was pressed against the break. You saw the lights."

"I'm sorry, sir," he says. His voice has softened. His hard face has dissolved into a sympathetic one. "I only vaguely remember the incident. It must have been some time ago, right?"

Ma died six months ago. Heriberto was at work when he got the call and he picked me up at the post office, where I was working the seasonal shift, sorting all those letters to Santa Claus addressed to the North Pole. The more I stuffed Christmas colored letters into bags, the more depressed I became, knowing they were going to get disposed of at the end of the day. The crayon scribbles and homemade stamps were heartbreaking. So when Heriberto arrived, the expression on his face as devastating as the Santa Claus letters, I nearly collapsed. But even sadder than the sacks of blind childish faith, and even sadder than my once good-looking brother, who was getting as frumpy as the mail-bag stuffed with that undeliverable hope, was getting told by a man whose last name was Diamonds that the woman who never got to own a single precious jewel in her life was dead. We kept the urn hidden away among her collection of fake china until this afternoon.

I decide to let the guy off the hook.

"Yes," I say finally. "It was a while ago. I apologize, officer, I didn't mean to take up your time."

"No worries, son," the cop says. He pats me on the back, gently. "Just get back in your car and let us do our job here."

"Thank you," I say.

As I move down the rows of cars, a few drivers roll their windows down and ask me what has happened. I don't speak. Others regard me with the same wariness they had for the ice cream vendor. I'm slow-pacing it back through the stopped traffic, which is surreal enough, but now I'm mulling over the signs: the ice cream vendor, the cop, Ma. Me. We have all crossed paths again. There has to be a message here that I'm not quite reading.

"Read the signs," Ma used to say. And I used to grin, humoring her the way we had learned to do, Heriberto and I, because she was our Ma, and she was dying.

"Is that what you do with the sunset?" I asked her once.

"When you get to be as mortal as me, you claim kinship with everything that comes to an end. All I have left in me is the patience to wait for the stars."

"One of these days I'll drive you out of the city," I told her. "So that you can see them big and beautiful. Here they're nothing but pin-pricks in the sky."

"But they come," she said.

By the time I get back to the car, traffic patrol has begun to direct the cars away from the accident site.

"What was that all about?" Heriberto says.

"Careful, careful," Catarino says. "Let's try to ease out of here in one piece, okay. God, I hate LA traffic."

When we pass the damaged cargo truck, the mute vendor is sitting in the police squad car with a water bottle against his lips. He doesn't see me. The driver of the truck is nowhere in sight, and the injured have been taken away rather quickly because this is an inconvenience on the impatient highways of LA.

"So is the goal sunset or what?" Catarino says.

"You know how it is with doña Angelina," Heriberto says.

He's right, but he doesn't understand why Ma came up with all these little idiosyncrasies, as if she were suffering from OCD. She would never schedule appointments on odd-numbered calendar days, she wouldn't wear red, she answered the phone only after an even-numbered ring, and she didn't read books with images of flowers on the cover. These were all things under her control. She also always prayed during sunset. She never revealed who she prayed to, since she wasn't a practicing Catholic. Mesquite's rearview mirror holds Buddhist beads, but there's a small statue of San Martín de Porres in the glove compartment. The only votive candle in the house is a relic of our father's and it bears a picture of Elvis. And though there's an Elvis tape sticking out of Mesquite's player, I never played it. I never bothered to remove it either, after I inherited the car. Come to think of it, I never heard her play her Elvis music in the house either. Our little house in Eagle Rock was always quiet because of the migraines, both hers and Heriberto's.

At sunset, Ma would step out to the backyard and face west, her fingers woven and pressed to her chin. The strange blood disease with the unpronounceable name had turned her skin blotchy, and the dusky light would bathe her with a fiery sheen. But she had been doing this, she said, since I was a child. When she became too weak to walk herself outside, I'd roll the wheelchair to the window, which is why Heriberto made sure her room looked out the right direction. "For religious reasons," he had explained to the hospital administrators. And Heriberto said they thought we were Muslims making sure we could locate Mecca.

"There are no stars to be seen out here in the summer," Heriberto whispered into my ear as we stood behind Ma one time. "Not with this smog."

"I know," Ma said. "In the fall the Santa Anas will take pity on me and blow the pollutants away. But I can still sense the stars there, glowing behind the sheet of dirty air."

When I tried to hum "Twinkle Twinkle Little Star," Ma swatted my knee. Heriberto snickered. And then we all fell silent, wishing for stars.

We veer off the 5 and onto Los Feliz Boulevard, swerving around to get to Griffith Park. The parking lot is relatively empty, but the tennis players are in full swing. The small path that leads to the bike trail lies just behind the courts.

"Why the LA River and why at this godforsaken spot?" Catarino says. I'm following close behind with my arm wrapped around the heavy urn. We cross through the shrubs and come out the other side, near the metal footbridge.

"When Ma was a young girl, she used to take care of her old tía in Atwater Village," I say, motioning with my chin.

Tía Lupita wasn't really a blood relation, but she took in Ma since neither of them had any other relatives in California, which is why neither of them wanted a funeral. They believed the saddest thing that could ever happen to a Mexican was an empty wake. After Tía Lupita was cremated, Ma dropped her ashes at this part of the river.

When the three of us stand at the footbridge, an awkward silence envelops us.

"What now?" Catarino says, looking down at the small stream of water running beneath us. The bridge vibrates with our weight.

I open the urn and look in. "I suppose we drop the ashes in?" I say.

"We should mark the occasion somehow," Heriberto says. "Otherwise it's going to seem like we're dumping trash. Know what I mean? Catarino, you're our guest. Say something first."

"Me?" Catarino says.

"Go ahead," I say.

"Well, all right." Catarino clears his throat. "I'd like to thank Angelina for allowing me to be part of this ceremony. Indeed I'm flattered. Though I didn't get to see her as much these last six or seven years, I have to admit she was often in my thoughts. I'm very saddened by her passing and hope that she's in a better place, at peace, and that she's looking upon us now and that she's as proud as I am of her two handsome sons."

Flushed, Catarino steps back though there isn't much room on the bridge to move.

"Thank you," Heriberto says, his voice cracking. "Helio?"

I look out at the river dense with debris and a few growths of plants that sprout out of the cracks in the concrete. I hadn't given much thought to a eulogy, and I'm by no means as articulate as Catarino, who socializes a lot more than I do. He once told me it was a necessary survival skill for Latinos in white-dominated spaces like the universities. Ma liked that about him—that his strength came from his skull. She said he was a perfect match for Heriberto because my brother's fire organ was his heart. I'm sure she told Heriberto what rules my nature, but the catch is we're not allowed to tell each other.

I want to keep the speech sweet and simple. I'll let Heriberto deal with the more complicated stuff. He always has, frankly, everything from the finances to my college application. Part of me would love to thank Heriberto at this point, or at least acknowledge him for taking care of me all these years. But this afternoon is not about brotherly love; it's about closing the chapter of our lives called "Our Ma."

I take a deep breath and stare up at the sky. "I'm here to say good-bye, Ma," I say.

I don't get any further because of Heriberto's burst of unrestrained sobbing. Catarino moves in to comfort him and this makes him bawl even louder. At first I'm touched by this display, but five minutes later it's clear Heriberto's not going to stop and that this moment has opened up a pain inside him that only Catarino can assuage. I'm strangely disaffected, perhaps because

I can see through the exaggeration of the act—the staged break-down that was planned from the start, from the moment Catarino stepped into the car.

"Oh, God, I need you. Oh, God, I need you," Heriberto keeps repeating in Catarino's arms. Suddenly, Ma's ceremony seems anti-climactic. So I tip the urn over and watch the ashes plop down on the narrow stream of water that we insist on calling a river. I toss the metal urn in for good measure and it doesn't even make a splash, though the din of the metal makes a quick complaint.

I watch Heriberto sink into Catarino's body, their black attire melding into one mass.

We walk to the car and Catarino and Heriberto take the back seat. Catarino keeps rubbing my brother's back all the way to Eagle Rock and Heriberto mumbles apologies and pleadings into Catarino's shoulder.

The drive home is uneventful. I park Heriberto's Jetta right behind Mesquite and hand Catarino the keys.

"This one's for the front door," I tell him.

"Aren't you coming in, Helio?" Catarino says.

He doesn't wait for an answer and proceeds to lead Heriberto to the house. They go in and shut the door behind them. I push in the key to Mesquite's door and am surprised to hear the ice cream vendor's bell. But it's not the mute vendor who tried to strangle his boss just a few hours ago. This is someone else. The lettering on the cart reads PALETAS JALISCO. How quickly the business of moving on.

I sit behind the wheel and close the door. Ma's scent still lingers inside Mesquite. Perhaps it has permeated the seat coverings. In here I will tell Ma that I've changed my major once again because I still don't know what I want to do with my education. Or my life for that matter. That Catarino has returned to take Heriberto back to the East Coast, where he'll learn to sip Manhattans and poke fun at Midwesterners. That I can't shake the habit of closing people off, even though I'm as curious about people as I am about cars. That I think I know what she was doing when she was facing the sunset because I do it myself all the time—look for signs of salvation.

Catarino comes out after another twenty minutes. He's stripped down to his undershirt and his ribcage shows through the sides. His arms are long and sunless, and the trendy design of a tattoo wrapped around his bicep looks florescent green against the pale skin. I roll the window down.

"I think Heriberto will be okay," he says. "I gave him something from the medicine cabinet. I hope it's a sedative."

"It is," I say.

"How about you, are you okay?"

"Fine," I say.

"Are you joining us?"

I think about it for a few seconds. Catarino has slipped back into his old role again. He's the finicky worrywart that Ma's illness didn't allow her to be. I suppose it won't be that bad to get looked after for a while longer. Heriberto sure as hell needs it.

"Yes," I say, finally. "But I need to stay in the car a little longer. Know what I mean?"

Catarino bends down and plants a kiss on my head, and then walks back toward the house, assured.

"Cata," I call out. He turns around. "Do you believe in coincidence?"

"Odd question," he says. After a brief pause he continues: "I think I do. But I also believe we make ourselves see what we want to see. To make ourselves feel better."

Catarino walks inside the house. I roll the window up, adjust the seat, and push the Elvis tape into the player. No music plays. The only sound I hear is the magnetic strip rolling. It's the blank end of the tape. In a moment it will begin playing the other side, but in the meantime I turn the volume up and listen to the static, trying to make sense out of it, maybe discover something, maybe a hidden message since I have just figured out what Ma was doing in the car in the final moments of her life. She wasn't trying to go anywhere; she was trying to get to this tape, the only connection left to her husband, who never came back—she was going to listen to the end of some sad song as she waited for the last time for the stars to come.

Haunting José
Seattle

Don't ask if I believe in ghosts. I refuse to, even as I lie here listening to the strange sounds coming from inside the walls. If this were my old apartment I'd dismiss the noises as the everyday chatter of an old kitchen: the overworked wires in the stove, the pipes beneath the sink, shrinking or expanding in response to the season, the refrigerator creaking with the burden of its own weight. No ghosts there. Only the echoes of living.

My family, on the other hand, can't get enough of ghosts. They'll sit for hours in the evenings, spinning tales of spectral visitations and paranormal activity—memories of moving objects, hearsay of haunted houses, postpartum possessions, demon dwellings, et cetera. Each time I hear the stories they come with a little more flourish and flare than the earlier versions. That's why it took me so long to lose my fear of the dark, and why, before I became a grown-up and an atheist, I recited every memorized prayer in the catechism—the Ave Maria, the Credo, the Lord's Prayer, et cetera—before I could sleep. Those prayers were like a nice Catholic shield against my grandfather's hoof-footed, chicken-legged, goat-horned, pitchfork-carrying dwarf devils that wandered the shadows after sundown, searching for errant children.

All through my college years I've never taken home a friend or a lover, afraid that my grandfather would come over and commence to entertain his captive audience with his long-winded, implausible, unbelievable stories. I'd be embarrassed to place a friend in a situation like that. Or worse yet, what if my guest witnessed one of my mother's many superstitions—odd, unrecognizable ones like her habit of crossing herself whenever the clock chimes to the hour, or lighting the candle on top of the television whenever the Pope appears on the screen. Even other Mexicans don't behave this way.

I would never think to tell my mother about the sounds in my new studio apartment. She'd either want to rush over to bless every corner with one of her crazy concoctions of oil and cactus extract, or she'd bring it up at the next gathering of ghost telling I happen to stumble upon. "José's new apartment is haunted. Isn't it, José?" she'd say, and then my grandfather would pounce on it, never letting up until I fabricated some acceptable narrative around the whole thing.

There isn't really anything worth talking about anyway. I'm simply unfamiliar with the new place and its noises. All living spaces have them, I've discovered. My old apartment channeled it through the appliances because I spent many an evening preparing an exquisite meal that would earn me an exquisite roll in the hay. That's why I don't date vegetarians. I've also discovered that the best aphrodisiac is meat—steak, preferably, but in moderation. It must trigger something primal in a man when combining the two acts, eating and fucking, so close together. They always come back for seconds.

They also tend to sleep quite soundly when all is said and done. Derek here is snoring like a bull and keeping me up. I could light a firecracker in his ear and he wouldn't budge. It's a miracle I can still hear the sounds inside the walls. Outside, the wind is blowing. But the glass must be bulletproof or something because I can barely detect the rustling of the leaves. I'm not sure yet if this is better, the silence of the outside world. In my old apartment the window was a thin glass and I could hear the passersby stumbling home late at night, arguing all along the sidewalk, or jabbering in their cells to friends in later time zones. This random eavesdropping was like an urban lullaby that eased me into dream. Not that Seattle needs another lullaby: the traffic and the rain are good enough. Maybe that's why I'm having trouble sleeping tonight—I can hear no street noise, and it hasn't rained in a week, and Derek here snores like he dances, without rhythm.

There it is again.

The sounds are coming from *inside* the walls, not through them. I know the difference. Through plaster and brick the noises that carry are the neighbors'. In the old apartment I was wedged between Mrs. Hillerman and a Seattle cliché, a musician. Mrs. H always fell asleep with the television at high volume, apparently never forgetting to pop off her hearing aide—the same powerful little amplifier that pressed her to bang on my wall when she could hear my stereo playing. On a bad day, the old lady would be yelling into the phone to one doctor or another, or to the nurse who came over to administer some injection, and the guitar player would be composing insufferable tunes that I've only heard in mediocre musicals played at the local coffee shops. At times like that I fled my tiny Capital Hill haven and found myself on my mother's couch in that old house across the lake. Why my mother chose Queen Anne I'll never know. There are plenty more inexpensive neighborhoods. Certainly, more inexpensive towns. But no, mami and gramps had to follow me here to Seattle and blow the settlement money again on an old fixer-upper that doesn't have a single glimpse of a body of water.

But I digress. My point is that I can tell when it's a human-made sound and when it's something more independent of our obnoxious species. The studio must be made of a thicker material, because I can only hear my neighbors murmuring, even when their voices are loud. No wonder I had such trouble hammering in the nails. I came this close to purchasing a drill. My neighbors here are much quieter—a reflection of their class status, no doubt. But the lack of noise also makes the place feel isolated, empty, and lonely.

Technically I now live in Madrona, where the homes are as big as palaces, but tucked away demurely behind extravagant foliage, as if apologetic about their size. I can still climb on the Number Two bus to Queen Anne, but it's a much longer trip. It's also a longer drive to the university, where I hope to earn my master's in English in a year or two. However long it takes, my family will be patient, just as they were when I was completing my bachelor's—two years in San Diego and two more years in Tucson. But they follow my tracks from city to city, afraid they'll lose sight of me.

There it is again. It's as if the walls are inhabited. Maybe by those tiny aberrations I've seen in old horror flicks—little green bug-eyed monsters that worm out through the vents to antagonize the new inhabitants of their domain. They're beating on the wall to keep me up, to exhaust me into leaving and giving this place back to them. Or maybe it's muttering I hear, the leadership counsel plotting my overthrow. Maybe they're farther along in the plan by now and are giving last-minute instructions to the minions—the miniature henchmen who will have miniature statues erected in honor of the successful coup. Am I listening to myself? I sound just like my grandfather.

"Derek," I say into Derek's ear, not bothering to whisper.

"Huh, what?" Derek utters, half asleep.

"I can't sleep with all this noise," I say. Derek rolls his eyes around as if searching to zero in on the culprit.

"I don't hear anything," he says. He turns around and presses his body against mine. I can feel his penis growing against my leg.

"That's not why I woke you up," I say. "You're snoring too loud."

"Sorry," Derek says. He yawns, showing me his set of perfect white teeth. "Relájate, José. Tenemos clase mañana."

One thing I detest is when non-native speakers address me in Spanish, especially if they're white. And I don't care if Derek is black and as fluent as I am, it still bothers me. I nudge his arm off me and go sit on the chaise. Above it hangs that Alfredo Arreguín poster my mother gave me for my twenty-fourth birthday. She says Arreguín is from Michoacán, just like our family, and that he's exiled out here in Seattle, just as we are. Exile. Is that what this is?

Exile. The dictionary says: 1. Banishment; *also*: voluntary absence from one's country or home; 2. A person driven from his or her native place.

I toss the dictionary back on the coffee table. Derek has started snoring. And the sounds are here again, coming from inside the walls. Maybe the walls are not inhabited by physical beings at all. I'm not claiming ghosts, I'm claiming something else, something that's not as simplistic, or sensationalistic. Then suddenly there's a crack and I jump. I look behind me, expecting to find a fracture, deep and jagged, running down from the ceiling, but find nothing. I'm scaring myself with my own nonsense. Still, I climb back into bed and into the comfort of Derek's body heat. That and my body blanket of tattoos is all I need to keep me warm. I place my hand along the curve of his hip and eventually, miraculously, I fall asleep.

My eyes open. I believe I've slept a few hours, but when I check the clock across the room I'm dismayed that I've been tricked by a two-minute submersion into the deep unconsciousness. And now I'm wide awake.

Maybe I'll read poetry. That's always boring. But the thought of turning on the light at this hour makes my face hurt, so I opt to leave my old *Norton Anthology* alone and collecting dust at the base of the bookshelf. Instead I go back to the chaise, to the Arreguín poster of salmon leaping in and out of visibility through the ocean waves.

This time I'm not as jittery when I hear the sounds coming from inside the walls. It's as if I'm getting used to them. When my grandfather talks about his ghosts, he speaks of them so casually, as if they're old friends dropping in to visit. Unlike my mother's visitors, grandfather's ghosts are spirits unknown to him, complete strangers with whom he had no earthly connection. It's as if all those years that he worked in Baja as the entrance attendant at a parking garage, opening and closing the heavy aluminum doors for tourists and locals alike, has earned him the trust of every citizen at the gates of the Otherworld. Random ghosts walk through, and many of them take a pause in their journey to exchange pleasantries with my grandfather.

"Had a fellow here last night," my grandfather will confess without warning. "A poor soul from Oaxaca, who lost his life in a factory. He's going back to his homeland to ask his relatives to ship his body back. Give him a proper burial among his people."

And then just as abruptly my grandfather will scratch his chin and reach across the table for a helping of tortillas.

My mother, on the other hand, claims it's all our dead relatives that get in touch with her, my father included. Old Tía Mariquita came once to reveal where she had hidden her cache of jewelry. My mother sent word to our cousins back in Michoacán and we never heard back from them. My mother says it's because they found the gold and are afraid she'll want to collect her share for relaying the message. I think it's because they dug through half the courtyard by the time it dawned on them what fools they were, following instructions from their crazy aunt up north.

Cousin Braulio came to pay her a visit also. He was our lay-about relative who drowned in a bucket of water. The story is he came home late one night and was too drunk to bother going into the kitchen to pour a glass out of the cooler. So he knelt down to lap it up from the bucket that had been collecting rain all evening. It was a deep bucket, and a heavy Braulio. He passed out with his head in the water and that was the end of that. We all accepted that explanation, and so did the authorities, who had had their run-ins with this town drunk before. But the version his ghost came to tell my mother made everyone in Braulio's household nervous, enough to have them shut out our branch of the family tree from theirs.

"Josefina," my grandfather asked her. "Are you sure that's what he said?" Even he understood the ramifications of that disclosure.

"Positive," my mother answered. But that wasn't enough for the authorities to reopen the case, and the death of Braulio remained an accidental drowning, not a murder.

These two visits were enough to instill confidence in my mother that she was not out of her mind and that she needed to pay close attention, and even heed those communiqués from the great beyond. So when she claimed that my father had come to tell her that she must let *me* guide her way through the rest of her life, she made it her mission to move to the same city shortly after I do. We started out in the Caliente Valley, where I was born, then made our way to San Diego, and then Tucson, and now Seattle. What allows her to pick up and leave, dragging my retired grandfather with her, is the money we got after the doctors fucked up my father's kidney surgery and put him in a coma, a state he died in weeks later. All I remember from that time, besides my poor father's frozen body, is my mother sitting at his side, praying, hoping, and frightened about staying behind in the country he had brought her to, where I had been born.

Now they follow me, mami and gramps—my father's father. As per my father's instructions, they need to be near me, or near enough. I'm the last of the bloodline. I'm precious and the last thread weaving them to this physical world.

If I pursue a PhD, perhaps I'll spare my family another move and simply do it here at the University of Washington. Although it's a peculiar arrangement, this keeping up with my every move, I don't dare defy it. My mother has been through enough. She has certainly given me the space to be who I am. Not only does she overlook the whole gay thing, she's never objected to my tattoos. I have six, but only two are visible to her—the orchid on my nape and the Guadalupe Posada skeleton on my left forearm. Derek here has made love to the other four: the butterfly on my shoulder blade, the hummingbird on my hipbone, the crown of stars around my pierced nipple and the swallow on my lower back. So it was with slight trepidation that I informed her I was leaving Capitol Hill.

"You're moving?" my mother said in alarm, her face shriveled up so quickly she was on the verge of tears.

"Just across town," I said. "No further than before." I could see her shaking. I could see her crumbling at the thought of being at the mercy of my capricious, nomadic lifestyle.

"This is a big town," she said, her body deflating with resignation.

Despite myself I reveled in a perverse pleasure. But guilt quickly set in, and I hugged my mother to comfort her, to reassure her that I would never leave her behind. And then I went outside to break the news to my grandfather, and to watch him go through the same state of distress.

Derek stirs in his sleep. He has bent his legs and pushed them up toward his belly. I won't be able to fit my body into his. I suppose I can climb into the other side and spoon him, but that's not why I let a man spend the night. I try to imagine my parents in bed all those years before my father died. I try to imagine how my mother, a widow for almost a decade, has managed the emptiness of her bed without him. Is it any wonder she resorts to these fantasies about the spirit world? It makes her own world that much less vacant.

My mother will always live in fear, I hate to admit. The only change I see in her is in her aging: every year she's grayer and the frown lines on her forehead and around her mouth become deeper with worry. I'm not sure that she was built to survive in any place, but she's doing it somehow, stubbornly sticking to life like a parasite. It's disheartening, but the more time passes, the less I love her. I can feel this loss in my blood. I can feel it thinning out. One day I'll bleed and the fluid will be colorless, transparent as a ghost's.

After this much angst, it'll be disappointing to find out that it's only mice inside the walls, or some infestation of termites—a whole colony of them clustered into one large pulsing presence. I'm beginning to understand the need for imagination—the need to believe that perhaps it's a restless being trapped behind the wall, like in an Edgar Allan Poe story. He's trying to tell me something, this ghost. They insist on doing that to humans because unlike other ghosts, we the living still have mouths and we can savor a secret or a revelation.

Have I inherited my father's side of the sensitivity to the spirit world, and is it a stranger come to say hello? Or am I more like my mother, attuned to the souls of our departed loved ones, and has my grandmother or even my father come to warn me to knock it off, to stop playing mind games with my poor, living family?

I rise from the chaise and am guided to a spot on the wall where the sounds seem to emanate the loudest. In my weariness I believe I see the wall bubble out like a belly at the moment of exhale. I press my ear and two hands against the cool surface, and then I flatten the rest of my body on it. There's indeed a heartbeat. To get the full effect, I strip off my boxer briefs, my penis sinks into the cushion of my groin. I remain fixed against the wall for a while longer and let my own beating heart communicate with whatever's behind that barrier.

My grandfather contends that there are two types of ghosts: the good ones who will haunt you until you chase them off by asking politely or with obscenities, if the first method doesn't work; and evil ones who come to exercise their last bit of harm before descending into their hell. Those can only be dispelled through a Catholic cleansing.

I believe my guest is a good ghost. But I won't ask him to leave. For a change, I want to be haunted by the dead, and not the living.

"José," Derek calls out to me from the bed. I can see the accent above the *e* of my name float above his body like a feather from the pillow gone free. "What are you doing?"

I don't answer. I pretend not to hear him, even when he repeats the question. I don't want to explain why I'm standing here in exile with nothing on except my body blanket of tattoos that makes me look like a decoration affixed to the wall.

Road to Enchantment

Albuquerque

The message reads: "Esmeralda is dead," a crude drawing of a cross just beneath it. A pair of dancing shoes with stiletto heels dangles from one of the arms. In spite of myself, I can't help but think of Dorothy's house atop the wicked witch, legs jutting out with the pair of ruby slippers sparkling like blood drops.

I look up from my desk, expecting Cecilia to be peeping from a window as she waits for a response to her joke. The last time she pulled something like this was on my birthday, when she left a pornographic card with a paper penis that popped out when I opened it. At any other workplace I could laugh it off, even share it, but not here, at the Montaño YMCA Daycare Center, where people drop off their five-year-olds at seven A.M. and then pick them up in the afternoons, expecting that nothing more alarming than a nosebleed or a finger painting accident transpired during the day.

The message is handwritten on the eggshell stationery from the law firm where Cecilia is temping this month. She must have dropped it off on my desk while I was out in the back making sure that no one's sandal disappeared into the sandbox.

Suddenly, the weight of the message hits me. Five years ago Esmeralda had watched Cecilia and me walk out of the bankrupt dance studio for the last time. I never heard from her again nor did we seek each other out because our farewell that day was final. There was no next day, or another chance, or an again. And now here she is, the poor woman, in the shape of an unadorned note. I look over at Maggie, who looks back at me with the startling telepathic ability she has of sensing when I need her attention. Her face looks like a robin's egg against the dirty blonde straw of its nest.

"Is something the matter, Art?" she says. I never like that she says my name that way since she's the art teacher, not me. None of the children look up from their projects—pasting dry pasta on their stick-figure houses.

"I need to make a quick call, okay?" I whisper. On my way to the back room I turn on the CD player and let the center fill with those cheesy playtime songs that even the children roll their eyes at. But I don't do it for the kids; I do it because Maggie loves to hum along to them, and this way she will not be tempted to eavesdrop.

I dial Cecilia.

"Montrose and Associates," she answers in her low, fake sexy voice.

"Goddamn it, why didn't you pick up the phone and call instead of leaving me this stupid note? How did you find out anyway?"

"Calm down, Arturo," she says, "It's not like we're getting invited to the funeral or anything."

"That's not the point," I say. "And I didn't appreciate your little drawing either."

"I knew that was too much," she says. "I couldn't help it. Anyways, I can't stay on the line long because I'm addressing all the holiday cards for the firm, and I want to get them done so I can leave early. But I'll drop by your place this afternoon, vale? I'll bring some wine."

"Red," I say, glibly.

"Red," she repeats, and then hangs up.

For the rest of the afternoon I'm distracted. Even the munchkins realize it when I do a shoddy job at calling out the images during picture bingo. Maggie walks around with a piece of elbow macaroni stuck to her blouse and I don't chuckle at it, even though the children keep pointing it out with hand signals. Any other day I would have joined in the fun, like when we all worked collectively to create a portrait of a cow using paper cups and saucers. The closer we got to completing it, the more we realized our model had been Maggie, not the storybook Bessie we had been reading about.

"Art," Maggie says as she packs her homemade tote bag with supplies. The last child had been picked up. "The Rio Valley YMCA crew is getting together this weekend for a bowling game. Care to join us?"

"Are you kidding?" I say.

"No," she says, deadpan.

I feel for Maggie. The only social life she looks forward to are these gatherings with the other awkward daycare providers from the sister branches. Cecilia and I ran across them during one of their outings to the Cottonwood Mall. We were there to shop for shoes; they were there to volunteer to run the blood pressure testing booth for the health fair.

"Will you look at that?" Cecilia said, pointing them out to me. "I think it's so empowering to see the mentally disabled be productive."

"I'll pass," I tell Maggie. "I've got a funeral to go to this weekend."

"Oh, my gosh!" Maggie says, raising her hand to her mouth. "I'm so sorry, Art."

"Thank you," I say.

As I step into my car I catch Maggie looking out at me through the office window. It's her turn to close up, and I suspect she actually stays until seven P.M. On my shift I'm out with the last kid, which most of the time is closer to six. I also suspect that Maggie actually takes home all of those art projects the kids give to her, the ones they know even their parents will toss out after a day or two. I imagine Maggie's wall looking like those college campus billboards I used to staple dance-lesson fliers on—a chaos of color, except the messages and images on hers are indecipherable finger paintings, potato prints, tissue collages, Crayola scribbles, and construction paper cutouts.

The drive down the I-40 is a bit congested, so I take the city streets to my apartment down by the campus. Though I never went to the University of New Mexico, I have always chosen to live near it because the student housing is cheaper. And the reason I never left Albuquerque after leaving the dance studio was because I thought the gorgeous skyline over the Sandia Mountains was going to sustain me. I've never encountered such beauty before, not in my ugly old town of Caliente in Southern California, where the only good thing that ever happened was a visit to my high school dance club by a ballroom dancer named Esmeralda.

"You've got the hunger," she told me after watching me do my interpretation of Orpheus. And a year later, when I gained my independence from my foster parents, I followed her to the Land of Enchantment.

The first thing I see when I open the door is the last traces of the spider plant on the kitchen window. Jimena has finally had her way with it.

"Jimena," I call out lazily. But the cat will not respond. Because of my long shifts at the daycare center I thought I would feel guilty not giving her the affection she deserved as my pet, but a month after taking her off Cecilia's hands, I know it is she who's neglecting me.

"Don't let her hurt your feelings," Cecilia warned me when she brought the orange tabby over after she moved into a place that didn't allow pets. Cecilia had been trying to cover up a failed home perm by sporting a beige summer hat with an off-white scarf wrapped around the crown.

"You look like a rolled-up condom," I told her.

When Cecilia put the carrier on the floor, Jimena waltzed out nonchalantly, taking quick ownership of the kitchen window, shoving the leaves of the spider plant to the side.

"She'll be no trouble at all, I promise. And thank you so much, Arturo. You're a life saver." Cecilia gave me a peck on the cheek. "And have you given any more thought to Walter?" she asked, coyly.

"I'll take your old pet, Cecilia," I said. "Your old boyfriends are a different matter."

But I did end up dating Walter, a divorced drugstore manager, because he was lonely and upset at his discovery that he didn't like women after all. And since I was the only gay man he knew, and only then because I was his ex-girlfriend's best friend, it was up to me to teach him something about being gay. He took me out to dinner twice and we tried to have sex once, but only because he was curious about the whole "penetration thing." That's how he referred to it. And when I asked Cecilia about Walter's performance with her she cackled away and said, "Seriously now, do you think I would go to bed with him?"

According to my timing, Cecilia will be busting through the door in about thirty minutes. She'll have forgotten the wine, so I'll have to break open one of my cheap offerings, or worse, I'll have to drive out to the Walgreens at the corner, where Walter works. I shake my head, uncork a bottle of Merlot, and pour myself a glass in order to preempt Cecilia.

Now that Esmeralda's dead, I wonder what will happen between Cecilia and me. Our friendship was created in response to this woman. The most graceful of ballroom dancers, Esmeralda was married to her business partner, Xavier Reynolds, the owner of the studio, the place she won eventually in their divorce settlement. As the newest addition to the company, I didn't feel obligated to leave with Xavier Reynolds after the big split. Others did. I stayed behind because I admired Esmeralda, and I had faith in her dream. Besides, I had a feeling Xavier Reynolds wasn't too pleased with my abilities and would've let me go sooner or later.

"Fuck this ballroom dancing shit," Esmeralda announced to the new members. "We're going Latin!"

The studio had always generated funds teaching ballroom dance to amateur competitors—aging socialites and retired couples with the time and money. We did Latin dance on the side, doing shows at the Native American casinos, or guest stints at the university dance program, where the dominant scene was flamenco. Esmeralda wanted to shift the balance, keeping a few ballroom clients and taking more Latin dance gigs, expanding our repertoire to include danzón and tango. That was when Cecilia came into the studio, her hair billowing around her head like a storm cloud ready to burst with rain.

From the moment I saw her I sensed an air of pretense in Cecilia. A tall and fair-skinned Chicana from LA, she had trained in Santa Fe and had lived in Spain the previous summer, returning with an affected Spanish accent and a "vale?" tacked to the end of every other sentence. She wept at the end of her audition in keeping with the character of the tragic matriarch from a flamenco interpretation of Federico García Lorca's *The House of Bernarda Alba*. Esmeralda hired her because Cecilia's was a theatrical performance people would devour.

"I don't know, Esmeralda," I voiced my concern. "She looks kind of flaky to me."

"We'll give her a month," Esmeralda assured me. And a month later, Cecilia and I became inseparable.

Suddenly I have the urge to go through the bottom drawer of the dresser, where I stuffed away all of my former life. It feels appropriate to do so now that Esmeralda is gone. Many of the photographs in my album show me frozen in space just after I jumped up to do my signature 360-degree spin. Even the studio brochure featured my trick on the cover. Of course I could never teach anyone else to do this because my students were mainly older people who risked dislocating a hipbone or breaking an ankle.

I keep a few videos of some performances we did, but I rarely watch them. I have only the photographs of me in glitzy outfits that complemented Esmeralda's faux feather dress hems and sequined skirts. When I tangoed or danced flamenco with Cecilia, my small, tight-fitting jackets made me look like yet another accessory to her fabulous polka dot dress.

I'm not ashamed to admit I was not the best dancer, more of a teacher than a performer. I was prone to forgetting my steps, which is why I was placed upstage in the group numbers. In expensive engagements Xavier Reynolds made me the understudy.

In the last pages of my photo album the changes in Esmeralda's costume are obvious. She shows no cleavage because she has no breasts. The necklines have been moved higher up and the hems have exploded with ruffles and fuller feathers—anything to draw attention away from the flattened chest. She wore falsies only once, but they were never secure enough for Esmeralda, who feared they would shift or fall in the middle of a performance. She had the double mastectomy during the off-season without informing anyone. And no one was more painfully aware of her missing breasts than me, her most frequent dance partner. When she pressed her body against mine for the first time she pushed herself into me almost deliberately, as if that was her way of letting me know.

"Are you all right, Esmeralda?" I asked. But she didn't answer. She simply danced, lighter on her feet than she ever was because, recovered, she was stronger.

"There's my kitty cat!" I hear Cecilia greet the cat in the living room. I start shoving everything back into the drawer. My eyes, I realize with alarm, have watered.

"I'll be right out, Cecilia," I say.

"I'll pour myself a glass of wine, vale?" she calls out.

When I walk out of my room I walk in on Jimena rubbing herself on Cecilia's pantyhose.

"You poor thing. Doesn't Arturo give you any love?" Cecilia says. She's wearing a navy-blue skirt with a matching jacket. Her hair is a cascade of long black curls that make her look more energetic than she really is.

"So how are things back at the Y?" she says.

"Typical. As long as no one has an allergic reaction to anything, we're golden."

I notice Cecilia has spilled wine on the counter as always, and has used my white linen napkin to wipe it off.

"You've always had the patience of the gods, that's for sure. I think I would strangle a child to death if he didn't stop whining or crying or talking," Cecilia says. "That's why I left you a note this morning; I didn't want to stick around to watch one of those kiddies vomit."

"But you did have time to stand around and draw me a pretty picture?" I say. She grins, caught at her lie.

"You're looking so pale," Cecilia says. "Are you eating well?"

I give a nervous giggle. "Yes, of course I am. Shit, you know how it is with work and all," I say. I take a sip of the wine. "And don't try to distract me. I'm still pissed off at you."

"Oh, that," Cecilia says. "Can you believe she lasted this long?" My throat tightens as I swallow another sip of wine.

"She finally succumbed to the cancer, poor thing."

"Who told you she had died?" I ask.

"Xavier Reynolds."

"Xavier Reynolds?"

"It turns out he's seeking advice from the law firm I'm working for this month, because his family's trusted attorney works there," Cecilia says. She downs the wine and then taps on the lip of the empty glass to signal her desire for more. I grab the bottle and pour.

"He's getting another divorce, and this time he doesn't want to get shafted," Cecilia says.

The crass way Cecilia sometimes words things bothers me. She was no different on the dance floor. Even on such a simple exercise as the first copla in the sequence of sevillanas, she would step so close to me that I had to lean back to keep from knocking knees. When we performed with castanets, her floreo was aggressive. Her hands would come too close to my face so that the wood nearly bit my ear off.

"Well, in reality Xavier Reynolds didn't have much use for the studio since he was planning to relocate to Santa Fe," I say. "It made perfect sense for Esmeralda to keep it."

"Don't get so defensive, Arturo," Cecilia says. "I think it's so cute that you still get touchy when we talk about her."

"She's dead now," I say. I feel an odd surge of electricity go through my body. It makes my hand tremble as I pour more wine.

"That she is," Cecilia says, solemnly. "Though Xavier Reynolds didn't seem that torn up about it."

"How did he tell you?" I ask.

"Well, you know. He came in and I brought him coffee. I recognized him right away, even though he's shed most of that gray head of hair he had. Well, that's not true. I remembered him only after I read his name in the appointment book. He was sitting there fidgeting with the *National Geographic*, so I thought I'd let him know who I was.

"'I used to dance for Esmeralda Manríquez,' I blurted out.

"'Did you? You look like a dancer,' he said. 'Do you still dance?'

"I told him I had given up dancing years ago and that I had left the company at the same time you did—"

"You mentioned my name?" I interrupt.

"Well, yes but he didn't remember who you were. We spoke briefly about what great things Esmeralda had been doing back then, and then he said that all those pain-numbing drugs Esmeralda had been doing down there in El Paso had finally caught up with her." Cecilia concluded her story with a lengthy gulp of wine.

"El Paso?"

"Apparently that's where she's been all this time," Cecilia says.

"What else did he say?" I ask.

"Then he was called into the office and he took off for lunch with the lawyer. He didn't even say good-bye."

"Shit, poor Esmeralda," I say.

Cecilia lets out a giggle. "Poor Esmeralda? Are you joking? Have you forgotten what a cruel bitch she was?"

I feel my blood gushing up to my cheeks.

"What, are you operating on a selective memory, Arturo?" Cecilia's voice reaches a lower pitch. "She all but beat us with that goddamn stick she used to keep tempo during warm-ups. Don't you remember how she liked to poke us with it when we were down on the floor, trying not to cramp? And don't even deny that she slapped you around once or twice. Jesus Christ, she broke your nose!"

I stutter a reply. "I—I had forgotten most of that. Except for the nose." I rub my face.

"Well, remember all of it before you start shedding tears over Esmeralda. We dumped her ass on the same day two years ago. And I swear to God she would have shot us down if she had had a gun. To this very day the thought of going back to dance sickens me because of the hell I went through with Esmeralda."

"You never told me that's why you never went back to dancing," I say softly.

"It's always been the same reason as you. What did you think, that I enjoyed unemployment benefits and some of these half-assed jobs I get every now and then through the temp agency? I don't have a college degree and neither do you. She ruined our careers, Arturo, don't you know?"

"I know I've had too much wine," I announce before I stumble away to my bedroom. I push the door behind me but it doesn't close completely. A warm pain begins to grow in the pit of my stomach and a thread of bile quickly works its way up to the back of my throat. I thought I had forgiven Esmeralda. Come to find out that the only thing I managed was amnesia.

"Are you all right?" I hear Cecilia call out from the living room. After waiting patiently for a response she adds, "I'll come by after work tomorrow if you want, vale? We have to make plans for Christmas."

Jimena meows. I hear Cecilia refill the cat bowl with kitty chow. "Bye, bye, Paloma," Cecilia says to the cat as she shuts the door behind her. And it dawns on me that I have been calling my new pet by the wrong name.

I usually don't go out to the bars on weekdays because I have to open the daycare center at seven A.M. sharp, which means I have to be out of the apartment by six-twenty, the latest. An early riser I never was, until this job. But tonight I feel like having a drink in a public place because it makes me feel I'm not succumbing to the pathetic stages of alcoholism I used to see in my foster parents.

The Ranch down on Central Avenue is the queer cowboy bar where men my age usually congregate. It's a place to be left alone if you give the right signals. There are also signals for getting someone's (or anyone's) attention. This time, as I walk through the large wooden doors, I have no choice, because Walter is standing next to the pool table, a scrawny stick figure of a man with a beer sweating in one hand.

"Artie!" Walter yells out. The cowboy hat and the black boots are new. The awkward rush across the room is the same old one.

"Fancy running into you here, Walt," I say, kissing him on the cheek. The jukebox is blaring out country tunes and a few couples are line dancing on the floor. The rectangular bar is the center of activity, especially on a slow night like this.

"Let me buy you a drink," Walt says. "What will it be? Wine, right?"

"Actually," I say. "I'm in the mood for something stronger. I'll take a shot of whiskey."

"Sounds serious," Walter says. "Man trouble?"

At this point I know I won't be able to get rid of Walter. But I'm not sure I want to either. Unlike Cecilia, Walter likes to give me all the attention. Only after I take my first sip of the whiskey at the bar do I feel like telling him anything. At least with Walter I won't have to explain the whole Esmeralda history, because he was one of the many dance students at the studio way back when, a connection that allowed him to chat up Cecilia into a date in the first place.

"I just found out Esmeralda died," I say. "Remember her, from the studio?"

"No, can't say I do," Walter says.

I stare blankly at him.

"Which one was she, the chubby blonde with the calves?"

"That was Jimena," I say, and I feel as if I have bitten my tongue. So that's where I got that name. I'm spared any further explanations to Walter, however, because a cowpoke comes over to ask him for a dance. I'll have to remember to congratulate him for getting the hat. Had I had a chance to tell Walter which woman Esmeralda was, I would have told him that she was one who became like a mother to me, except that unlike the mothers I knew, she got carried away sometimes, striking me across the face when she was overworked and frustrated on those nights it was becoming clear she could not support the dance studio. And she was the one I waited for all along because, up until today, she was the one who was still alive. My birthmother had died when I was five. So had my birthfather. I have no memory of either of them. And my foster mother died of liver damage not long after I moved to New Mexico. Only my foster father was still around, keeping his eye inside the bottle because it was incapable of roaming anywhere else in the room. I don't care to remember either of them. But Esmeralda. She was dead. And that made me the orphan all over again.

By the time I arrive at the daycare center, two pairs of anxious parents are already waiting for me. According to the weekly logs, these are also the last parents who sign out their children before closing time.

"Good morning," I say to the parents. "Good morning, munch-kins." The children are more awake than the adults and show more enthusiasm, giving me hugs or gifts of small candies. The routine is this: the kids get dumped on the activities carpet, the parents scribble signatures on a yellow sheet, the children play inside, then out in the back as the rest of the children trickle in, and as soon as all twenty-four children are accounted for, Maggie serves them breakfast, usually jelly sandwiches with chocolate milk or cereal and toast. The front desk receptionist doesn't come in until nine, but she's usually late. Maggie, on the other hand, is always early.

"Good morning, Maggie," I say as I walk behind her. She's squatting on the carpet with the few early birds.

"Oh, Art," Maggie says. "Are you going to need some personal time off this week?"

"For what?" I ask.

"For . . . your recent loss," Maggie says, whispering.

"Oh," I say. I walk to the back room without answering her.

The morning goes by without incident, except that one of the kids accidentally kicks another, and we have to turn the event into a lesson about paying attention to our surroundings. The kid that got kicked gets a consolation prize over all the fuss—the privilege of holding the door open for group exits and entrances.

Annie, the absentminded secretary and child psychology major at UNM, comes in late.

"Midterms," is all Annie says by way of explanation.

A few of the young girls who admire Annie, claiming that her daily garb of diaphanous clothing and flowers in her hair make her look like a fairy, come scrambling up to hug her. She returns each embrace halfheartedly as she makes her way to leftover plate of finger-sized jelly sandwiches.

I raise my hand to signal to the dozen or so children present to be quiet. They all raise their hands to show me that they're paying attention.

"We're going out to the playground now. I need to see two lines at the Baby Lion Door," I announce. The children scurry to the door with the lion cub poster stapled to it. The morning's kickee takes his place in front of the line and holds the door open. I follow the last child onto the playground.

Outside, the children disperse to the jungle gym, the swings, and the sandbox. I pace back and forth on the playground, ready for any minor emergency. But all the time I know I'm invisible, just another adult fading in the background.

"Paloma," I call out. Still the cat doesn't respond to me. Perhaps she's resentful of my misnaming her all along and correcting that mistake is useless at this point. I drop my mail on the counter, covering up the dry purple ring of yesterday's wine. A crisp gold-toned letter grabs my attention. At first I think it's another one of Cecilia's notes from Montrose & Associates, but this one's from another law firm. In Texas. I open it immediately. Esmeralda has remembered me in her will.

I drop on the easy chair, let my feet rise. I wiggle my toes. My feet are the ugliest feature on my body. All that build up of calluses has scarred my ankles, the backs of my heels, and my little toes. My legs kept their musculature after all this time off the stage, but I have since gained a few pounds. And sadly, my feet have aged. They don't belong to a twenty-five-year-old who hasn't traveled much and who has only known two homes, Caliente, California, and Albuquerque, New Mexico. I've never been on a plane. I've never had a boyfriend, though I've dated plenty, mostly undergrads from the university. And the closest I've come to a significant other is Walter. God, I'm pathetic.

The letter burns in my hands until Cecilia arrives.

"What do you think this means?" I ask her. I don't even give her time to kick off her shoes.

"It means you better hope she didn't spend it all smuggling painkillers across the border," Cecilia says. "Pour me some wine, will you?"

"Can I just call them and ask how much? Or do I have to go all the way to El Paso to find out?"

"Well, you can hire an attorney to take care of all that for you," Cecilia says. "If you want I can put in a word for you at Montrose."

I'm dizzy with excitement. I suddenly see myself quitting my job, buying a better car, then packing a few things and heading back to California. I finally admit to myself that I have been stuck here all this time. But back to what? I look down at Cecilia.

"Hey," I say. "Why don't we both ditch this dump?"

"Dump? I happen to like it here."

I wait for the answer I want.

Cecilia's eyes widen. "You're serious?"

"Yes. Why don't we pack up and move to LA. We could get back to dancing and stuff."

"Well, we're still in good shape," Cecilia says. She then shakes her head. "No, impossible."

"Come on!" I plead with her. "It'll be like old times. The good ones anyway. I mean, fuck, Esmeralda owes us that. Isn't it so fucking appropriate that her dying has given us a chance to pick up what we left because of her?"

"You don't even know what she left you. I seriously doubt she had a fortune stashed somewhere. She would have used it to save that sinking ship of a studio."

"Well, I'm going to find out. And if it's enough to get us the hell out of here, we're going, vale?"

Cecilia's eyes light up. She lifts her glass. "Vale," she says.

The next day I sneak a phone call to the law firm in El Paso from work, because I have no long distance service at home. They're unable to release any information until I fax them an ID. I use my lunch hour to do that, expecting them to call me back immediately, but they don't. I call them again to ask if they've received it. The secretary says "yes" in a disinterested tone that makes me want to throttle her. I realize then what a perfect match Cecilia is for her position at Montrose and Associates.

The next time the phone rings it's naptime. The children are all scattered on their mats, some of them beneath the floral print blankets that make the floor look as if it has sprouted daisy bush upon daisy bush. The CD player plays classical music at low volume. Maggie knits on the rocking chair. She's wearing those funny white shoes that look like grown-up versions of little girl shoes with the strap and perforated designs. Annie, with her wilted purple morning glory pinned to the side of her head, signals me to take the receiver.

"Hello," I say.

"Mr. Mendoza?" the voice asks. I know immediately it's from the El Paso law firm.

"Yes," I say nervously. I become even more anxious as they reveal the nature of the will. Esmeralda Manríquez has indeed named me her heir. There's the matter of settling her medical debts, but the amount is still notable. It's enough to fuel the car all the way to California. It's enough to struggle in LA for a few months until something comes around. I call Cecilia right away.

"Pack up your shit," I whisper into the receiver. "We're leaving the Land of Disenchantment and heading to the Golden State."

"Congratulations," Cecilia says. Her voice carries the same disinterested tone as the El Paso secretary's.

"What's the matter?" I say.

After a brief pause Cecilia let's the bomb drop. "I'm not coming with you."

"What? Why?"

"Well, Xavier Reynolds is still around, and he offered me a chance for an audition at his studio up in Santa Fe," she says.

"Santa Fe?" I say in disbelief. "I'm offering you a chance to come to LA."

All I hear on the other end is Cecilia tapping her nail against her teeth.

"Don't do this to me Cecilia," I say. At this point I'm aware that both Maggie and Annie are listening in. But I can't stop myself. "You know I can't do this alone."

"Yes, you can, Arturo," she says. "You'll be fine without me."

"Then give me a good reason why you're not coming with me?"

"How do I say this nicely," Cecilia says, and then adds, "I can't. Arturo, you're a shitty dancer. You know that. And you're better off investing that money than blowing it on a pipe ass dream that you can still make it on the stage. I mean, you could barely hold your own in a mediocre Albuquerque studio. They're going to laugh you right out of town in LA. And I'm sorry if the truth hurts but you're not thinking—"

I hang up. Maggie and Annie are staring at me. My face feels bloodless. I turn away and pretend to be fussing with the sign-up sheet at the front desk.

When Cecilia comes knocking on my apartment door that afternoon I don't answer it. I sit on the floor with my legs crossed until she gives up and leaves. My phone is unplugged. The only sound I hear for the next hour is the cat scratching at the litter box. The smell is repugnant.

At eight o'clock that evening I pick myself off the floor and head for the Walgreens on the corner. I conclude that if Cecilia won't come with me, then maybe Walter will.

The streets on this side of Central are all named after colleges on the East Coast. Harvard, Yale, Cornell, Columbia, and Vassar, where I live. I imagine the college kids who also live here have fantasies of actually getting into those fancy colleges. It was never a choice for me, not with my crappy grades from high school.

My foster mother used to ground me whenever report card time came around. But the punishment didn't really do much since I chose to stay home on weekend nights anyway, except when I had a show. She let me make those, sending me off with a half-assed scolding for my C-average GPA. By the time I got home, both she and my foster father were passed out drunk. They never knew if I had made curfew. And I could sneak a date in and out of the house without them finding me out.

When I get to Walgreens, the florescent lighting hurts my eyes. I ask one of the freckle-faced cashiers for the manager, and she pages Walter.

"A laaa, are you, like, his boyfriend or something?" she asks. I can see her gum when she talks.

I ignore her. She rolls her eyes at me.

When Walter sees me, he does that awkward rush across the floor that makes the freckle-faced cashier titter.

"Artie, what a surprise," he says. "How are you?"

I realize then what a fool I'm making of myself. Of course Walter is not coming with me because I'm not even going to bother asking. Instead I give him this nervous look that lets him know I'm telling him one thing but hoping he can read between the lines.

"Sorry to bother you at work, Walt," I say. "I came by to say good-bye."

"What? Are you going out of town or something?"

"I'm moving out of New Mexico."

"What? When?" Walt gives me that look of genuine disappointment.

I can't stop myself. I don't know what I'm about to say until I say it. And it all comes out so irreversible. So true.

"You're not in trouble with the law or anything, are you?" Walter's voice is low when he says this, and the look of genuine concern on his face makes me want to reach over and kiss him on the lips.

"You're too sweet," I say.

After a brief moment of awkward silence, he shrugs and says simply, "Well, you've got my number, and you know where I live. And if you ever come through here again, you know where I work. I'm certainly not going anywhere."

I reach over and hug him. "Thanks, Walter," I say. I feel an ache in my chest and I'm unable to say anything else.

As I leave Walgreens I make a mental list of things to take with me: a box of dance memorabilia, my wine opener, my good shoes, the cat. And before I know it I'm calling Maggie at home. Her silence to my announcement tells me she will go into a deep depression. Not because she loved me or anything like that, but because disruptions in her routine send her spinning out of orbit. She's like a child that way, always the happiest when she has structure. Walter, on the other hand, went back to his job with only the hint of sadness, the kind that will melt away when he realizes that he won't miss me that much after all. The munchkins will forget about me by next week.

In the seven years I have lived here, I haven't accumulated that much, and it shows by how quickly the room empties out when I remove a few key items: the CD player, the cushion with a wool slipcover from Peru—an old gift from Esmeralda. Everything else is forgettable, easily disposable. I imagine the landlord shoving everything into a plastic garbage bag, enraged at the audacity of my act: abandonment.

I feel like a thief, or a murderer on the lam. Even the cat begins to sprint each time she sees me, but she doesn't escape the kidnapping. I throw her into the carrier but leave her water dish and food sack behind. The adrenaline is really pumping by the time I shut the door for the last time, the keys inside.

"This is it," I tell myself. My little car sits on the parking lot, not even weighed down by my possessions. In a few minutes I will be the heaviest thing inside.

As soon as I'm out on the main drag and stop in at the ATM to withdraw some cash, I feel the urge to make more dramatic decisions. The cat howling in the back pushes me toward one. Ten minutes later I'm in front of Cecilia's door.

"Arturo—Paloma," she says. "What's going on?"

"I'm moving on, that's what," I say.

"What? Moving where?"

Cecilia stands at the door without inviting me in, sensing perhaps that this is a quick visit, that she's about to get her cat dumped back on her. I place the carrier at her feet.

"Arturo," Cecilia says, all affectation in her voice has vanished. "You're scaring me."

"I'll drop you a note," I say, and leave her standing there with her mouth open. I march back to my car, turn the ignition and head out to the road.

When I take the I-25 south instead of veering back to the I-40 west to California I recognize I have made yet another impulsive decision. I am heading toward El Paso. Perhaps I'm following Esmeralda once again because she's the only one who has given me any direction. Perhaps I'm now entering that state of grief called shock, in which I move mindlessly toward the next hour. Maybe I'll shake it off and suddenly turn back to Albuquerque, pick up the cat and break into my apartment. But I doubt it. This is a tornado I have climbed into, and the feeling of uncertainty exhilarates me. Who knows where I'll land? Who knows what wonders await me at the end of this road?

The Abortionist's Lover
New York City

for M

When he slips under the covers at night, my lover's hands are cold and clean as the bathroom mirror. But they're no reflection of mine. They don't match my hands in either pigmentation or dimension. His are white and small—harmless looking things. Their compactness keeps his profession a secret. I will let him touch me, I will let him feel me, and I will let him pinch and prod me, to remind him that his fingertips are not desensitized, though they're completely sanitized. The warm points of his desire, I will show him, have not scrubbed off.

"Fourteen procedures today," he mumbles as he walks into the bedroom. The lights have been dimmed in anticipation. I'm already naked. I hear him remove his clothes, tap one of the computer keys to wake it up, though he knows he shouldn't do this—check his email on a Thursday afternoon. The screen projects its blue glow against the wall. His shadow towers over me, and then everything goes to black when he shuts the laptop. And suddenly his hands. A creature of routine, he expects the following program this day of every week: sex at six-thirty, dinner by seven-thirty, bedtime at ten.

"Procedures," he calls them, and it makes me want to scoff. But it's this skill that has insured him a job at the Bronx hospital, and what pays the mortgage for his penthouse in the Meat-packing District.

I turn to face the tight square of the window, picturing the traffic on Fourteenth Street as Adam stretches out on the bed. I've seen him naked so many times I can reconstruct his body through memory. His arms are thin and his nipples are red as blood drops against the pale skin. The navel spills out a thin trail of hair from its opening, a brown mole sits shyly on the hipbone—on his left. He is circumcised, and the first thing he does is reach over to pull my foreskin back, stimulating my erection.

Even after a year of this ceremony I've not learned to stop thinking, when we have sex, about what he does at work—perform "procedures" on poor women, Puerto Rican, Dominican, Haitian, Black. Any one of those women could be my sister Dalia back in México. Except that here these "procedures" are legal. All of them done carefully, hygienically by my Jewish doctor from a wealthy family in Chicago.

He wraps one leg around mine, and then fits his chin into the curve of my neck to run his tongue along my skin. The tickling forces my thighs to press his knuckle deeper into my crotch. I reach back, weave the long, silky strands of his blonde hair into my fingers, and invite him into me. When he pumps the lube bottle on the nightstand, I'm temporarily shaken out of the moment. The spurting sound is clinical and obscene. But then he enters me so smoothly, my body locks into place with his so perfectly, that I dismiss those thoughts of "procedures" and women and tiny fetuses that have met their end at my lover's hands. The more he thrusts, the more I forgive him. Maybe I will come before him, maybe he will come before me. This is the only part that goes unplanned. The bed squeaks, picking up the pace to catch up with our quick succession of moans. The more we sweat, the quicker I want this to end, so I recall a time when I actually enjoyed the sex, when it was still spontaneous, before he made it a duty—mine, in exchange for living in his home without paying rent.

I ejaculate first this time, and my semen oozes out between his fingers. I reach over for the box of tissues.

"Gracias, Papi," he whispers in my ear. His breath is hot and garlicky. How strange that for everyone else the mouth becomes odorless in the throes of passion.

Adam's breath is always bad, as if he's rotting from the inside. I once brought it up politely, after watching the tenth person wince in Adam's face. And he wasn't embarrassed about it, not even apologetic. He said it was a side effect of the pills he was taking to fight his receding hairline. I suggested he carry mints. He suggested I carry a first-aid kit, which I would need it if I ever brought it up again.

I follow Adam to the bathroom where the light's too bright and hurts my eyes. As he stands over the toilet to pee, I turn the shower knobs. On one side of the tub, the shampoos for his type of hair; on the other side, products for mine. We share the body soap.

I am no longer squinting by the time we step inside the tub. Adam wraps his arms around me. I can feel the wet tip of his penis. In a minute I will wash it for him with the soft sponge. He will scrub between my ass cheeks with the loofah. And now that it's visible in the light, the tattoo along my collarbone will guide his finger across my chest as if he can feel the wings of the inked-in streamer of bird silhouettes. We will lather each other's heads and dry each other off with matching towels. And in between I will let him kiss me. Since we're the same height, all of these reciprocal activities give the semblance of equality, or even love. But we are far from either.

"I had this patient today," Adam tells me as I stir the pot of lentil soup over the stove. He slices the bread loaf. We're in our robes. Mine is white and his is blue. "Big fat cow. I mean, the only way I could tell she was pregnant was after studying the sonogram. I was expecting to see a tumor in there. Or maybe a huge mass of fecal matter. But instead I found a baby."

"Would you mind terribly if we changed the subject," I say.

"Oh, pobre Papi," Adam says in that gringo accent that annoys me. "Have I hurt your little ears?"

"We're about to eat," I say. "I don't want those images in my head."

"I'm a doctor," he says. "I speak doctor talk. You want meaningless chatter? Go back to your lazy artist boyfriend in that tacky railroad apartment in Williamsburg I pulled you out of."

" 'Big fat cow' is doctor talk?" I say. "Hmm . . . sophisticated. I'll have to grab the medical dictionary to look that one up."

"You know how much your sarcasm annoys me," he says.

"If you don't like my company then maybe you should eat alone tonight. I don't feel like fighting," I say, resigned.

He comes up behind me, grabbing hold of my arm before I'm able to move. "And I don't feel like watching you walk away from me tonight. So you just stand there in front of the stove like the little bitch that you are and stir the fucking soup before I shove your face in it."

The exaggerated threat makes me giggle. "Wow," I say. "What tough guy flicks have *you* been watching? Isn't it a little early for an Oscar performance?"

He tightens his grip on my arm. "You're hurting me, Adam," I say. And when I look into his eyes I see someone else completely. "What's the matter with you?"

"I'm tired of you," he says, no emotion in his voice. "I wish you would leave me."

"And I wish you would let me," I say.

Without warning, I feel the hot sting of his fist across my face. It's the surprise of the blow that knocks me down, not the force. Adam drops beside me immediately. "You see what you made me do?" he says.

I'm stunned into paralysis. He rolls me over on my stomach and lifts the robe up over my ass. He continues to coo apologies and to kiss the back of my neck as he squirms his way on top to penetrate me. The adrenaline has excited him, and though I'm not prepared to receive him, I let him exhaust himself. I let his breath distract me from the pain.

Fortunately, the second round is shorter than the first, but he feels a sense of accomplishment anyway. When he's done, he sits up and leans against the wall and lets out a deep sigh. He keeps one hand on my calf, caressing it as if that's all the comfort necessary. I remain pressed to the wooden floor.

"Get up, Lorenzo," he commands, because he wants to forget what just happened, but I don't budge.

"I hate it when you play your little games," he says, his voice more severe this time. He nudges me with his foot. "All right, get off the floor, you look ridiculous."

I want to rise but I'm unable to, it's as if I've slipped out of my body, relinquishing control. I'm not even able to speak.

"Stay there then," Adam says, and steps over me as he walks away. So this is where it is, I think to myself. And yet I'm unable to narrow down what *it* is: our relationship? my life? the terrible karma I put out in the world come back to roost?

The lentil soup on the stove is now boiling over. I imagine it evaporating into the night, going dry and eventually hardening, making of the pot a stone with crystals in the center, a beauty worthy of a museum, the only thing of value left within reach.

On Friday mornings I have my own routine, which has become more urgent today. Adam is on call for twenty-four hours at the hospital and won't be back until early Saturday, when he'll drop dead asleep until the afternoon. I clean up the mess he left in the kitchen after he made too much noise this morning fixing his lunch, dinner, and midnight snack to go. And then I scurry about, taking care of all the small errands before my lover comes over: drop off the laundry, pick up the dry cleaning, do some light grocery shopping at the Chelsea Market. I pick up a bento box and hope there's a bottle of white wine chilling in the fridge. But red will do. I notice with much resentment that I have to maneuver around more baby strollers each month. Everywhere white babies.

Back at the penthouse, I put away the dry cleaning, refill the sock and underwear drawer, and stock the kitchen cupboards with the market purchases. I finish washing the pot I left soaking all day, and then I dry the glassware and the spoons with the odd stems shaped like green bean pods. I shuffle around the magazines on the coffee table and hide the extra pairs of slippers in the hallway closet. When I even out the stacks of CDs filed beneath the sound system I have completed my tasks: erased all evidence of anything out of place and eaten up the hours until Jaysen rings the buzzer around noon.

The elevator at the end of the hallway hasn't closed yet by the time I'm unzipping Jaysen's pants. He stands at the doorway passively, letting me stretch open his fly to reach in. It's a beautiful cock, long and thick at the base, the shaft narrows down to the head, which points out like the tip of an arrow. I take it flaccid into my mouth and swirl it around with my tongue. Adam never lets me take his penis if it's not erect. It's an insecurity I've only seen in white guys.

"I guess you're horny," Jaysen says. The tone in his voice alarms me; he sounds disinterested. I look up at him, pull away.

"Something wrong?" I ask. He doesn't answer.

I've been dreading this moment. It's the part in the affair where the married man finally succumbs to regret or guilt or shame or a combination of all three. It's the part where he thinks he should turn himself around and make right by his woman, breaking off the illicit meetings with his whore, cleansing himself, or so he believes, of the dirty kisses, when all he's really doing is ending one chapter to move on to the next—another fool who'll start a romance from scratch, long before it wears thin with monotony.

"I see," I say. It's the serious breakup, because he doesn't even let me finish the blowjob.

"I'm sorry, Papa," Jaysen says. "It's just that things are getting bad at home."

"Of course they're bad," I say. "Why else would you come over to let me suck your dick?"

"Look, I don't want problems, okay? I get enough of that shit already," Jaysen says. He zips his pants and throws himself on the couch.

"I'm in the mood for a drink," I say. "How about you?"

"I'll take whiskey," Jaysen says.

"That serious, huh?" I say. I pour him a double shot of Maker's Mark and hand it to him. I step back into the kitchen to mix a martini.

"What happened to your face, anyway?" he asks.

I'm startled by the revelation. All morning I've been running around the streets of Chelsea and not one look to betray the visible traces of rage on me.

"I fell," I say.

"Don't bullshit me," Jaysen says. "He kicked your ass didn't he? Was it because of me?"

"Don't flatter yourself, hon," I say, walking to the living room slowly, to keep from spilling my drink. I take a sip. "It's none of your business anyway."

"All right, all right," he says. We drink the cocktails in silence. Meanwhile, the world of car horns and fire truck sirens continues outside without us.

"Would you like another," I ask him, reaching over for his glass.

"I'm good," he says.

"I know you're good," I say. "What I want to know is if you're ready."

"I take it you are?" he asks.

"Well," I say. "Since this is good-bye."

I snuggle up next to Jaysen and place my hand on his crotch. "So what do you say? I've had a shitty week myself and I'm about to be left behind by the best piece of ass in both Upper and Lower Manhattan. I've got to have something juicy to tell the girls the next time we go on a cigarette break at Bloomie's."

"You sure do have a way with words, Lorenzo," he says.

Once we've had our quickie, I lie back on the couch with my pants around my knees as Jaysen walks into the bathroom to clean up. The water runs in the sink. The clouds are gathering behind the skyline, and I make a mental note to take my umbrella to work. In a minute I will dress in my retailer's black, I will walk five blocks to the Lexington express train because the weather's good and I will step out onto the platform at the Fifty-ninth Street stop, which leads to the lower level of Bloomingdale's. But before all this I will walk out to the terrace and talk myself out of jumping.

"So what is it, really?" I ask Jaysen when he comes back to the couch, a fresh shot of whiskey in his glass. He's slightly apprehensive that I haven't pulled my pants back up and keeps looking away politely.

"Why is it over?" he asks, taking a sip of his whiskey.

"Do tell," I say.

"I'm having a baby," he says.

"How do I know it's mine?" I ask.

Jaysen frowns. "Look, could you cover yourself up?" He takes a cushion and places it over my crotch.

"Well, congratulations, Jaysen," I say. "I think you'll make a wonderful mother."

"Damn," Jaysen says, exasperated. "You can never take anything seriously, can you?"

"Not today," I say. "Everything's falling apart around me."

"You know," he says. "We would have made a good couple if neither of us were married."

"You mean, if both of us dared to leave our spouses?"

"Same difference."

We sit on the couch, finishing our drinks in silence. Jaysen's lunch hour will end soon, and he will have to go back to the coffee shop. The ice in his whiskey has melted completely so that not even the tipping of his glass makes a sound.

I stand on the terrace. Beneath me is Fourteenth Street. There is always foot traffic, day and night. No matter what hour I choose to fling myself over the guardrail, chances are somebody will be around to bear witness to the tragedy. Once Adam and I dropped maraschino cherries on pedestrians and never once hit our targets. A mathematician or a physicist might have. The only time we come out here anymore is to breathe in the cool autumn air. Even a penthouse can be as oppressive as any shoebox apartment after a while. My mother has a saying: "Jaula, aunque sea de oro, no deja de ser prisión." I always thought it was a Mexican woman thing, this perspective of marriage and society as prison.

But my mother's still serving her time. My sister, on the other hand, got out the hard way.

The setting: Morelia, Michoacán, mid 1990s. The players: my beloved sister Dalia and a husband who cheated on her with other men. The conflict: a shitty marriage. The plot: my sister punishing her husband by terminating her first pregnancy. The twist: a botched abortion. The closing scene: unwritten. Dalia remains in a coma, and her husband, my mother warns me, is still out looking for me.

"And what's he going to do when if he finds me? Kiss me to death?" I asked my mother over the phone the last time she called.

"He says he's going to kill you," my mother said, her voice so soft and sullen, as if she believed his threats. And then she adds, her voice shaky: "Please promise me you won't come back. And if it's an emergency, there's always your cousin Meño in California."

California. Never been there and, like a true New Yorker, I've developed a prejudice against all things Californian, like suntanning. And I certainly can't imagine myself traipsing around with my farmworker cousins in the town of Caliente. Caliente, for heaven's sake. What do people do for fun in Caliente? Pelt grape?

As I look over the edge of the building I call out Dalia's name to the wind. If I were standing next to her at the hospital she still wouldn't hear me, no matter what those doctors say. My mother, who has faith in things invisible like God and the subconscious, visits my sister every week and speaks to her, tells her that I miss her and that I'm sorry. The last part is not true. I am not sorry I told her about her husband, who from the days they were dating had his eye on me. At first I thought it was all in my head, wishful thinking and silly adolescent fantasy—what had gotten me through many nights of compulsive masturbation. And then one evening he was in my room, my dream materialized.

"Shh . . . " he said to me, though it was quite unnecessary. I knew it would be a secret between us—that and the warm hand crawling under the covers, my erection already waiting for his touch. I came almost immediately upon contact, and it embarrassed me. But when he bent down to kiss me on the lips, the first kiss I'd ever received from a man, I knew that he understood, and that he'd give me another chance to do better.

I thought these exchanges would end when he married Dalia, but he expected them to continue. And when I put a stop to them myself, he started to hate me because he was forced to seek his pleasure elsewhere.

"Are you sure about this, Dalia?" I heard my mother say over afternoon tea.

"Positive," Dalia said. "You know a wife senses these things."

I pictured my mother nodding her head in agreement, having been through the same bullshit with my father, though she never left him. But neither did he affront her with the additional shame of being a faggot like the son she helped move out to the north, worlds away from her husband's line of sight.

Fourteenth Street and Ninth Avenue is my favorite intersection, connecting Chelsea with the Meatpacking District with the Village. When I finally pour out into the bustle I'm simply another anonymous body in motion. The only people I make eye contact with are those I'd like to sleep with. And there are plenty of beautiful men to choose from.

As I make my way to the north side of Fourteenth, I'm grateful for having decided on Manhattan as my hiding place. This is the city where people come to disappear from the old identities and to reappear with new ones. I arrived a scared teenager on a student visa with a fetish for the English language and American things, and now I'm a twenty-seven-year-old college dropout, but fit and versatile. This goddamn island is my oyster.

"Lorenzo!"

I turn my head to check who has called. No one steps forward to claim responsibility for shouting out my name. I keep walking. Maybe it was simply the wind carrying back a plea from Dalia from so far away.

The best perk about working as a retailer at Bloomie's is that I'm just as desirable as the merchandise. That's how I met Adam.

And Robbie before him. And Ahmed before that. And on Fridays after work, the other queens and I head out to the O.W. or to the Townhouse, to drink and flirt and poke fun at the dumb tourists whose eyes go wide as clocks when they find out that Bloomingdale's is actually affordable. But I'm not feeling it tonight. After a first round of cocktails, my energy begins to wane.

"Girl, I got a hot number tonight," Kenny says. He works in women's jewelry. I'm stuck down in the basement, dusting off the designer labels and putting up with the bitchy queens who have saved all season for a Kenneth Cole outfit to go with the leather shoes from Century 21.

"Well, call right now," Martin dares him, pulling out his cell phone. He's the youngest of the group and he circulates among the perfume counters like a frazzled bee.

"Are you kidding me? And kill the play I'm getting from that dude in the trucker hat?"

Martin and I turn at the same time to face a drunk patron nodding off at the end of the bar. We burst out laughing.

"Oh, my God, I think Dillon has herpes or something," Kenny says.

"You're kidding?" Martin says.

"I'm going to Google-image it tonight, and if it's what I think it is I'm going to cut it off while he's asleep," Kenny says.

"Fidelity is so not queer nowadays," Martin says, shaking his head.

My mouth drops open. "This from the cunt who doesn't even bother wearing panties anymore?" I say.

"Hey, it's convenience," Martin says. "That way I don't have to look for them in the dark."

I roll my eyes and Kenny lets out one of his attention-grabbing hoots. These are the most superficial friendships I have, but after today they're also the only fun I have left. We gravitated toward each other because we've made a pact never to bring up the hard truths of our miseries. No one talks about Martin's anorexia, or Kenny's teeth, which are showing faint traces of green. No one inquires about my sunken eyes, and the telltale bruises on my face.

"You know what, girls?" I say. "I think I'm calling it a night."

"You're kidding, right? The party's just getting good," Kenny says.

"I'm sorry," I say. "Man trouble."

"Say no more, sister," Martin says. "Go home, get your beauty sleep, and Prozac your headaches away."

"I'll try," I say. I kiss them both on the cheek and walk out.

"And next time, sweetheart," Kenny adds, pointing at my bruise, "a little more makeup on the cherry stain."

"Bitch," I say, and then wave good-bye.

A few blocks up I arrive at the Hot and Crusty, hostile with Upper East Side sociopaths and intoxicated businessmen. I find Shiraz fending them off with his disarming looks.

"Cup of coffee, two sugars, and cream, please," I tell him. I check my watch. Quitting time for him is midnight, in an hour.

"How are you, my friend," he says. "Haven't seen you around here lately."

"I'm doing fine," I say. "Busy. But I'm free tonight." I wink.

I sit with my elbows on the crumb-filled table for the next hour. The line of customers grows and shortens quickly at fifteen-minute intervals. To pass the time I pretend I'm reading a book from Adam's shelf. But what I'm really doing is going over what's about to transpire after midnight.

Shiraz and I walk down from Second Avenue to Central Park and grab the first dark spot we can find. All the way there we chitchat about harmless things like work and the weather and the rising price of a subway ride. But as soon as we're out of view he tackles me with a bear hug, knocking the wind out of my body. I don't have time to breathe again before Shiraz pins me to the ground, his right arm wrapped around my neck. He's adept at one-hand maneuvering. I've seen him work his skill over sandwich preparations. Somehow he has unbuttoned our pants and pulled them down at the same time. He guides himself inside me. My lower back feels the hairy bristles of his stomach.

"You little slut," he spits into my ear. "It's what you came for, isn't it?"

I squirm beneath him, wanting to tell him to ease up, just a little, but he has cut off my breathing. I open my mouth and nothing comes out, except the hollow sound of strained air escaping. I'm wondering how long after I pass out will I come to. It would be embarrassing to wake up in the daylight like this, my pants around my knees telling the whole sordid story. Or what if I never come to and meet up with my sister in that nebulous limbo where those stuck between the living and the dead must gather. How would I explain what took me there?

"So you *are* the promiscuous little faggot my husband told me about," she will say. And how could I deny it.

But when I black out there is no such encounter or dream. When I wake up, it is only about an hour later. Shiraz has run away, scared shitless that he fucked me to death. I pull myself together, brush the leaves off my shirt, and stumble to the nearest bench for a rest. A cruiser on his way to the rambles mistakes my pose for a solicitation and grabs his crotch while he walks by. I ignore him.

I suppose that a soul search is appropriate at a moment like this, but I don't care for one. I know exactly what I'm doing anyway—punishing Adam for being cruel and Jaysen for leaving and Dalia for marrying that prick and Shiraz for . . . for being so goddamn irresistible in that little white hat. Contrast it against the freshly-baked bread and he's completely edible. Ha, ha.

When I wipe a tear off my face I'm stunned. Have I been crying all this time? It is almost two-thirty in the morning. In five hours Adam will be home, expecting to sleep peacefully, and to wake up rested for an evening on the town, maybe a movie at the Angelika, maybe a browse through the Strand, maybe a stroll along the pier, where he will apologize profusely for the fifth or sixth time for having raised his hand to me. He will give me a pair of cuff links. And I will take his generous hand and kiss every knuckle, rub it against my cheek to assure him that it is meant to be in service to the women who might otherwise hurt themselves without the attentiveness of a doctor like him. I have heard the stories and I have known instances of women who turn to unhealthy and unsanitary alternatives, in places where procedures like the ones he performs are not available. He is not a bad man, my boyfriend. And I will forgive him as surely as I know he will forgive me for taking that leap from the penthouse terrace. But he'll have his peace of mind because it's not really me who jumped, but that person who I became when I set foot in New York City, that terrible glutton seduced by all the hungers accessible to him, he who didn't seek out his cousin Meño from Caliente, California.

And the man I used to be, inexperienced, clumsy, but pure as light, will return to his origin, a chair next to his unconscious sister, where he'll hold her hand and ask for forgiveness, for having conjured up the most stupid fantasy of all: that when she left her husband, she would also understand why her little brother took her place beside him, after jealousy drove him to expose his lover/brother-in-law. Who would have imagined that she was carrying life inside her belly? Who would have imagined that by plucking out the fruit she would also fell the tree?

And if her husband comes knocking on the door, a weapon hot and heavy in his fist, I'll welcome the fury, because from the beginning I've been making sure that the blade of the knife is going to set the birds on my body free.

I'm suddenly relaxed, resting on the silence of the night as if what had weighed it down is gone. I lift my body off the bench, turn right on the cobblestone sidewalk along Fifth Avenue, which is long and quiet and dark, but it too reaches an end. A breeze nudges me forward. Above me the leaves rustle and resist. I'm not alarmed when in the wind I hear my name again—"Lorenzo!" This time I don't turn around to check where it's coming from because its origin, now and forever is me. It's one of the places I'll never be able to escape.